WHERE SHADOWS BURN

Where Shadows Burn

by

Catherine Hunter

Catherine Hunter

Where Shadows Burn

published by Ravenstone
an imprint of Turnstone Press
607 – 100 Arthur Street
Winnipeg, Manitoba
R3B 1H3 Canada
www.TurnstonePress.com

Turnstone Press gratefully acknowledges the assistance of the Canada Council for the Arts, the Manitoba Arts Council and the Government of Canada through the Book Publishing Industry Development Program for our publishing activities.

Portions of this book appear
in *Prairie Fire* magazine, Vol. 20, No. 1, Spring 1999.

Cover design and artwork: Doowah Design

Interior design: Manuela Dias

Author photograph: Patrick Iveniuk

This book was printed and bound in Canada by
Hignell Book Printing for Turnstone Press.

Canadian Cataloguing in Publication Data

Hunter, Catherine, 1957–

Where shadows burn

ISBN 0-88801-231-4

I. Title.

PS8565.U5783W48 1999 C813'.54 C99-920064-X
PR9199.3.H8255W48 1999

Acknowledgments

Many people helped during the long writing of this book. Thanks to Kevin Hunter for reading the very first draft; Zoya Niechoda for generously sharing her knowledge of dramatic costuming; Susan Rempel Letkemann for the title; Brian Janzen for encouragement; Kathie Axtell for editorial suggestions and driving lessons; my colleagues and students for their various strange interpretations of *Hamlet* (and for listening to mine); Anne Marie Resta for long-distance corrections and late-night casting assistance; and Melody Morrissette for her patience, insight, and invaluable advice.

The verse on page 188 is from the anonymous poem "Donal Óg" (Ireland, c. 1650), translated from the Gaelic by Lady Augusta Gregory.

Many thanks to Jennifer Glossop and Marilyn Morton for being true professionals and caring editors.

Special thanks to Linda Holeman, for her sharp and gentle reading of the earlier version, and especially for giving me that gift a writer needs most—a friend who won't let you give up!

This book is for my mother, Doreen Hunter,
who helped me write my first novel,
when I was eleven, and started all of this.

if you had let me rest with the dead,
I had forgot you....

why did you glance back?
why did you hesitate for that moment?
why did you bend your face
caught with the flame of the upper earth,
above my face?

—H.D. "Eurydice"

Chapter One

Kelly Quirk held the black telephone receiver away from her body and stared at it, as if it were a poisonous snake. She shook her head to clear her thoughts. Then, gingerly, she raised the phone to her ear again.

"Hello?"

No answer. Only the sound of distance—traffic, perhaps, or ocean waves. White noise. She listened for a while, too long, before she replaced the receiver in its cradle.

She could not believe what she had heard. It was a mistake. Yet the voice had been clear enough. First, the mechanical, recorded message: "Will you accept a collect call from . . ." and then the name.

The name.

She had distinctly heard those syllables in that deep, familiar voice. *"James Grayton."*

She sank down onto the couch and for a few moments surveyed her living room blankly. With its plush upholstery, reams of curtains, rugs and pillows, this room was a kind of refuge for her. Soft earth colors, no sharp edges. On the surface, it looked as warm and comforting as always, but everything had changed. She let her eyes travel through the room, across the many paintings and carvings that James had made with his own hands.

James Grayton. Beloved James. If she closed her eyes she could see his youthful face, his dark-green eyes flecked with gold.

Her husband.

Her late husband. Dead this past year and a half. These sixteen months and ten days.

DARL GRAYTON WAS STUFFING his six-year-old son into an oversized tiger suit, impatiently pushing the boy's arm through a striped sleeve.

"Dad, you're hurting me!"

"Sorry, Alex. Sorry. But we have to go, okay? We have to get you to Angel's by five if you want to go trick-or-treating, and Dad's got a lot of things to do first."

"What things?"

"Things." Darl stood up and smiled at his son. "Hey. You look pretty cute."

Alex frowned. "Auntie Kelly said I'd look fer— I'd look scary."

"Ferocious," said Darl. "She said you'd look ferocious. Come on, let's move." Grabbing Alex's overnight bag, he hurried his son out of the house. Once in the truck, he paused only to help Alex secure his seat belt and lock the door.

They spent the afternoon driving all over Winnipeg, running errands. It was getting late by the time Darl navigated the maze of potholes on Angel's run-down street. He parked the truck carefully and pulled two large bags of groceries from the back.

"Do I have to go to Angel's?" Alex asked. He dragged his heavy knapsack along the gravel path as he trailed behind his father up to the front steps.

"Yes."

"Couldn't I go to Kelly's house?"

"Kelly's coming with me tonight. Come on, Alex. You had fun here last time, remember?"

"No," said Alex. But Darl didn't hear. He was knocking on the peeling paint of the front door.

KELLY KNEW SHE SHOULD get up. She should tidy the house and finish her sewing and get ready for the party.

Yes, she really should restore order to this room, she thought. It was impossible to find anything lately. Her usually immaculate house showed signs of the hectic pace of the past week, the carpet full of tiny threads and probably pins as well, the coffee table strewn with teacups and half-read books and the toppled pieces of a chess game she and Darl had abandoned days ago. A light dust coated the chess pieces, including the empty spool they'd used to replace a missing white knight. The loose ends of the costume she'd been working on lay scattered across the couch.

She picked up the mask she planned to wear tonight. The sad face of a beautiful young woman stared back at her, two bright teardrops suspended on her cheek. The mask needed only one last touch—some sparkles at the eyelids. Kelly knew she had a tube of glitter in her sewing box.

But she didn't move.

ANGEL SMILED VAGUELY as she opened the door. "Hi there, Tiger. Oh, Darl, thanks." She relieved him of one of the grocery bags and drifted down the hall toward the kitchen. Darl followed, his shoes sticking to the linoleum as he walked. He cleared aside a stack of dirty dishes to set the groceries on the kitchen table.

"Where's Paul?"

Angel gestured toward the basement stairwell. "He's

practically living down there. God knows what he's doing."

Darl grimaced. Both Kelly and her sister Angel had married unstable men. Kelly had married Darl's brother, James, and Angel had married Paul. Paul was trouble. Always had been. In high school, when Paul was arrested for breaking and entering, Darl tried to talk some sense into Angel, but she refused to listen. She made a mess of her life, and now Darl brought the groceries, while her husband moped in the cellar.

"So," he said. "You sure you're up for Alex tonight?"

"Yeah. We're gonna knock on every door in the neighborhood and then come back here for a super sugar rush." She smiled at Alex, who was hanging back in the doorway. "We'll have fun."

Darl hoped so. Sometimes he hesitated to bring Alex over here, but he knew Angel loved children. Alex's presence seemed to lift her spirits, lift the fog that had enveloped her ever since she lost her own baby to crib death almost four years ago. When Darl worked the midnight shift at the Riverside Clinic, or on those rare occasions like tonight when he went out late with friends, Alex stayed overnight in the baby's old room.

"You'll check the candy?" he asked.

"Of course, of course. Get going, you worrywart. Aren't you taking my sister on a hot date?" Angel led him by the sleeve back outside and walked him to his truck.

"You sure you've got everything you need?" he asked.

"We're fine. Go. Have a ball." She waved and turned back up the path.

"There's steak in there," he called. "And broccoli. Make sure he eats his broccoli."

Darl watched Angel disappear into the house. Through the back of her T-shirt, her shoulder blades stood out in sharp relief. She'd shaved the back of her head, and her bony neck stuck out of her collar like the neck of a stick doll. He hoped she would be tempted by the steak.

The front lawn was a disaster area, and he knew he should do something about that, too. The garden was tangled with brown, overgrown vines. Angel hadn't even tried to plant anything this summer. Just let the wind blow seeds into the yard. A few poppies had sprouted and bloomed, but otherwise there was nothing but dandelions, crabgrass and thistles. Now, everything was matted and had started to rot. It would probably stay that way all winter, under the snow. Maybe by spring Angel would get her energy back, but Darl doubted it.

IT WAS A MISTAKE. Surely it was a mistake. Perhaps it was somebody *calling* James Grayton. Some canvasser or insurance salesman with an outdated phone book. That had happened, once or twice, in those first few terrible months after his death.

Or it was some prankster with a sick sense of humor.

Or perhaps Kelly had imagined it. Her brain had garbled the message, so that she'd thought . . . No. She was over that.

She hoped she was over it.

For a whole year after James's death, she'd refused to give up the fantasy that he was still alive. Plagued with visions of her husband, she saw him everywhere, on downtown streets, in restaurants, driving past her in cars. Sometimes she would follow a complete stranger for blocks because he bore a resemblance to James. She would return to neighborhoods where she thought she had seen him and haunt the streets, searching. But that, she now knew, was a form of insanity.

With the help of Dr. Leon Chartrand, Kelly had finally come to admit that these sightings were hallucinations. James was gone. Still, it took a long time to rid herself of recurring dreams that James was still alive. Sometimes in those dreams she could feel her body filling up with sweet, nearly unbearable relief. Then she woke up, and the moment she opened her eyes, she wanted to die. She wanted to run to the top of the bridge and throw herself off. Thrust knives into her heart, set fire to the whole damned world and drag it into hell with her.

Those were common dreams among the bereaved, Leon Chartrand told her. As long as she knew the difference between dreams and reality, she was all right. But this was little comfort to Kelly. Every night she dreamed James alive and every morning she had to learn again that he was gone. Every morning the pain of grief was hotter, fiercer.

Kelly remembered that pain well. She didn't ever want to feel it again. It had taken all her strength to pull herself out of grieving, to accept that her life must go on without James. But she had done it. Finally, she stopped seeing Dr. Chartrand. Her friends began to trust her judgment again. In these past few months, she could feel herself growing stronger and stronger.

And now this.

DARL DROVE HOME and hauled his own groceries into the house. He still had a lot of chores to complete before he could dress for Sam and Lila's party. He was looking forward to seeing Kelly tonight, though it was hardly a "hot date," as Angel put it. He didn't see much of Kelly these days. She was always running around, working too hard, busy with her sewing projects. Or maybe she was seeing Joe Delany again.

No. He dismissed that last thought immediately. He knew Kelly too well, had known her since they were kids. He spoke to her every day. It was inconceivable she could be seeing anyone without Darl hearing of it. And Joe Delany had blown his chances with Kelly, anyway, by trying to move too fast.

With Kelly, a man had to be careful. He couldn't push. Darl had seen what she was like when she was pressured. She dated a couple of guys this summer, but the minute they got serious, she retreated, cut them off. She was far too stubborn, or, no, she was skittish. Like a nervous colt. She was wary of men—of love—and for good reason.

As he put the vegetables away, Darl cursed his younger brother, not for the first time. What a complicated mess James had made of their lives! What damage!

He moved into the living room and began to pick Alex's toys off the floor. Alex had been painting with the watercolors Kelly gave him for his birthday, and had left his little glasses of color, all of them muddy now, on the newspaper Darl had spread to protect the carpet. This morning Alex had painted a large picture of a little boy, standing in front of an apple tree with giant red apples, a yellow sun. A self-portrait, Darl thought.

He removed everything from the mantelpiece and ran a damp rag across it. Then he replaced all the knickknacks—photographs mostly—which he kept there for Alex's sake. The illusion of a family.

He picked up the largest framed photograph, taken the day that Alex was born. There they all were, crowded together in the hospital room. Happier days. James and Kelly. Angel and Paul. Sam and Lila. Himself and Diane. The fickle Diane, whom he married on impulse, without even getting to know her. He sighed. He had to admit he was partly to blame. He had a tendency to push, he knew that now. But he had learned it too late. Diane was gone. She wasn't cut out for family life, she said, or at least not for family life with Darl. When Alex was only three, she had left Darl for another man. A professional wrestler, of all things. "The Hooded Masher," or something like that.

"Sounds like a kitchen appliance," James had said.

Damn him.

WHEN THE TELEPHONE RANG again, Kelly was still sitting on the couch, lost in thought. She realized, as she jumped at the first ring, that the room was growing dark.

She grabbed the receiver and fairly shouted into it.

"Who is this?"

"Kelly? What's the matter?" It was Lila.

"Nothing, I'm . . . Nothing. What's up?" Kelly glanced at her watch. Six o'clock. Lila should be up to her ears in preparations for the party tonight.

"Oh, it's disaster central around here. You wouldn't believe it. I'm just calling to tell you that I talked to Taylor Grant today, and I had a fabulous idea."

Lila was famous for her fabulous ideas. The party tonight, a fundraiser for her husband's art gallery, was the latest in a long line of schemes she devised to help her friends and family. Kelly had the feeling that she was about to become Lila's next project.

"Oh no," she said.

"No, really. It's great. You know you need work, and—"

"I have work," Kelly interrupted.

"I mean *real* work. The kind you should be doing. Not this kind of piecemeal stuff, children's plays and costume shop consignments. I'm talking real theater. Shakespeare. The good old days. Come on."

"Which one?"

"*The* one. *Hamlet*."

"Wow. In Minneapolis?" Kelly knew that Lila had been dying to snag the position of costume designer in Taylor Grant's upcoming production of *Hamlet*.

"You bet. I got the job. Taylor says I get to pick an assistant, and I pick you."

"Me?"

"You. I told Taylor I can do most of it myself, but I need you for the special effects. You know, like that great job you did with Caliban and Ariel?"

The Tempest. That had been two years ago. A lifetime ago. Before Kelly had lost her ambition.

"I told him I need you for the ghost, especially," Lila continued. "Nobody can do those otherworldly things like you can. And this is a big production, and I mean big. A real chance to show off your talents and get your career back on track. And you know who's starring? Michael Black."

Lila waited for a reaction, but received none.

"Kelly? Remember Michael Black? From New York?"

"He's from New York?"

"No, he's from . . . I don't know, Europe somewhere. But we met him in New York, remember? On the set of *Rising Heat*?"

"Oh, the movie star."

"Jesus, Kell. You do remember that he asked you out."

"That was four years ago," Kelly said. Many men had asked her out in New York, when she was a rising young designer. But she had been too wrapped up in James to pay attention.

"Anyway, I got to run. Things are insane around here. I'll tell him you'll do it?"

"I'll think about it," Kelly said.

"Think hard," said Lila. She hung up.

Hamlet. It might be a good idea, Kelly thought. She felt a twinge of excitement. A good sign.

She finished the mask with a splash of glitter, laid out her costume and stepped into the shower. If she hurried, she'd be ready when Darl arrived. She took a deep breath and let the water run over her face. She was just tired, she told herself, from working such late hours, hunched over the sketchbook or the sewing machine. Too much stress. Tonight she would relax and have fun.

When she stepped out of the shower, she felt better. Refreshed. She toweled herself dry, then reached into the closet for the most comfortable shirt she owned. James's worn blue denim, which hung down to her knees. The one she had mended so many times it was seamed through like patchwork. She often slept in it when the nights were cold, and she felt the need for it now.

But it wasn't there. It should have been hanging among her nightgowns, where she'd seen it just yesterday. She searched through every garment, but it was not to be found.

Still wrapped in the towel, Kelly lay down on top of the bed and curled herself into a ball. How could the shirt be missing? What had she done with it?

She wanted that shirt more than anything in the world. She wanted everything that had belonged to James. She wanted James back.

She tried to fight it, but she lost. The pain came coursing through her veins with all the force of a tidal wave.

Chapter Two

Finally, Kelly forced herself to get up and dress. A small part of her wanted to stay curled in bed for the night, but she knew that was dangerous. Too easy to become like her sister Angel, a pale ghost of a woman, living in the past.

She stood before the full-length mirror in her bedroom and inspected her costume. She was a mermaid tonight, in a long flowing dress of dark-green velvet, heavily decorated with scales of emerald sequins. Filmy wisps of silk and chiffon seaweed trailed from her shoulders. She wore her dark hair long and loose, a pearl-encrusted comb nestled in the thick locks.

She adjusted the loops of pearl necklaces that hung at her throat. The jewelry was overdone, and the pearls were plastic, but Kelly was not aiming for real glamour tonight. She knew the theater crowd would provide plenty of genuine glamour, and she would never feel comfortable trying to compete on their level. She always felt slightly nervous among Lila's friends, who were all older and more sophisticated. They were nice enough people, she reminded herself. They just belonged to a different world. It was a matter of social class, James had always said. Her background hadn't prepared her for the social life her career sometimes demanded. Tonight she felt more jittery than usual. This was the first big party she'd agreed to attend since James's death.

Well, at least it was a costume party. She could always hide behind her disguise. She picked up the mask and held it over her face. There was something haunting about the forlorn features of the mermaid. Kelly remembered the story of the Little Mermaid she'd read as a child. Appropriate, she thought wryly. The Little Mermaid couldn't fit in, either. She couldn't walk without pain, or speak, or be with the man she loved.

Kelly lowered the mask and gazed at her own face. White skin, rarely exposed to the sun. Pale-blue eyes. A worried forehead. She ran her fingers across her lips, remembering her husband. How he used to touch her.

When the doorbell startled her, Kelly flashed a quick practice smile in the mirror before greeting Darl.

"Wow," he said, as he took in the full impact of her costume. "You look stunning." Slowly, he raised a hand and brushed the hair from her temple in a gentle caress.

"You too," Kelly said. She hid her grin as she ducked away to retrieve her coat from the closet. Despite Darl's eerie vampire cape and fangs, he was less than frightening. His kindly face completely ruined the effect, she thought.

AT THE PARTY, KELLY LET DARL take her coat while she made her way through the crowd, looking for her hosts. In the gallery's kitchen she found Sam but no Lila.

"Great outfit." Sam smiled and kissed Kelly's cheek.

"Thanks. Where's yours?" Sam was dressed simply in a sweater and jeans. "Or are you just an artist?"

"Very funny," Sam said. "I was supposed to be a pirate, but I never got a chance to get ready. Look at this." He pointed at the back door, and Kelly saw with a shock that it was completely boarded up. "Someone broke in here last night. Found the door smashed open this morning when I got here."

"Anything stolen?"

"I don't know. Can't tell yet. They made a mess of the storage room. I'm looking for volunteers to help sort it out tomorrow. Check the inventory. How about it?"

"Sure, Sam. Gee. You all right?"

"We're fine. Angry, I guess. This neighborhood ..."

"I know," she said. The gallery was right in the inner city, where crime was growing worse every year.

"Anyway," Sam said, "Lila made me promise not to worry about it until tomorrow. She's been planning this night for months. So grab a drink and get out there and party. What's-his-name—Joe—is here and he's looking for you."

"Joe Delany?"

"That's the one. You're not seeing him any more?"

"Not much," Kelly said. She didn't want to see Joe at all any more, but she didn't elaborate. She poured a drink and headed back out to the gallery. There was Joe, his eyes searching the room, watching the door every time it opened. She turned in the other direction. Not that Joe wasn't a sweet guy and a talented artist. He was just too insistent about getting into Kelly's life. He asked too many questions about her childhood, about her marriage, her plans for the future. He was one of those men who gets a little too close for comfort. She turned her back to him and watched the crowd.

All the guests were elegantly and outrageously attired, and many wore masks. Kelly realized she probably knew several of them, but she recognized very few. Was Taylor Grant here? There was something familiar about the extremely tall man in the devil's mask and red cape. She watched him as he danced with a very convincing Marilyn Monroe. Despite his size, he moved gracefully, twirling his tiny partner with ease, bending down to whisper in her ear, making her laugh. They were obviously intimate, and Kelly turned away just as Sam appeared in the doorway.

"Ladies and gentlemen," he cried dramatically, "we have a visitor!" He gestured toward the studio behind him.

Five gold-ringed fingers with long red nails slithered slowly out between the strands of beads across the doorway. Lila entered, wearing a long flowered dress, a black shawl, and thick, magenta lipstick. Gold hoop earrings grazed her shoulders, and gold bracelets clattered on her wrists as she rubbed her hands together.

"Who will come into my tent and hear his future? Who dares?" she cackled in a high voice.

"This Gypsy crone," Sam announced, "has come begging at the kitchen door. I told her she'll have to earn her supper. She has offered her black arts for our amusement."

Lila beckoned to Kelly. "Come, my child of the sea."

"Oh no," Kelly laughed. "Am I your first victim?"

Lila smiled mysteriously. She took Kelly by the elbow and led her through the beaded curtain into the darkness of Sam's studio. At first, Kelly could make out nothing but amorphous shapes and looming shadows. As her eyes adjusted, she saw white sheets draped over the easels and potter's wheel. In the middle of the room, a space had been cleared for two chairs and a table covered in heavy brocade; it held flickering candles, a crystal ball, and a piggy bank.

"Very spooky," she said. "Where'd you get the crystal ball?"

"A family heirloom."

Kelly inspected it and discovered it was a goldfish bowl, filled with silver confetti. Lila consulted the bowl with a furrowed brow. She placed both her hands around it and pretended to glimpse something.

"Ah," she said, "I see a man coming into your life."

"That's *all* I need."

"You doubt the power of love?" Lila wiggled her eyebrows and made Kelly smile.

"I don't doubt the power of love," Kelly said. "It's the man I'm not so sure about."

"Ah, you young girls today. You mock the forces of the universe. There are changes coming that you cannot resist. They are stronger than you know. Lend me your palm. No, no. Your right hand."

"But I'm left-handed."

"Foolish girl. That makes no difference. Give me your right hand."

"But you're supposed to use the left one. I read it in a book on palmistry."

"Hush, child. You dabble in things you do not understand. Let me concentrate. This line here, it is peculiar. This is the line of life, and this other line follows it like a shadow. What does this mean? You lead a double life? Don't shiver, little one. There is nothing to be frightened of. It could mean a life companion, a soul mate who will come into your life. See how the two lines run together, here toward the wrist? I told you you will meet someone."

"I just saw Joe Delany again," Kelly said dryly. "I hope it's not him."

"What? No. Perhaps it is someone you have known a long time, and yet—" She looked genuinely puzzled.

"What is it? Lila? Come on, cut that out."

But Lila was serious. "Someone you know and yet you do not know," she said.

"Oh, great."

"Yes. Two souls who cannot recognize each other. But here, see? You come together at last." Lila smiled.

Kelly looked down at her own hand. "The lines come together," she said. "But look—they split apart again. What does that mean?"

"That is mysterious," Lila admitted. She peered closely for a minute and remained silent. Then her face turned red with embarrassment.

Kelly realized with a start that Lila had suddenly thought of James. Of course. Lila was cursing herself for coming up with this dumb story, so ridiculously, so painfully true. It wasn't the future she'd been reading. It was the past.

After a long moment, Lila lifted her face and looked at Kelly. There was an apology in her eyes, but she said nothing about James.

Kelly tried to smile. "I told you we should have read the left hand."

"Perhaps you're right," Lila whispered. But she fixed her friend with a hard stare, as if she suspected Kelly of concealing something from her. "Kelly? I mean it. The part about mocking the universe. There are forces at work you don't understand."

AS KELLY DANCED WITH DARL to a slow, romantic tune, she tried to dismiss her friend's predictions. Lila was taking her own play-acting a little too seriously, getting carried away. Yet some of the things Lila had said were disconcerting. A line that followed her own lifeline like a shadow? This was odd, especially since Kelly could almost feel another presence lately. Sometimes she sensed she was being watched. In her absent-minded state, she had misplaced so many things she was beginning to suspect some unseen hand was removing them from her house. James's hand? Had she really heard James's name over the telephone earlier this evening? Impossible.

She rested her head on Darl's shoulder. She knew what he would say. It was superstitious nonsense. There were no such things as ghosts. Her imagination was running wild again.

Sensible Darl. She squeezed his hand, and he responded with a warm smile. He was proud of her lately, and he was so relieved to see she was getting on with her life. She could never let him guess she wasn't perfectly fine.

ALTHOUGH THE PARTY WAS STILL going strong at midnight, Kelly was tired. She wanted to go home, but Darl insisted on sampling the buffet first.

"Don't you have an early shift tomorrow?" she asked.

"You have to eat," he said. "I'll get you a plate."

Years of experience had taught her there was no use arguing with Darl when he wanted to feed her. She waited, watching the dancers sway to the "Tennessee Waltz." The devil still danced with Marilyn Monroe, who pressed herself tightly against him. Kelly admired the authentic detail of her costume, the beauty mark, the famous sleeveless white dress and white pumps.

"Marilyn lives!" Sam commented, as he and Darl returned, laden with too much food.

"Well, sure," Darl joked. "It's Hallowe'en. The night the dead return to earth."

Without warning, Kelly felt the pain again, and she nearly dropped the plate he handed her. Darl, intent on refilling their wineglasses, didn't seem to notice. Kelly was grateful. She buried her head for a minute in her hands and tried to compose herself. *The night the dead return to earth.* The phrase echoed in her mind, blocking out the chatter of voices. *Return to earth. Return.*

No.

She couldn't indulge in this. She had to sit up, be sociable. Be sane.

When she raised her head, she was looking straight at the devil man, and he, it seemed, was looking straight at her. The music stopped for a moment, and he stood, long arms crossed, head to one side, as if regarding her with intense curiosity. But the mask obscured his expression completely, and when the next song began, he bent his attention once again on his dance partner.

"Let's go." Kelly tugged at Darl's sleeve.

He turned to her again. "Did you eat?"

"Yes," she lied. She pushed the plate out of sight.

DOWNTOWN WINNIPEG WAS EMPTY. Cold and deserted. Bits of litter flew through the wind tunnel of glass office buildings. A train rumbled into the station by the river. Kelly stared out the truck's window as they drove across the bridge into her neighborhood, St. Boniface. Across the black river, the long yellow cross of the hospital burned against the night sky. Beyond it, she could see the enormous round gap in the Cathedral's stone tower, where a long-ago fire had shattered the stained-glass window, leaving an empty stone ring that hung over St. Boniface like a dark moon.

They drove past the hospital, and as always Kelly couldn't help looking up into the windows of the east wing. The psychiatric ward. She shivered.

Darl reached across the front seat and took her hand. "Don't," he said gently. "Don't."

Chapter Three

Kelly was deep in a dream of James when the doorbell rang. James was turning in the air before her, slowly, displaying his scarred body. His neck was bent back and his arms hung loosely at his sides. Sunlight streamed from the sky, bleaching his skin, blinding her. She could see him lift his head. He moved his lips, speaking to her.

"James!" she called. "What are you saying?"

She heard her own voice. She was wide awake. Yet James continued to turn, his body becoming transparent until she could see right through him. Then he was gone. She was staring at the cracks in the ceiling. The doorbell rang again.

In a fog she opened the door for Angel and Alex.

"Hi, Auntie Kelly!" Alex threw his arms around her neck and proceeded to kiss her, first on one cheek, then the other. It was a ritual greeting she'd taught him when he was only two, and he never failed to remember it.

Alex settled himself in his favorite spot on the living-room rug, beside the shelf of colorful toy animals James had carved from wood. Alex loved to play with them, putting them through the motions of eating and sleeping and racing and fighting.

Kelly and Angel moved into the kitchen. Kelly brewed a pot of strong coffee. She needed to clear away the wisps of the vision that hung in her mind. While her back was turned, she heard the scrape of a wooden match, then smelled the strong, unmistakable scent of marijuana.

"Angel! Alex is here!"

"So I'll blow it outside," Angel said. She propped the window open a crack and leaned her forehead against the glass. "Darl said there was a break-in at the gallery."

"Yeah. Poor Sam."

"But you guys had a good time?"

"It was all right."

Angel smiled. "It's good to see you and Darl going out together. Finally."

"Well, it doesn't happen often." Kelly poured two cups and sat down across from her sister. "I don't see him—or Alex—much since I started working again."

Angel took one last toke and crushed the joint between her fingers. "You two should get together," she said.

Kelly sighed. She had heard this before.

"I mean it," said Angel. "What are you waiting for?"

"Angel, he's my brother-in-law."

"Not any more."

Kelly glanced away. "It wouldn't be right."

"Seems right to me." Angel shrugged. "What you guys been through, you should hang together. James'd want it."

What would Angel know about what James wanted? Kelly wondered. Angel didn't even know what she wanted herself any more. Didn't even know *how* to want, just how to need—a drink, a toke, a fight with Paul.

She watched her sister scratch at the dry skin on her elbow, then run her hands through her near brush-cut. She remembered when Angel's hair had been long and thick. Strawberry blonde. A pale version of their mother's hair, as Angel had always been a pale version of their mother.

Maggie Quirk.

Kelly could still describe her perfectly, although she had not seen her in four years.

As a child, Kelly had stood outside the downtown hotels describing her mother over and over again: the Brooklyn accent, the auburn hair that fell like flame across her freckled forehead, the color that bloomed high on her cheeks, as though she always had a fever. Have you seen her? Could you ask her to come out?

If Maggie was there, she usually came to the door willingly enough. She'd stand on the doorstep, squinting in the sunlight, while Kelly begged favors. Maggie would give her grocery money, or sign a note from school, and then she'd disappear again into the cool, dark prison of the pub. Kelly would return to the apartment, to the cleaning, to the cooking. To Angel.

Poor, sweet Angel. Kelly watched as her younger sister gazed out the window at the first snowfall of the year. The large white flakes drifted slowly through the air and Angel stared. As a child she had loved the snow, had clapped her hands in delight to see it fall. But there was no childlike wonder in her face now. Now she watched with a dull, hypnotized expression, her eyes vacant.

Alex interrupted the silence by running into the kitchen.

"Kelly, where's the dragon?" he asked urgently.

"It should be right there, with the others."

"But it's not! And it's my favorite!"

So they looked. But the little green dragon with spiked tail and webbed wings was lost.

Kelly questioned Alex, perhaps a little sharply. Had he taken it outside? Had he played with it in the garden? But Alex was adamant. He had never taken the dragon anywhere, he said. Kelly had already noticed the tiger missing, and the little spotted horse. It seemed that every time she dusted, there was one fewer member of the menagerie. Now the dragon. James's favorite.

"Well, don't worry. It'll turn up," she said.

"It'll turn up when you least expect it," Angel said.

Alex resigned himself to playing with the less exotic animals, and the sisters returned to the kitchen.

"How's Paul?" Kelly asked, trying to switch the subject.

"Crazy," said Angel. "Getting crazier."

Kelly thought about this for a while. "Violent?"

"No. Just ... weird." She looked at Kelly. "You know what he did?"

"What?"

"He bought a gun."

"Oh God! What in the world for?"

"Says he hears intruders. In the night. Says someone is out to get him—or me."

"That's just dangerous," Kelly said. "He could shoot someone by mistake. He could shoot you, for God's sake."

Angel laughed. "He's convinced we need protection. You know what he said?"

"What?"

"He said he never used a weapon when he, you know, when he used to, you know, break into places. But nowadays they all have them—kids with knives, climbing right through your window. Your friend Sam there, he could have been killed in that break-in."

"Well, you have to protect yourself," said Kelly. "But a gun!"

"I know. Crazier and crazier." Angel pulled a red thread from the tablecloth and wound it tightly around her finger until the fingernail turned white. Kelly looked at the ragged cuticles, the hangnails, and the sight made her angry.

"Well, look," she said. "I have to get moving. Sam wants me to help him clean up the gallery. Are you taking Alex home?"

"Yeah. Darl gets off at three. Do you mind if we stay here till then? Paul's in a hell of a mood today."

"Not at all," Kelly said. "Of course." She would have to talk to Darl about this, and soon. Alex would no longer be allowed in Angel's house, she was sure of that. Darl would certainly never allow Alex anywhere near a gun.

As she started the car, Kelly smiled, thinking of Darl's earnest approach to fatherhood. "Mr. Responsibility," James used to call him. And it fit. Darl had raised Alex all alone, and done a good job of it, though it hadn't been an easy road. When Diane left, Darl was forced to quit medical school. Now he juggled shifts as an intake worker at the clinic, night courses in pharmacy and, she thought guiltily, hundreds of little chores for herself and Angel. But he managed it all, and still had time for his son. Alex was thriving, healthy and happy. And he was so good it was almost unnatural. There weren't many men who could be loving, full-time parents. Or at least Kelly wouldn't know about it if there were.

She had never known her own father, except through Maggie's tales, which revolved solely around his striking looks, the blue eyes and coal-black hair Kelly had inherited. And Angel's father was a fading memory, indistinct in her mind from Maggie's other boyfriends. Angel's father had made his mark on their life by moving them from New York to Winnipeg—and then disappearing.

The only reliable male presence around her childhood home had been Darl himself. Darl had been Maggie's one and only faithful admirer. He had loved her from the moment he met her, when he was eleven years old and tumbled off his bicycle on the sidewalk in front of their apartment building. Maggie was sober that day, and in a mood to be sympathetic. Her hair shone red and gold in the summer light as she bent over the small boy, wrapping his scraped knee in her handkerchief, telling him how very brave he was.

From that day on, he was a frequent visitor at their apartment, helping Maggie hang out the laundry, sweeping the snow off the steps in the wintertime, walking the girls to school.

When he was only a high-school boy, he sometimes stayed with them all night, when Maggie went missing. When she came home drunk, it was Darl who spoke to her, helped her into bed, listened to her rambling tales of woe. Kelly could hear their voices, Maggie's harsh, bitter complaints and Darl's soft answers, through the wall of her bedroom where she lay comforting Angel. In the morning she'd find Darl asleep on the sofa, his usually neat clothes hopelessly wrinkled.

Eventually, Darl's infatuation with Maggie had turned to pity. But he remained loyal to the girls. Although he was only two years older than Kelly, he watched over her and Angel with a fatherly concern that they were grateful for. He spent almost as much time with her family as he did with his own.

Kelly had first come to understand why he did this when she visited Darl's house, a dark little bungalow at the end of the street behind the Cathedral. She slowed her driving now, as she passed in front of it on her way to the bridge. There was the sagging porch, where Adam had stood, smoking his foul cigars. There was the toolshed, its charred walls still standing.

She accelerated. Darl was right. There was no point living in the past. But she couldn't shake the memory of the afternoon she had first glimpsed her future husband in that yard. It was the first day of school, grade four, and she was waiting for Darl. She had been examining the spiderwebs strung across the windowpanes of the toolshed. There seemed to be hundreds of them, ancient and cloudy and tough as spun cotton. In the midst of the thick layers, a desiccated grasshopper lay on its back, as though resting in a hammock, stick legs folded across its chest. Fascinated, she moved closer, then let out a scream when a sudden movement behind the glass startled her. A small hand raised the burlap curtain in the window of the toolshed. A dark face behind the streaked and dusty glass appeared and was gone.

"Who was that?" she asked Darl, when he emerged from the bungalow.

"That's my brother, James," said Darl. They walked down the sidewalk, away from the house. He looked over his shoulder to make sure no one was listening. "He's grounded."

THE GALLERY STORAGE ROOM was in worse shape than she'd expected. Sam and Lila and several of their friends, including Joe Delany, were standing around in the entrance, just looking at everything. Crates had been turned over and some had burst open. Paintings had been ripped from the shelves and strewn around the room.

"Holy Mary," Kelly said, as she lifted an easel and revealed a demolished papier-mâché Madonna. "Did they take anything?"

"We don't know yet," Lila sighed. "After cleanup comes inventory. We just don't know where to start."

For a minute they all remained standing, staring at the confusion. Then Sam reached over and grasped the other end of the easel Kelly held.

"Might as well start here," he said.

They turned their attention to the papier-mâché figure. Her head was caved in, and one hand dangled, torn at the wrist.

For some time they all worked silently, letting out only the occasional curse when they came across something ruined.

"Who would *do* this?" Kelly wondered out loud.

"Some jealous artist," Joe suggested.

"Doing what?" asked Sam. "Trying to steal the secrets of my success? Ha!"

"Some nut case, probably," another friend said. "Just did it for no reason—mad at the world."

"Kids," said Lila. "Come Hallowe'en they'll smash up anything." She groaned. "So much work!"

It was late in the evening by the time Sam came up with a list, and it was surprisingly short. Missing were two boxes of jewelry, the petty-cash box, and a set of drawings. James's drawings.

"Those pictures he did of that crooked house," Sam said. "Remember, Lila? That series he was working on before he—" He stopped when he remembered Kelly was present.

But Kelly knew the drawings he meant. A crooked house with its front wall open like a doll's house. A demon hand, like a flame, slithering down around the roof, searching inside among the crooked furniture. Two small, twisted figures huddled beneath the stairs. The finest drawings her husband had ever made in his brief life.

"I've got to go," Kelly said. "Tired."

"I'll drive you," Joe offered.

"Thanks," Kelly said. "But I'm driving myself."

"Call me about *Hamlet*," Lila reminded her.

"Right," Kelly said.

Sam walked her out to her car. When they were out on the street, he asked how she was doing.

"I'm fine," she told him. She wasn't sure whether this was true or not.

"It takes a long time." He touched her shoulder. "I'm sorry about the drawings. But, you know, there are always going to be things that bring him back to mind."

Right, Kelly thought. Like breathing.

"We all miss him," he said.

"I know."

"The healing will continue to happen, Kelly. Have faith. You think it won't happen but it will. The mind is miraculous—a miraculous machine."

"It's a dangerous machine," she said. "Sometimes ..."

He waited. "What?"

Kelly wanted to talk, but felt something holding her back. Fear. It wasn't only that James was gone, it was everything. The silence on the telephone line, the dreams that were not dreams, the way that James's things were being lifted out of the world, beyond her grasp, as if all evidence of his life on earth was vanishing.

"I don't know," she said. "Just—the mind can play tricks, you know?"

"I know. You mean James?"

"Well, his mind—but mine too, sometimes. Sometimes I'm scared."

"We all get scared," Sam said softly. But it was small comfort.

"Thanks, Sam. I'll see you."

She drove home slowly. What in the world was going on? Were James's drawings so valuable that someone would steal them? He had died so young; surely they weren't worth that much money. Who would want them, besides Sam or herself?

Or James.

If she told Sam that, he'd think she was going off the deep end again.

She walked up the dark sidewalk and entered her house, feeling very alone. There was no one she could talk to. No one she could tell. She thought again of that mummified grasshopper swinging in its transparent shroud. She pictured herself suspended there, paralyzed, the thick white membrane of the web closing slowly over her throat.

IT HAD BEEN A LONG TIME since he had stood outside her house like this, looking in. He saw the hall light go on, then the living room, then the kitchen. She had a habit of peeking into every room when she came home alone, especially at night. Especially when she was agitated. And she was pretty agitated these days.

She turned on the lamp in the bedroom, a soft red glow. He could see her moving toward the closet, placing something on her bed. Probably a nightgown. She went into the bathroom and he waited.

He was good at waiting. He should be good at it. He should be a regular expert on waiting by now. A Zen master. He chuckled to himself. Master of nothing, master of absences. Silence and shadows. Disappearances.

The bathroom light went out, then the living room. She was walking through the house, turning them off, one by one. Nothing now but the glow from the red bedroom lampshade. She took off her sweater and began to unbutton her blouse, and then she stopped. She walked to the window and drew the curtains closed. He could see nothing more.

He stayed there in the lane until the bedroom light, too, was extinguished. Then he sighed. He wished he could go home to sleep, but he couldn't sleep any more. He had become a creature of the night.

IN THE DREAM, JAMES STOOD TALL and naked in the sun. She could see him clearly, though he was far above her on a rocky cliff that reached up past the clouds. The sun was gleaming on his shoulders, and then suddenly he was diving and she was falling with him, all the long way down, heart in her throat, and she was awake, her head pounding, blood rushing in her ears, sitting straight up, staring in the darkness.

Yes, the mind was a miraculous and dangerous machine. Although she had never seen James at the edge of that cliff, the image was clear as a photograph, imprinted on her imagination. The forest, the river, the rocks.

James's compact, muscled body.

She still felt drawn to that body, though it no longer existed. James had hard, wiry arms and strong hands that could pitch a baseball with lightning speed or strum a guitar with easy grace. She had loved to touch him, skimming every surface of his body, while he told the tale of every childhood scar, the four small circles on his belly, where he'd fallen on a garden rake, the stripes across his back, where the branches caught him when he fell out of the crabapple tree, seven years old. She touched his eyelids, his collarbone, ankles, the high arch of his foot....

Kelly leaned over and turned on her bedside lamp. Why would the past not leave her alone?

Because early one morning, a year ago last June, James had thrown away his body, as if he owned it, as if it were his to dispose of as he wished.

Against her will, she lay in her empty bed and remembered, once again, the terrible events of the time James left her.

Chapter Four

The first signs of James's breakdown went unnoticed. Kelly was in New York that winter almost four years ago, working on the set of *Rising Heat* with Lila, while James stayed in Winnipeg, preparing for his first show at Sam's gallery. He was only twenty-three, young to be exhibiting his work, but Sam had faith in him.

Kelly and James had never parted before. The intensity of their relationship shocked their friends and family. "You'll starve to death," Darl cautioned, when they married so young. Even Angel, hardly the model of responsible living, told Kelly dryly that a person couldn't live on love. But the two lovers were lucky. On Sam's recommendation, James won a scholarship to the School of Art, where he quickly built a reputation as a gifted and promising student. Kelly apprenticed in costume design with the local theaters, and when she had enough experience, Lila began to take her on out-of-town assignments. The New York trip was Kelly's opportunity to break into the lucrative world of movies, and she was determined to make the most of it. She would miss James, but they both agreed it was worth it.

At first James called her every evening, full of news about his work, about friends and family, Darl's progress at university and his hopes of entering medical school. He kept her informed of the antics of their two nephews, baby Allan and two-year-old Alex. Kelly responded with gossip about the rich and famous. She had never encountered such self-important people as these movie stars. And she complained about her mother, Maggie, who had chosen this particular time to come back to New York and expected Kelly to help her find an apartment.

But gradually the phone calls became depressing and repetitive. James missed her, wanted her to come home. Often he had little else to say. Then one evening he appeared on the front stoop of her Manhattan apartment, unshaven and incoherent. He often became distraught when he worked too intensely, she told herself. He was just tired. But James could not sleep. He clung to her all through the night.

The next day he showed up on the movie set, disrupting everything, insisting Kelly come home with him. She refused. She was angry. First he had kept her up all night, and now he was making a scene. She told him to leave, but this only made things worse. James began to shout at her, declaring for all to hear that she didn't love him any more. A couple of the stage-hands had to toss him off the set.

Kelly was mortified. For the rest of the day she worked with her head down, avoiding eye contact with the cast and crew. That night she came home to find a letter of apology from James. He was exhausted, he said; the strain of his upcoming show was killing him. He was sorry. He had gone back to Winnipeg and hoped she would forgive him.

"It's a sweet letter," Lila agreed, when Kelly let her read it. "But something is definitely wrong with that boy."

James seldom telephoned after that. Sam reported that he wasn't working. He was drinking every day. He couldn't finish anything, and finally the show had to be canceled. Then one night James drank a fifth of whiskey, swallowed a bottle of pills, and drove Paul's motorcycle straight through the plate-glass window of a car dealership on Portage Avenue.

Kelly returned to Winnipeg immediately.

She remembered with anguish the terrible sense of betrayal she felt at that first suicide attempt. That James could take his beautiful body, the body that belonged to her, and just break it like that enraged her. All the way home on the plane, she imagined what she would say to him, how she would punish him. But when she arrived, she was not allowed to see James. She was allowed to see only Dr. Chartrand.

Dr. Leon Chartrand was a bony, nervous man, with long braids of black hair, very young for a psychiatrist. He had been brought to the hospital from the Riverside Clinic, on a psychiatric consult because of his specialty. But Kelly didn't know, then, what his specialty was.

Dr. Chartrand was kind but unshakably strict. James was in a state of exhaustion, he said. He would need at least two weeks of complete rest. No visitors. Not even Kelly.

"I'm his wife," she argued. "I have a right to see him. I have a right to know how he is."

"His physical condition is good," the doctor said. "Beyond that, I can't discuss this case with you. I hope you can understand, Ms. Quirk, that your husband is going through an extremely difficult time. We need to respect his wishes."

"*His* wishes?"

Leon Chartrand nodded. "He's refusing all visitors. He doesn't want to see you," he said.

Kelly didn't believe it.

BUT IT WAS TRUE. Two weeks turned into four, and Kelly was frantic with worry and confusion. She was living alone for the first time in her life, and James was living in the east wing of St. Boniface Hospital. Every day she walked over and stared up at the windows of the psychiatric ward. Every day she asked to see him and was refused. Every day she returned home alone.

When Allan died in his crib, and Angel turned into a zombie, Kelly had no one to turn to. While Angel berated herself endlessly for her baby's death, Kelly tried to reassure her she was blameless. But she saw in Angel's eyes her own sense of guilt. She had failed to read the warning signs. She had been blind to the one person she loved more than life itself.

Finally, James agreed to see her. Leon Chartrand summoned Kelly to appear in his office. Against her protests, he insisted on being present at the meeting.

Kelly threw her arms around James when he walked into the office. She felt the sharp bones of his rib cage against her breasts. He smelled of disinfectant. What had they done to him? She wanted to take him out of there that second, bathe him and feed him and bring him back to himself. But it wasn't going to be that simple.

James held her lightly. He patted her back the way an absent-minded parent might comfort a small child. He disengaged himself from her arms and said, "I'm sorry."

For the first time in their life together, Kelly sensed that James was far, far away from her. He knew something, had seen something, without her.

"Where have you been?" she whispered.

"I've been—like—in hell." It was no ordinary use of the word. He meant it. The real place, the fire that burns and gives no light.

"Tell me," she said.

James shook his head. "I'm not taking you down there."

"I'm going down anyway."

A long silence. Then James reached out his hand. Not to Kelly, but to Leon.

Leon closed his hand around James's hand so tightly she could see the veins stand out in his forearm. They gripped each other. Leon told him to breathe deeply. He said, "It's safe here. Go ahead. Speak to her."

And so she stepped down into the underworld with James.

Is that where he was coming from now? The underworld, where shadows singe the skin and there is no sky?

Kelly got out of bed, although the sun had not yet risen. She moved through the house, turning on all the lights, as if to chase away the specter of her husband.

Why was he returning now? He appeared every night in her dreams and would not always leave her when she woke. It seemed he was trying to tell her something. But what could possibly be left to tell? When James was alive, he had told her everything. She'd held him in her arms as she listened to everything. She listened until her throat filled up with bile, with flame. She had followed him down, she thought, every step of the treacherous way.

The stories came slowly at first. James related them to her in a detached voice. After Kelly had left for New York, he had been plagued by nightmares. He dreamed his father, Adam, was chasing him, and he woke shaking with dread. He dreamed continually of Adam threatening to cut off his head with a sword. Fearing for his sanity, James fled to New York City.

Where Kelly turned him away.

When James started to suspect the dreams were actual memories, he wanted to end his life. But instead of killing him, the motorcycle crash was his salvation. It led him to Leon, and Leon helped him to face the truth. It was all true. All the dreams were true, even the one about the sword. As Kelly's stomach churned, James and Leon explained to her that Adam had done it all. He had kept his youngest son in a constant state of terror. Because when Darl was out of the house, when Eleanor was sleeping, Adam would have his way with James.

Lying in bed with Kelly, James moved her hand across the four small scars on his belly. "He pinned me against the toolshed wall with a pitchfork," he said. "My father told the doctor I fell on a rake. My mother believed it. Darl believed it." He looked in her eyes, tears beading his lashes. "How did I come to believe it, too?" he whispered.

He was bewildered by the workings of his own mind, that miraculous, dangerous machine. How could he have layered over the story of his life with another story, so carefully matched that the seams never showed?

It was repression, Leon explained. Deep repression. Unable to handle the memory of the abuse, James let it sink into his subconscious mind, disguised it in dreams, tried to blot it out with alcohol. But it all returned with a vengeance as soon as he was vulnerable.

Without asking, Kelly knew what had made him vulnerable. She had abandoned him when he needed her most.

THAT SUMMER BLURRED into an endless series of visits to the hospital. Kelly spent every evening she could with James, listening to the stream of memories that surfaced with sickening speed. She didn't want to hear it, but she listened. James needed her help.

Kelly needed help, too. But there was no one she could talk to. James made her promise that she would keep the most shameful details confidential, and she wouldn't have dreamed of betraying his trust. Everyone was told that James was having a "nervous breakdown," a vague term, but they all accepted it. No one was terribly surprised. James had always been intense, unstable. "High-strung," Maggie had called him.

Darl was engrossed in his own problems, the pressures of school, a small toddler and a wife who was rarely at home. He began to realize Diane was seeing someone else, and he channeled all his energy into keeping his family together.

Diane visited James often. Kelly was always uneasy when she arrived at the hospital to find Diane there, holding James's hand. Leon said this was a good sign. James needed to let go of his obsession with secrecy. It would not only help James, it would also relieve some of the burden from Kelly. But Kelly felt strangely jealous. Of course she wanted the burden lightened. Yet she was also reluctant to share James with anyone. She was especially disturbed when Diane sat in on their private sessions with Leon.

One day, James revealed, his mother told him Darl was dead; Adam had killed him because he wouldn't cooperate. She showed James the heart of a calf and said it was his brother's heart. Adam would kill James, too, if he didn't behave. James believed that story for two whole days. Two days of terror. And Eleanor let him believe it. When Darl finally walked in the door, she had merely laughed.

"God!" Diane began to sob, and James embraced her. Kelly and Leon watched in silence while they rocked in each other's arms. Diane's breath came in hard little gasps. "Where was Darl?" she asked. "Where *was* he?"

Kelly knew exactly where Darl had been. At her place, teaching Angel how to tie her shoelaces, helping Kelly with the housework, oblivious to the sadistic games that were played out in his absence, in his own house.

Leon thanked Diane for coming. Family support was crucial, he said, and difficult to get. Family members were usually deep in denial, especially if, like Darl, they had never suspected the abuse. Diane could not convince Darl to come to the sessions. "He just can't handle it yet," she said, eyes full of tears. "He won't even talk about it."

But Darl did talk about it to Kelly. He was deeply concerned about the situation, though he concentrated his concern more on Kelly than on James.

"He's wearing you out, Kell. You're so involved with him you can't see straight. You're too involved. You always have been." He sighed heavily. "Artistic temperament," he said ironically. "That's one thing you two have in common. James was always freaking out over something. I had to hold his hand. He used to cry, for Christ's sake, every time Dad raised his voice. He never learned to stay out of Dad's way and they—he and Dad—just didn't get along."

"Didn't get *along*!" Kelly cried.

"Okay. Okay." Darl held up his hand. "I admit it. Dad just plain did not like him. Dad was a bastard, if the truth be told. He had a mean streak. I barely speak to him myself. But James is . . . he's still obsessed with it."

Kelly thought about Leon's comments on denial. Don't try to force it, he'd said. Don't expect the family to believe it, not all at once, if ever. If the truth was too painful to face, he warned, Darl might turn away from James entirely. Kelly couldn't risk that.

"James has got to let it go," Darl said.

James, however, could not let it go. He was released from hospital, but it was weeks before he was able to stop telling the horrible stories of abuse that consumed him. Kelly listened and listened until she felt she couldn't listen any more. The stories came so thick and fast, and they were sometimes so bizarre she began to think he was making them up, hallucinating. He woke from terrible nightmares, crying and moaning in shame, not letting Kelly near him.

Then, almost as suddenly as they had started, the hysterical episodes eased off. James cut back on his sessions with Leon. The stories stopped. Kelly was getting her husband back, the man she'd fallen in love with, the strong one. Her love was healing him, he said, and she believed it.

James emerged into the upper world again. Light and air. He bought new art supplies and began to draw for the first time in ages. He junked the work he had been planning for the show and began instead the series of dark drawings of the house, the torture chamber. He was working out his pain through his art, and it was a healthy sign.

"James is an artist; he needs to express himself in images," Leon said. "The talking cure can go only so far."

Kelly was relieved. She was heartily sick of the talking cure.

"THE TALKING CURE," Darl said doubtfully. "Repressed memories. I don't know, Kell. I've been looking into it, reading up on it at school. It's called false memory syndrome. The therapist looks for abuse. He wants to find it, therefore he finds it. They put the patient in a hypnotic trance, they give them drugs. Chartrand had James on Valium, didn't he? And when they're highly susceptible, the therapists plant these ideas in their heads."

"But James remembers everything in such detail."

"That in itself is suspicious, don't you think? You know yourself those details are fantastic. Diane told me some of them. That one about the calf's heart is right out of a book of fairy tales we had in the house. *Snow White*. And the sword? Right out of King Arthur. James was always freaked by those tales of knights and dragons and damsels in distress."

"Those old stories scared him?"

"Everything scared him," Darl said. "He was hopelessly suggestible. And Chartrand played on that. Most of those stories—they're cobbled together from the bits and pieces of my brilliant little brother's vivid imagination."

Kelly reserved judgment. She was never sure if James's memories were true or false. But to be honest, she didn't care much about the theoretical side of things. The point was, Leon had cured her husband.

LIFE WAS GOOD AGAIN for James and Kelly. Angel reached a certain point of recovery, gaining a tenuous hold on reality. She would probably never be herself again, but at least Kelly was no longer afraid she would die from grief. Paul dealt with his son's death in his own way, retreating into silence, spending hours alone in the basement with his tapes and his recording equipment.

Then it was Darl's turn to suffer. Diane, who couldn't seem to handle the responsibilities of motherhood, took off to New York to stay with Maggie, whom she viewed as a kind of mother-in-law. This move irritated Kelly and Angel. Maggie was never available for her own daughters, yet she welcomed Diane with open arms. Darl was optimistic, though. He saw Diane's trip as a sure sign her affair was over. He never discovered who the man was, but he was so relieved he didn't care. Despite the added workload it meant for him, Darl approved of Diane's "vacation."

Then Maggie called. "You better get your ass down here," she told Darl. "Your wife is stepping out with another man." It was the wrestler. Diane had met him in Maggie's neighborhood bar. He was a friend of Maggie's, but when Diane started staying out all night with him, Maggie's loyalty to Darl took over.

"You better take some time off and come down here and straighten out your marriage," Maggie ordered.

"I can't, Mags," Darl said. "I have exams. Try to talk some sense into her, will you?"

At the Christmas break, he flew to New York, while James and Kelly took Alex into their home. Darl left with high hopes, armed with photographs of Alex. But in January, he returned in defeat. His marriage was over, he admitted. Diane didn't want him, and she didn't want Alex. She was moving in with the wrestler, the "Hooded Slicer," or whatever his name was, and if Darl wanted to file for divorce, he could go ahead.

When Diane left him, Darl seemed to fall apart. He found single parenthood impossibly hard at first. He neglected his studies and finally dropped out of school entirely. Kelly was full of sympathy for him, but James was cool toward Darl, almost cold sometimes.

"What you need is a job," James told his brother. "Get out of the house. They need someone over at the Riverside Clinic, you know. You should go down and apply."

Kelly wished James and Darl could be more empathetic. She didn't understand their attitude toward each other.

"Men!" Angel commented. "Tough guys. Paul's the same."

Kelly could only sigh in answer. But she had to admit, finally, that James was right. Darl took the job answering phones at the clinic, and it seemed to do him good. Gradually, Darl regained his good humor, and the two brothers came to an uneasy truce. They resumed their regular fishing trips with Sam and Paul. Sometimes they took Kelly out to the clubs, where they took turns dancing with her. But more often they stayed home. Darl and James would sit hunched over the chessboard for hours at a time, while Kelly played with Alex. She was content. She had her two men back. Three, if she wanted to count Alex.

Kelly had one whole year of happiness.

Then suddenly, everything exploded in one horrible night.

IN THE EARLY HOURS of the morning on the day of James and Darl's last fishing trip, James left the house while Kelly was sleeping and committed an unspeakable act.

While Adam lay passed out, drunk, in his usual place on his living-room sofa, James crept inside the bungalow, sprinkled the upholstery with lighter fluid, and lit a match. The fire spread quickly. The couch cushions caught, and then the blankets, and then Adam's shirt. By the time the smoke alarm went off, Adam's entire upper body was in flames. The neighbors reported that Eleanor ran out of the house, the sleeves of her nightgown on fire, screaming for help. She was unable to lift Adam's heavy body from its burning bed.

When James left the burning house at dawn, he drove directly to his brother's place, picked him up as planned, and then proceeded to pick up Paul and Sam. The four friends traveled east into Ontario, with James silent all the way.

When they found a campsite, James left Paul and Sam to pitch the tents and gather firewood. He took Darl aside and confessed what he had done. Then he hiked off through the woods, higher and higher above the river, until he was standing at the peak of a high, thin waterfall, far above the rapids.

Kelly could picture him there, could not stop picturing him there. She had heard three versions of the event, from the three men who witnessed it, each from a different angle down below. Each version was the same. James had roared like a wounded animal. One final cry of rage and despair. His startled companions had turned and looked up. Too late. James had already jumped. All they saw was a glimpse of the falling body, brief as a flash.

Everyone agreed he was dead. "Every bone in his body must have been broken," Sam said. "Crushed by the rocks at the bottom of the falls," Paul said. "Washed out to the lakes," Darl said.

All Kelly knew was that he was gone. Despite her love for him, the so-called healing power of her love, he had stood up there and let his shame win, just let himself go. Never to be found. Father and son in hell together.

EXCEPT ADAM SURVIVED.

Adam walked with a limp now, and his reconstructed jaw would always bear a patch of yellow, grafted skin. But he would never admit that James was responsible. At the inquest he refused to implicate his son. As far as Adam was concerned, the whole ugly incident had never happened. The fire was an accident. James died of some vague, natural cause. Or James was only gone, not dead. "Since Jimmy disappeared," he'd say, as though his son were simply lost and would return.

In Kelly's weakest moments, she believed this too.

Chapter Five

Alex was excited. All the way home from school he held tightly to a large paper bag and wouldn't let Kelly look inside it until they got home. Then he could conceal his news no longer.

"I have something to tell you, Auntie Kelly," he said, as he tracked snow into the kitchen.

"Hold on," Kelly said. "Give me your stuff and take your boots off." She'd come to Darl's house to make dinner and babysit while he attended his evening pharmacy class, and she was looking forward to it. She knew she needed to be around people, people she loved, to get her mind off its recent morbid fascination with the past.

Alex handed her his lunch box and a fistful of crumpled papers. She smoothed them out and looked at his latest drawing. In crayon, he'd made the figure of a boy standing under an apple tree beside a bright yellow house. A sun beamed down. Red apples hung from the tree. The boy was almost as large as the house. He gazed out of the picture with a comically stoic expression in his eyes, one hand behind his back, the other across his mouth.

"This is nice," Kelly said, following him out into the hall. "What's the boy doing?"

"That's me," said Alex. He tried, and failed, to hang up his coat. The hook was too high. "Guess what?"

"What?"

"There's going to be a show at school, at Christmastime, and Mrs. Chan says I get to be the magician."

"A magician! Wow!"

"Yeah, and I have tricks and everything." He held up the paper bag.

"Show me."

Alex ran to his room to prepare while Kelly put away his things, fastening the picture to the fridge with a magnet. She wanted to finish getting the meal ready, because Darl would be home soon, and he'd have less than an hour to eat before his night class. By the time Alex returned, she had slipped a macaroni and cheese casserole into the oven.

Alex performed magic tricks while they waited for Darl. Most of them were simple card tricks, and he managed to do about half of them correctly. He also had a tiny magic box that he used to make things disappear. He performed this over and over, with a quarter, a marble, a key, and one of Kelly's earrings.

When Darl arrived, he sneaked up behind Kelly and laid his freezing hands on her neck, making her scream.

"Ack! Get your cold hands off me! Grow up!"

Darl laughed and bent to tease Alex instead, tickling his tummy. Alex shrieked and ran from the room.

"He's happy," Darl remarked, as he hung up his jacket.

"I think he's glad to have me here when he gets home," Kelly said. She had been the most constant woman in Alex's life, she realized. Last year, when she'd been too depressed to work, Darl had paid her to care for Alex every day. Alex had kept her from sinking too far into her own grief. And Darl had kept her from sinking into poverty.

"I've missed him," she said, "since I've been working again."

"He misses you, too," Darl said simply. "So do I."

Kelly smiled at him. "You know I appreciate everything you did for me last year, Darl. Everything you do for me. I don't know where I'd be without you, but …"

"Fortunately for you," he said, grinning, "you'll never have to find out."

"But I'm glad to be back on my feet."

"Yeah?" He began to set the table. "What are you working on now?"

"Well …" Kelly hesitated. "Lila might have a job for me. A big one."

"Doing what?"

"Shakespeare. My all-time favorite. I might get a chance to do *Hamlet*."

"That's great." But he sounded skeptical. Perhaps he didn't think she was ready for it.

"*Hamlet: Prince of Denmark*," Kelly emphasized, trying to stir up his enthusiasm. She tried to sound confident. "The most brilliant play in the world."

"*Out, out brief candle*," Darl quoted.

"No. No. That's *Macbeth*."

"Whatever," said Darl. He laughed. He went to find Alex.

"HOW'S ANGEL?" DARL ASKED, as they were finishing their dinner.

"Oh. Angel." Kelly ladled more green beans onto Alex's plate, and Alex quickly hid them underneath his macaroni. "Paul is, you know …" She rolled her eyes at Darl and touched a finger to her temple.

"I know." Darl shook his head. "I don't know what's going on with him these days."

"He was always strange," Kelly said. "Ever since he got out of J-A-I-L."

Alex looked up, aware that he was being left out of something.

"Well, at least he's quit that," Darl said.

"I wouldn't be so sure," Kelly said. "You know what he's gone and bought?"

"What?"

"For 'protection,' or so he says."

"What are you talking about?" Darl asked.

"Daddy!"

"G-U-N," Kelly spelled. Behind Alex's back, she mimed aiming and pulling a trigger. Darl stared.

"I'm magic, Daddy," Alex said.

Darl continued to stare at Kelly. She nodded slowly.

"I can make a quarter disappear," Alex said.

"You can, can you?" Darl murmured, distracted. He had not taken his eyes off Kelly.

Alex could tell he wasn't listening. He lifted his fork and looked at his father through the tines. "I could make you disappear," he said.

"Honey, go get into your pajamas," Kelly said. "I'll read you a story."

"And brush your teeth," Darl added.

When they were alone again, Darl asked, "When did he get a *gun*? Jesus."

"A few days ago, I think. He's always been paranoid, but now I'm afraid he's really going off the deep end."

"If only she'd get away from him," Darl said. "Can't you talk to her?"

"It's no use," Kelly said. "And you know it. She stuck by him when he got arrested, and nothing we could say—"

"Yes, but she was nineteen then! And pregnant! There is no reason now for her to stick around. Jesus, he might shoot her!"

"That's what I said," Kelly told him. "She just laughed it off."

Darl stood up and began to pace. "She's out of her skull," he said.

"Hey!"

"Well, it's true. Anyway, look, I have to get to class. I'll be home by eleven."

He gathered his boots and slung on his jacket. Kelly watched him walk to his truck, shaking his head in annoyance. She didn't want to worry him. He had enough on his mind, but she'd had to tell him. It was a matter of Alex's safety, after all.

ALEX CHOSE *SNOW WHITE* for his bedtime story, and as usual he kept interrupting with questions. Were there really poison apples? Was that why Daddy threw away his Hallowe'en apples? Was there really such a thing as a magic mirror that could talk to a person?

"I don't think so," Kelly said patiently. "I've never seen one. This is just a story."

"I think there could be," he said. Kelly raised her eyebrows doubtfully. Alex nodded and nodded, his eyelids heavy. "I think there might be a mirror like that. We could have one in our house."

"That would be something," Kelly said. "I'd like to see that."

"You can't," he said. He shook his head sadly. He was so tired he could barely keep his eyes open.

"How about we finish this story tomorrow, okay?"

"Okay." He reached up and placed his small hands on her head. He pulled her face close and kissed both of her cheeks, one after the other.

"Good night, sweet."

"Good night, Auntie Kelly."

She turned off the light.

"I don't mind the dark," Alex said. "I don't mind it when you're here."

"Sleep tight," she whispered. She left the door open, so that the hall lamp would be visible, in case he woke in the night.

Kelly washed the dishes, vacuumed the living room, and put away Alex's toys. She made herself a cup of tea and looked around for something to read. Darl was not a big reader, so there wasn't much to choose from. Old textbooks. Diseases of the brain. Yuck. Car manuals. She picked up a movie magazine and leafed through it, finding an interview with Michael Black. Here was something she should read if she was going to be working with him. But it wasn't very informative. He gave stock answers to every question, dodging anything personal. Well trained by his publicity agent. She turned to the movie reviews, but they were boring, too. She yawned, wishing she'd brought along some sewing. She carried her tea into Darl's room. Maybe there was a book by his bed.

Lying open and face down on the pillow was a library book. *The Truth about Haunted Houses* by Jerry Pryne, Ph.D. What was he reading this for? She lay down, flicked on the bedside lamp, and opened the book to the spot where Darl had left off. "In cases of trauma," she read, "the energy of the psyche is unable to move on into death. Failing to separate from the body, it may hover near the grave site. This is why so many sightings occur in cemeteries. In cases of severe distress, however, the psychic energy may remain at the place of the traumatic incident, unable to leave the scene of the crime, as it were. This is the cause of most house hauntings. In fact, in seventy-five percent . . ." Kelly flipped through the pages, fascinated, until another sentence caught her eye. "In rare cases," continued Jerry Pryne, Ph.D., "the spirit may fixate on an individual, following the person from place to place, as if unable to tear itself away. Through historical research, we were able to ascertain that these incidents almost always involved a sense of unfinished business. The spirit lingers for a number of reasons, chief among them love, warning, or revenge. In the event of a painfully sudden death . . ." Kelly stared at the words, transfixed. *Love, warning, revenge.* Was James returning to warn her of something?

If so, he was being very cryptic about it.

Hungrily, she rifled through the book, searching for some answer. But she found nothing to explain the strange events of her own life, though she read until her vision blurred, the pages hit her face, and she was asleep.

THROUGH THE SLIGHTLY PARTED CURTAINS, the lamplight illuminated the reflection of her slender figure in the large mirror over the dresser. She lay partially on her side, the rise of one hip visible above her slightly bent knees. He couldn't see her features, though he drifted as close as he dared to the window. Her black hair had fallen across her face. Like a black waterfall, he thought. He imagined the heavy, silky texture of that hair between his fingers, imagined gathering it into a thick rope and twisting it around his wrist, pulling her gently toward him.

She slept. Unlike him, she could always sleep, no matter what disturbed her during the day. Her patterns were regular. No matter what happened, she followed her routines. Well. He would change all that. He watched carefully, trying to detect the rise and fall of her breathing. Yes. She was breathing evenly, steadily. Other than that, she did not move. She slept the sleep of the dead.

The wind picked up, and the snow that had descended so softly earlier that evening was whipped into hard little pellets that bounced as they beat against the frozen ground. The temperature was dropping rapidly. But he did not feel the cold. He stayed watching her for several minutes. Then, as a car slowed at the curb, he slipped into the shadows, out of range of the headlights.

WHEN KELLY WOKE, Darl was sitting beside her on the bed.

"Oh. I didn't hear you come in. Is Alex still sleeping?"

"Like a baby." Darl brushed the long hair out of Kelly's

eyes as she sat up. "He loves having you around," he said. "He really misses having a mother." He pulled her to him and wrapped his arms around her. She sat still, her eyes open, watching their reflection in the mirror. She could see her own face over Darl's shoulder, his broad back, his unruly, tobacco-colored hair. The illusion of herself in her husband's arms again. Her body grew tense.

Darl held her for a few seconds more, then gave up and released her.

"What's wrong?"

"I don't know. Just . . ."

"Hey. Can't I even hug you any more?"

Flustered, Kelly stood quickly and began to tidy up, gathering her untouched cup of tea, now cold, and the book about ghosts. "By the way," she said, "what are you reading this for?"

Darl looked embarrassed. "Oh, just for fun," he said.

"Do you believe in that stuff?"

"Nah. Do you?"

"No way."

They both laughed, nervously.

KELLY TRIED TO KEEP HER HEAD down against the bitter wind and at the same time keep a look out around her. Darl always warned her to be alert when walking alone after dark, even in their own neighborhood, even on this short walk home from his house. When she glanced behind her, a blast of arctic air swept into her face, making her eyes tear. She quickened her pace and reached her own street with relief.

But as she was turning the key in her lock, she sensed a dark shape move across the yard. She turned her head. Something fluttered around the corner of the house. She stood still, unwilling to call out.

Finally, she opened the door and stepped inside. The lilacs rustled, as if someone was brushing past the bushes that surrounded the house. The branches tapped against the back-room window and then fell still. She listened, watching her own shadow glide across the walls as the headlights of a passing car shone through the room.

The rustling grew louder. It was not the lilacs. It was definitely coming from inside the house. The back room. Someone was in the back room, shuffling through her papers. The papers rustled at intervals, as if someone was searching through them, pausing now and then to read.

She reached inside the kitchen drawer for a weapon. The bread knife? No, she couldn't. She chose a hammer instead and slid quietly across the linoleum. She flattened herself against the wall beside the door, hammer in her left hand, ready to defend herself.

Nothing happened.

No breathing, no footsteps. Only the eerie sensation of cold air, as if some deathly presence had entered the house. She braced herself, peered around the corner, and saw that the room was empty.

Papers were scattered all over the desk and on the floor. As she stood watching, a gust of wind sent the curtains billowing into the room. The frigid breeze lifted one page gently, sent it floating through the air to land at her feet. She closed the window. She picked up all the papers and piled them back on the desk, weighing them down with the clay flowerpot that Alex had made for her last Christmas.

Stupid. That book must have rattled her more than she realized.

It's just the wind, she said to herself as she undressed. Just the wind.

It wasn't until she'd settled in bed that she remembered closing every window before she left the house.

Chapter Six

Kelly had just returned from a fabric sale and was putting away her purchases when the telephone rang.

"Hello?" She was still nervous about answering the phone, although she had tried to convince herself the call on Hallowe'en was just some weird mistake. Crossed wires, her imagination.

"James Grayton," the voice said.

"What? Who is this?"

There was a soft click, then the words, "Work on what has been spoiled."

"Who is this?"

Another soft click, then that white noise again.

"Who is this?" she begged. "Who *is* it?"

But she knew it was her husband's voice. Her husband's words.

The line hung open, and she remained listening to the distant rushing sound.

She hung up, wondering if she was dreaming. No. There were her packages from the fabric store, there was her coat, where she had laid it across the chair, a light film of snow just beginning to melt on the shoulders.

Work on what has been spoiled. She knew the phrase. It was a hexagram from the *I Ching*, the Chinese Book of Changes that James used to consult every morning. Was he sending her some kind of message?

She hurried to the bedroom and pulled out the book and the small tin box in which James kept the three Chinese coins he used to toss to read his fortune. She flipped frantically through the table of contents. *Work on what has been spoiled.* The Chinese symbol was *ku*, the image of decay, worms breeding in a bowl of corrupted matter. The text spoke of guilty actions and neglect—

God!

She closed her eyes. Worms. Decay. She felt a sob rising in her chest. Was he speaking to her from his unmarked grave? For a long time, she sat on the edge of the bed, doubled over in pain. James had believed in the power of the *I Ching* to guide his life, to help him make decisions. Perhaps she should throw the coins herself, right now. See if they would offer any answers, any wisdom.

She opened the tin box and felt only a dull, almost expected sense of shock when she saw it was empty.

The coins were gone.

At least five or six of the little animals were missing. James's silver cigarette case was missing. A few of his smaller paintings were nowhere to be found. Worst of all, his pocket watch, the one she had bought herself and had engraved for him, had disappeared right out of her own jewelry box. Surely she wasn't this absent-minded.

The lost items were not random. Every one was intimately connected to her life with James. Every one had brought back memories when she saw it about the house. Now it seemed as if she had been sentenced not only to lose him, but to lose every reminder of him as well.

Tears gathered behind her eyes. So many things had vanished.

The way his body had vanished. Although Darl led the search party down the steep banks of the river where they all saw James plunge into the water, they found nothing. Not a shoe or a scrap of clothing. Just a scar near the top of the cliff, where he had scraped the clay on his way down. The water, the rapids, had swept him away, washed the earth clean of him.

The waterfall. As she drifted into sleep that night, it appeared in her dreams as a place of tremendous power. Magnetic force. One of the doorways to the other world. The world of darkness, where shadows burn and twist.

"I'M LEAVING FOR MINNEAPOLIS Tuesday," Lila said when she called first thing in the morning. "Have you signed your contract yet?"

"I haven't even met Taylor Grant yet," Kelly confessed.

"Didn't you meet him at the Hallowe'en party?"

"Never saw him. Was he there?"

"Yeah. With his whole entourage." Lila laughed. "Sorry. Guess I was too busy practicing my 'black arts' to introduce you around. But hasn't he called you?"

"I haven't spoken to him." Kelly was hedging. Taylor had left a message on her machine two days ago, and she still had not returned his call. Her career was starting to fall apart again, just as she'd been building it back up. Most of yesterday was spent staring into space, reliving the past. And for what? She knew what Lila would say: *you have to put the past behind you.* As if such things were possible.

"Why don't you come down to the theater with me on Tuesday? About one o'clock? I'm taking some preliminary sketches in for him then."

"Let's see." Kelly turned the pages of her daybook, knowing full well it was blank for weeks ahead.

"No. You have to, Kell. He's going to Minneapolis the minute his current play closes here. This is your last chance."

Last chance, Kelly thought. She should grasp hold of it. "Tuesday at one," she agreed. "See you there."

She said good-bye, then walked to the front window and opened the curtains. It was a crisp November morning, a bright blue Manitoba sky, clear and cold. Fresh snow had fallen the night before, covering everything. The sparkling whiteness of the scene made her wince.

It is time to make a choice, Kelly lectured herself. You can lie around the house for the rest of your life, inviting a ghost to haunt you. Or you can get over it. You can "move along," as Darl would say, and take this next step. *Hamlet* is the perfect vehicle. Think of the connections you'll make.

She watched as a wind picked up out of nowhere and rustled through the low hedge of young poplar trees she and James had planted along the front walk. She remembered how James had cared for those trees daily, watering them, staking them, even talking to them.

She could almost see him out there now. No, she *could* see him, wearing the patched blue denim shirt that had been his favorite, a mass of tangled, amber curls blowing across his beloved face. The wind whipped his shirt open and she caught a glimpse of his brown chest and flat stomach.

Strangely, she was not afraid. Not at first. James's appearance seemed perfectly normal to her. He looked so casual there, as though he had returned simply to finish his chores. He was walking around the house to inspect the trees, and he would return, any minute, to enter the house.

Then reality hit. She blinked.

She knew it wasn't really James. She knew it wasn't anybody. No one would be out there, no one *could* be out there in the sub-zero wind in a thin cotton shirt, an open shirt. She closed her eyes and rubbed them with her fists. Opened them again. Nothing but snow blowing over the yard, bowing the young trees toward the ground.

She sat down by the phone and looked up Leon's

number in her address book. It was still too early in the morning to call him.

Leon had saved Kelly's life when she was drowning in the abyss that opened up to swallow her after her husband's death. But she was a long time acknowledging it. At first she'd spent her sessions railing against him, cursing his stubborn insistence that James was gone for good. That there was nothing she could do about it.

The last time she'd seen Leon was June 21, at the memorial service they held a year after James's death. Kelly was outraged that Adam and Eleanor dared to attend. She refused to speak to them or even to return their glances, although when their heads were bent in prayer, she stared at Adam's face, feeling a perverse satisfaction when she saw that the burns had never healed properly. He was even more hideous than ever, with a patch of bright pink scar tissue on his upper lip.

After the service, she waited until Darl went out to his car, and then she flew at Adam in a fury, accusing him of killing James. She called him a murderer and a rapist and a monster. "And you," she hissed at Eleanor, who stood in stunned silence. "You're responsible, too. What were you doing sleeping all the time? Sleeping! While your little son was—" Leon grabbed her from behind, pulled her away from the startled, elderly couple, away from the shocked mourners, and dragged her into the parking lot.

She had raged in Leon's arms. "Can't we do anything?" she cried. "James is dead and Adam is walking around. Free!"

"There's nothing we can do, Kelly. You have to accept that."

"Couldn't we charge him with child abuse? You have the proof in your files."

"The files prove nothing, and besides, they're confidential."

"There has to be some justice! Couldn't I sue? Wrongful death?"

"Adam is not legally responsible for his death, Kelly. You know that."

"Yes, he is. He is. He is," she insisted, and kept on insisting, while Leon ushered her through the lot and handed her over to Darl, who drove her home without asking questions, and held her while she cried herself to sleep.

Kelly took a deep breath, remembering. The day after the memorial service, she had woken feeling stronger. Perhaps it was from venting her anger, perhaps it was the sense of closure provided by the priest's sermon, but whatever the cause, that day she had begun to accept her husband's death. She had taken an interest in her own life again, and in her friends. She had steeled herself against the pain, refused to give in. She had thrown herself back into her work.

But now, it seemed, she was slipping again.

It was nine o'clock. Leon would be in his office. As she turned from the window, she thought she glimpsed a blur of pale blue against the white snow. But she refused to look again. She would not let the vision seduce her. It was only her subconscious mind, as Leon had explained, projecting her own desires onto the walls and ceilings of her own house, her own yard. For a second, she thought about Jerry Pryne, Ph.D., and his theories of haunted houses. *Love, warning, revenge.* Then she lifted the receiver and started to dial.

Leon Chartrand was on the phone, talking to his grandmother, when Mrs. Krentz, the strictly businesslike intake worker, buzzed him on another line.

"You have a Kelly Quirk on line two," she told him. "Shall I tell her you are busy with a personal call?"

How did she know it was a personal call, the old bat? Probably eavesdropping again, Leon thought.

"Ask Kelly to hold a minute, please," he said pleasantly, then returned to his grandmother. "I'll be up to see you in a few days. You remember to take your medicine. Yes. Soon. Three times a day." He listened a minute, then repeated loudly, "Three times a day." He listened again, then sighed, and began to speak to her in the Cree language that she understood better than English. Hang Mrs. Krentz, anyway. It was none of her business. He was the doctor, he reminded himself.

When he was sure that his grandmother had understood his instructions, he pressed line two, but not without some trepidation.

"Kelly! Hello," he said heartily. He hoped she was not going to start in again about a lawsuit.

"Leon? Hi. How are you?"

"Fine. Fine. How are you doing, Kelly? Haven't heard from you for a while. Is everything all right?"

"Yes. Well, no. I mean ... do you think we could talk?"

"What's on your mind?"

"James," she said.

"Ah."

"Yes. I thought maybe we could talk a bit."

"Fine, fine. Why don't you make an appointment then?"

"Soon?"

"Whenever you need me," he said lightly.

"I need you." Her statement was simple and direct.

Leon felt his heart drop. He knew there was a lengthy waiting list for patients. "Right." He coughed and consulted his calendar. There was a budget meeting Tuesday morning he could skip if he had to. "Why don't you come in Tuesday morning? Eleven o'clock? I'm free then."

"I'll be there," Kelly said.

As he hung up, Leon called up a picture of Kelly Quirk in his mind. The pale, worried face, long jet-black hair. The most devoted—and the most attractive—wife of a client he'd ever known. James Grayton. He felt his head begin to ache, as he remembered James.

TUESDAY MORNING, Kelly was feeling better. She draped her coat loosely around her shoulders and ran out to check the mail, glancing hurriedly at her watch. She'd just have time for a quick breakfast before her appointments. She was not going to be late today, she told herself. She was going to be organized, sensible. Talk it out with Leon, then make it to the theater and make a good impression on Taylor. Lila was right. This was her last chance.

She dumped the mail on the table, poured a cup of coffee, and sorted through the envelopes. Bills, advertisements, a fat new volume from the book club. And a small parcel, wrapped in plain white paper. Some kind of free sample?

She ripped off the paper and discovered a wooden matchbox. It was used, and still smelled faintly of sulfur.

She slid back the lid.

Inside was the dragon. James's carved dragon, the one that Alex lost. It lay there in the box, surrounded by tissue paper, perfectly intact. Underneath, among the folds of paper, was the white knight from the chess set, the one that had been missing so long she couldn't remember when she'd seen it last. She emptied the box. There was no card, no message anywhere. The parcel had no stamps or postmark.

She held the dragon in one hand, the knight in the other. A cold tingling, like the tip of a fingernail tracing her skin, ran up the back of her neck.

Chapter Seven

The waiting room at the Riverside Clinic was a depressing place. Kelly sat on the edge of her chair, watching the other patients, some of whom shuffled around the room with the same awkward, drugged gait she learned to recognize when James was in the psychiatric ward. Others, like herself, more under control, sat biting their nails or looking listlessly at magazines. One young man seemed to be fixated on Kelly's face. He stared with a hungry, pitiful expression, and she moved across the room, out of his sight.

She was glad Darl wasn't working today. She didn't want to tell him, yet, about the growing suspicion she harbored. And she was glad Mrs. Krentz wasn't working, either. That old battle-ax gave her the creeps. She much preferred the young and cheerful Frances, who was standing up now, calling her name.

"How is everything, Kelly?" Frances asked, as she led her to Leon's office. "Winter getting you down? Oh—I mean, sorry. I didn't mean—"

"It's all right, Frances." Kelly smiled at the embarrassed young woman. She had shared many light conversations with Frances at staff parties she'd attended with Darl, and she knew it wasn't easy for Frances to separate Kelly's role as a casual friend from her present role as patient. Glumly, Kelly felt the old wall of professionalism intrude between them again. Just as it had when James was a patient here.

Leon Chartrand had gained a little weight since Kelly first met him, and he looked a little more harried, but he still seemed too young to be a doctor. He still wore his hair in two long braids that he tended to tug with his fingers when he was nervous. He often seemed nervous around Kelly.

"I need to know more," she said.

Leon indicated the files on his desk. "I've been looking over everything," he said. "I'll help you as best I can. But as I told you before, there is not a strong case here. Not much of this would hold up in court. It's all hearsay. A lot of conjecture, guessing. Even if I agreed—"

"It's not that," Kelly interrupted.

"What then?" He waited patiently.

"I called because I thought I was seeing things." Kelly stopped. "But now . . ." She rested her face in her hands a moment. Then looked up. "I think he really might be alive."

There. She had said it.

Leon's face betrayed no surprise, except for the slight rise of his eyebrows.

"Alive," he said.

"Yes."

"Can you tell me why?"

Kelly listed her reasons: the missing objects, the ones that returned, the telephone calls. But even as she spoke, she knew they sounded doubtful. She could hear the questioning tone in her own voice.

Leon swiveled his chair and gazed out through the window at the frozen river as he listened, his back to her. When she finished, he remained silent for a moment, then began to speak, without turning around.

"It's natural," he said. "You want to believe it. To be honest, I want to believe it. I share your sense of failure. But,

Kelly, we have to face facts. James was very sick. Fatally ill—that's the only way to think of it. He was sick and he died."

"But he was *not* that sick when he died," Kelly countered.

"It's not your fault." Leon turned around again and ran his fingers over the papers on his desk. "It's not our fault," he said softly. He flipped a folder open, and Kelly saw one of James's drawings inside. Before Leon could stop her, she reached over and pulled it out.

She studied the drawing in her hands, remembering every detail of Leon's interpretation. The walls of the house were crooked and thick. Distorted, because the body remembered through a haze of pain. Thick, because there had been no escape. The house was a world unto itself, insulated, isolated. A place where the split little boy writhed and cried out in silence. The two sides of James, the frightened one and the strong one who took over. He drew his child-self double, because he had been split in two. But he was putting himself back together. He was so close. This very picture was proof of that. Sam said this series was the best work James had ever done, and Kelly could see this was true. Anybody could see it. The lines were confident, powerful. The art was coming out of a place James had touched and seen and known. The wall that had severed him from his own body, his body's memory, was crumbling.

"He was healing," Kelly said, holding up the drawing. "You said so yourself, remember?"

They both gazed at the picture in silence.

Leon shook his head. "Psychological trauma is not a simple thing," he said. "James was a very, very frightened young man."

"But he was getting better."

"He was on his way," Leon acknowledged. "But sometimes . . ." He sighed. He took the picture from Kelly's hands and set it back on his desk.

"What?"

"Sometimes the healing is more dangerous than the sickness."

"I don't understand."

Leon tugged at his braids. Then he tried to explain.

"In these cases of sadistic abuse, the secrecy is nearly unbelievable in its power. Nobody must know. Not the grandparents, the closest neighbors, teachers. In many cases, like this one, even the other members of the immediate family do not know. Silence is enforced through deep, psychological terrorism so effective that eventually even the patient does not know. As James grew up, he concealed the truth even from himself." Leon tapped his finger on the image of the boy in the picture. "When it began to emerge—through the nightmares, through his art—he was at a very dangerous stage in his process of discovery."

He looked at Kelly. "I don't think you realize how much courage it took for James to tell. In a way, he was pronouncing his own death sentence."

"Death?"

"James believed that if he told, he would die."

"How could he really believe that?" Kelly asked.

"Consciously, James knew it wasn't true. But *subconsciously*, there was still a little kid inside him who depended on his parents for everything, for life itself." Leon tapped the side of his head, then the top. "Deep," he said. "It's buried deep inside. It's very much like brainwashing—or hypnotism. They sort of programmed him to self-destruct if he ever told. Protecting themselves."

Kelly felt herself grow numb as she listened to the rest of Leon's explanations. They had been through this before. James died from post-traumatic stress disorder. It was not only logical, it was even predictable. Such cases were often fatal. This was Leon's field of expertise, after all. He was writing a book about it. He should know.

His theories were very convincing.

If you didn't know James, she thought.

"Kelly." Leon's voice dropped, became almost painfully gentle. "It must be difficult, surrounded by your husband's things, so many memories. Even if you try to forget, you're surrounded by his presence, constant reminders. Don't you think it's possible you're misplacing his things because you want to rid yourself of them? To get on with your life?"

"I *was* getting on with it," Kelly said. "I was."

"Yes, you were. And James would want you to, Kelly. He loved you very much. You have to allow yourself to let go."

"If he loved me," she said suddenly, angrily, "he would be here right now."

"He *did* love you," Leon said. "Don't make any mistake about that. But you have to realize that inside James was a little boy so disgusted with himself he couldn't believe that anyone could love him back. Especially after he told."

"How could he possibly have believed that?" Kelly asked. She was crying, now. "I gave my life over to loving him."

Leon tapped the side of his head. "Deep," he said. "It runs deep."

WHEN KELLY PULLED UP in front of the theater, she remained sitting in her car. She dabbed at her makeup in the rearview mirror. Then she threw open her door and walked toward the lobby entrance with an air of determination.

From his particular vantage point, he couldn't read her expression, couldn't tell if she was filled with anger or with resolve. Whichever it was, he didn't like it. He wanted her unbalanced, unsure. He didn't intend to hurt her. Just to unsettle her, throw her off a bit. No. He definitely didn't want to hurt her. He'd have to be patient.

He had hurt a woman once. He remembered the fear in her eyes when she looked at him. It disgusted him to think of it. How he had to dispose of her. A thing like that could have ruined his reputation completely. Just when his life was going so well. When he was about to make a name for himself.

LILA WAS WAITING FOR HER in the lobby of the theater.

"Come on," she said. "Taylor's got only a few minutes for us."

"Do I look presentable?" Kelly asked. She had tried to repair the damage caused by her weeping.

"Fine. Beautiful," said Lila, without really looking. She pulled Kelly toward the office.

Taylor was a handsome, sophisticated man. His white teeth gleamed in his dark face as he shook Kelly's hand.

"Welcome," he said. "Very happy to be working with you."

He barely glanced at the resumé she handed him, and didn't ask any questions about her experience. Lila must have done a good job of selling her. He wanted to talk only about the play, which was set to open the sixth of January. Less than two months away.

"You know Michael Black," Taylor said to Kelly. It wasn't a question. He handed her a clipping from a Minneapolis newspaper, and she skimmed it quickly. A short article announced that the play was already virtually sold out. Timothy Sheer, artistic director of the Arcana Theater, was quoted, calling *Hamlet* "the most exciting production at the Arcana in ten years." Michael Black, apparently, was big medicine in the States.

"How in the world did you get him?" Lila asked.

"We were lucky," Taylor said. "Timothy knows his parents. They've been in the theater all their lives. Michael's father is an accomplished actor, well known in Europe, and his mother is a singer. Michael trained as a Shakespearean actor in London. Timothy directed him in several plays over there. Very pleased with him. No one ever expected him to go to Hollywood, I can tell you. I think his parents were appalled, really, when he ended up in all those dreadful films." Taylor grimaced. He obviously did not approve of popular cinema. "What a waste," he concluded.

Lila winked at Kelly. "I heard he wanted to get out of Hollywood for a while," she said. "I heard there was some sort of scandal—"

Taylor cut her off. "I wouldn't say there was a scandal," he said severely. His look warned her not to gossip. "But apparently, yes, word had it he wanted out of the movie business for a while. Hard to believe, when he was making so much money. But anyway, when we were casting this thing, Timothy suggested I call him. And Michael jumped at the chance, to my surprise—and delight."

"It's a big step backward," Lila said, "from screen to stage. I hope his ego can handle it."

"I understand he's very professional," Taylor said. "But like most talented people, he's used to getting his own way." He smiled at Kelly. "He gets what he wants."

For the rest of the meeting, Taylor lectured them on his interpretation of the play. He summarized the plot they knew so well. Hamlet's life is shattered when he is visited by the ghost of his father, the late King of Denmark, who tells him the terrible truth: the King was poisoned by the "serpent" who now wears his crown and sleeps in the Queen's bed. The ghost spurs Hamlet to his task of revenge—a task that leads to the madness and drowning of Ophelia, the death of her family, and finally the death of the entire royal family of Denmark, including Prince Hamlet himself.

Taylor spread Lila's sketches out for Kelly to see, along with some of the sketches from the set designer. Atmosphere was vital, he proclaimed. This must be a frightening play, the way Shakespeare intended.

Throughout the entire meeting, he asked Kelly only one question.

"So," he said, leaning suddenly forward, his face inches from her own, "you can do ghosts?"

"I can do ghosts," said Kelly.

"Real ghosts? Ghosts to harrow up the blood?"

"Oh yes."

"Good," he said. "There is something rotten in the state of Denmark, and we want the audience to feel it."

Chapter Eight

The evening that Darl returned to the graveyard shift, he dropped Alex off at Kelly's to spend the night. She offered him a cup of coffee to help him stay awake and asked if he had time to talk.

"A few minutes," he said.

Kelly parked Alex in front of the television and turned the volume up. She didn't want to be overheard.

"I went to see Leon," she told Darl.

He looked up, startled. "Chartrand?"

"Yes."

"Whatever for?"

"To talk about James. You know, Darl, I'm not sure Leon was right about him, after all. I want to take a look at James's files."

"Those files are long gone," Darl said. "After a patient dies, they're destroyed."

"Really? Well, he still has them."

"He does? That's not right." Darl sipped his coffee, frowned, and added sugar. "That guy's a quack," he said. "Those files should have been shredded months ago."

"Anyway, I wanted to see if . . . to get a better idea of James's state of mind when he—"

"You know his state of mind, Kelly." He reached across the table and laid his hand across hers. "He was out of his mind. Delusional. Paranoid. Suicidal."

"But he wasn't! That's the thing, don't you see? The night before the fire, he was perfectly fine. He was happy. He sat right here in this chair and told me he was happy." James had sat right there and sworn he loved her.

Darl glanced at his watch. "I'm really sorry, Kelly. I promised Frances I'd relieve her early tonight." He sighed as he stood up. "We'll talk in the morning, okay? I'll be here in time to get Alex to school, and then we'll talk."

"But, Darl—" She gave up. She wanted to tell him about the phone calls, the missing objects, but he was already pulling on his coat. He was calling Alex to come and get a good-bye hug. It would have to wait for tomorrow.

As he walked out the door, Darl turned and pointed a finger at her. "Don't even think about it till I get back, all right?"

"All right."

"Promise?"

"I promise."

But Darl did not get back in time to take Alex to school. At ten to nine, Kelly gave up waiting for him and drove Alex to school herself, apologizing to Mrs. Chan for bringing him late.

When she returned to the house, the message light was flashing. Probably Darl explaining why he'd had to work late. She reached for the receiver, but it started to ring before she picked it up.

"Kelly, it's Paul."

"What's wrong?" She knew that Paul would not be calling, especially at this hour, unless something was terribly amiss. "Is it Angel?"

"She's fine. It's Darl."

"Darl?"

"Yeah," he said. "He's had an accident."

Kelly felt a weight dropping swiftly through her body as if she were on an elevator, rising too fast. In a terrible moment of recognition, she knew that the recent series of fearful events should have prepared her for this. Something had been set in moton.

At the hospital, Kelly stared at the man lying on the green sheets. One half of his face was concealed by bandages, his head had been shaved, and his eyes were swollen shut. His face was a mass of purple bruises. She felt she was floating somewhere above this scene. She was barely able to realize that this was Darl, and that this had been no accident. It was a beating, Paul had told her as they'd waited for Darl to get out of surgery. He hadn't wanted to tell her on the phone, but Darl had been mugged sometime early this morning.

Now, in the recovery room, a sympathetic doctor was briefing Kelly and Angel on Darl's condition. As she spoke, she adjusted the flow of the IV hooked up to his arm. Kelly tried not to look at the black bruises where the needle entered the flesh. She tried to concentrate on the doctor's explanation.

"We think he'll recover fully," she was saying. "But with a head injury like this, it's difficult to tell. It may take him a long time to come out of this."

"He's in a coma?" Angel asked, her voice wavering.

"It's not a coma, technically," the doctor said. "But he is deeply unconscious. He's sustained severe—"

She was interrupted by the arrival of a young police officer Kelly had seen earlier in the corridor.

"You the girlfriend?" he asked Kelly.

"Well, I'm . . . yes," Kelly said, to avoid complication.

"Talk to you a minute?" He beckoned her into the hallway, where she leaned against the wall for support as she tried to answer his questions.

"Your boyfriend involved in any kind of criminal activity?"

"No!"

"Drugs?"

"No. He was ... he's perfectly respectable," Kelly insisted. "He works at the Riverside Clinic. You can ask them."

The cop scribbled in his notebook. "Any kind of feud, then?"

"Feud?"

"You know, did he have any enemies?"

"No. What are you saying? Isn't this ... ? They said it was a mugging."

"Pretty vicious mugging. Beating like that, it's, well, it looks almost personal."

"But it *was* a mugging, wasn't it? Robbery?"

The cop sighed. He looked at her skeptically, then seemed to relent. "Probably," he agreed. "Actually, it looks like a car-jacking. A passing motorist found him at the side of the highway."

"The highway?"

"North of town." The cop flipped through his notebook. "East of 59, alongside the floodway. He was just lying there, out cold. No sign of a vehicle."

"But he drove his truck to work last night. A white pick-up truck."

"Yeah, his wallet was in his pants. We got the license and registration."

"They didn't steal his wallet?"

"Like I said, looks like a car-jack. Hitchhiker, maybe. Looks like your friend put up a fight—hell of a fight, according to the doctor." The cop actually smiled at her. "I'd hate to see the bad guy," he said. "I imagine when we find him he'll need a few stitches."

The doctor emerged from Darl's room and overheard this remark. "I'd be expecting that bad guy to show up in Emergency somewhere," she said. "Our patient was covered with Type A blood, but he's Type O. Whoever lost all that Type A is going to need treatment."

"Well, you keep an eye out for him," the cop said. "And we'll keep an eye out for the truck." He handed the doctor a card. Then he gave one to Kelly. "Thank you, ma'am, that'll be all for now. You call me if you think of anything that might help."

"Okay," said Kelly. She felt weak. What was Darl doing out on the highway? Had someone forced him out there? Forced him to a deserted location and then . . . She didn't want to picture it.

She staggered back into Darl's room and collapsed into a chair beside Angel.

"He hasn't stirred once," Angel said. "It's been hours."

"God. What time is it?"

"It's three o'clock," Angel told her.

Kelly jumped up. "Alex!" she said. "I've got to pick Alex up from school." At the door, she wavered, looking back at Darl.

"I'll stay with him," Angel said. "You go. Take Alex home. I'll call you later."

"Okay." But she wavered again.

"Go! There's nothing you can do here."

Kelly nodded. The only thing she could do for Darl right now was to take care of his son. As she rushed into the parking lot, she checked her watch. She'd be late, but she knew Mrs. Chan would stay with Alex until she arrived.

PAUL PACED UP AND DOWN in the hospital corridor, impatient. He didn't like hospitals. Didn't like doctors and didn't like cops.

And he didn't like what had happened. Not one bit. It looked too suspicious.

He had managed to avoid talking to the police. But there were a few things he wanted to check. Things he wanted to do, just to be on the safe side. He looked at the hospital clock. Three-thirty. He had to get out of here.

The problem was, he couldn't leave Angel. She'd begged him to stay. She needed him. She'd become hysterical if he left for no good reason. He peeked into Darl's room and saw her there, keeping vigil. He sighed. He had to admit his wife was a sweet person. Weak, but sweet.

DARL DID NOT STIR, but in a small corner of his mind, he began to become aware that he had been dreaming. He remembered only jagged images. The truck in a ditch. Tall grasses waving above a thin layer of snow. The night sky filled with stars. Where had he been? He struggled to move, to sort out the nightmare, but the more he tried to rouse himself, the more jumbled the images became. He could barely feel his own body. Just a throbbing in his head, and a gentle warmth in one of his hands.

Someone was holding his hand. It was a girl's hand, long and slender. Kelly?

Then he heard Angel's voice. She was singing softly, a song he had taught her when she was a child. "Summertime." He recognized the tune, but the words were garbled, didn't make sense.

He felt himself sucked back into the nightmare. He saw himself hurtling through the air, under the stars, the long grasses coming up to meet him. Then a series of faces flashed through his mind, so fast and confusing he felt nauseated.

Angel? Angel, I have to tell you . . .

But no sound emerged. His lips were not even moving.

MRS. CHAN WAS MARKING PAPERS at her desk in an empty classroom. Kelly glanced down the halls, out into the playground. No sign of Alex.

"Mrs. Chan?"

"Oh, hello. How is Alex's father?"

"He's been in an accident."

"Yes, we know."

"You know?"

"There is no need to worry. Alex's grandmother picked him up this afternoon."

"His grandmother?" Kelly stared at the woman.

"Yes. She said she'd be caring for Alex until his father recovers." She paused, seeing the worry on Kelly's face. "Is Mr. Grayton badly hurt?"

But Kelly didn't answer. She was already heading toward her car.

SHE PULLED UP IN FRONT of the house and sat staring at it for several minutes. There it was, the dark little bungalow at the end of the street behind the Cathedral. The toolshed in the side yard, its window boarded up. James's prison. She wished he had burned it all to the ground.

There was no vehicle in the driveway. Luckily, Adam wasn't home.

When she knocked, Eleanor answered the door. She was a bulky, tired woman, with a face like an undercooked pancake, flat and sagging. Her dress was soiled and pulled too tightly across her broad waist.

"Kelly," she stated, in a dull voice.

"Mrs. Grayton, I've come to see Alex."

Alex heard her and came running to the door.

"Auntie Kelly!"

"What do you want?" Eleanor asked. She was, as always, slow to catch on.

Kelly opened the door wide and took Alex by the hand.

"You go jump in my car. We're going for a ride."

"I'll get my coat," Alex said.

Kelly spoke to Alex, but she kept her eyes fixed on Eleanor. "No, you just run in the car. It's warm in there. I'll bring your coat."

Alex obeyed, and once he was safely in her car, Kelly asked for his coat and hat.

"Adam won't like this," Eleanor said. But she handed them over.

"NO CHANGE," ANGEL REPORTED, when she called from the hospital. "Paul says we should leave and maybe he's right. I'm not even sure Darl knows I'm here."

"Why don't you come over?" Kelly asked. "Have you eaten? Come and have dinner with Alex and me."

"Maybe." Angel was reluctant.

"Come on. You have to eat. And we have to stick together."

She hung up. The message light was still blinking. She had forgotten about it. Maybe Darl's message contained some clue that would explain what had happened. But the message wasn't from Darl. It was Leon's voice that came on the line.

"Kelly? Leon Chartrand. If you're there, pick up the phone." A moment of silence. "I guess you're out. Listen, I want you to call me. I've been looking over these files, and I think there's something we should discuss. It might be very important. Call me at the office tonight. I'll be working late."

It was only five, and Kelly decided to wait until she was alone to call him back. She wanted to hear what he had to say, and she had a very personal medical question she wanted to ask him.

Angel bent down and gathered Alex in her arms the minute she arrived. "I saw your daddy," she said. "He had a bad car accident, but the doctors are taking good care of him." Her words of reassurance were less than convincing.

Paul said little. He spent his time pacing around the entire house, inside and out, checking the doors and windows.

"You should get an alarm," he advised. "The doors are

pretty tight, but someone could jimmy a window and get in here before you even knew it."

Angel caught Kelly's eye and nodded ruefully, as if to say that maybe Paul wasn't so crazy after all.

While everyone was eating pizza in the kitchen, Kelly excused herself and went to the living room to call Leon.

"Dr. Chartrand?" Mrs. Krentz repeated, in a clipped voice. "He's not in tonight. May I refer you to another doctor on call?"

"He said he'd be working late tonight," Kelly said. "Can you check his office?"

"I told you, he's not in tonight. He hasn't been in all day. Let me refer you—"

"No. No thanks." Kelly hung up, confused. Perhaps Leon had left the message the night before. If so, he must have called awfully late, after she and Alex were asleep.

With all the anxiety in the house, Alex could not get to sleep. By the time Angel and Paul left, and Alex was settled in on the couch, it was well past midnight. Kelly went into her bedroom, pulled out the top drawer of her dresser and laid it on her bed. It was full of personal papers. She was organized when it came to her files for work, but this drawer was a mess. Social insurance records lay jumbled among her other papers, Alex's drawings, old daybooks, the obituary of Angel's son, Allan.

The information she wanted had to be in here somewhere.

She sorted through the documents, paying particular attention to anything medical concerning James. She read through his old prescriptions, a copy of his release papers. His birth certificate. She stayed awake for hours, scanning them all carefully, but there was no mention, anywhere, of his blood type.

When the clock radio came on at seven, Kelly slept through it. When she finally woke, the nine o'clock news was being announced. Alex was standing beside her bed. "Won't I be late for school?"

She switched off the radio, fearing some sensationalized report of the mugging. "You're going to have a holiday today," she said. "You just climb in here with me and cuddle for a while."

Alex jumped under the covers and hugged her.

"Hey, it's going to be all right. Daddy will be okay. He just needs to rest at the hospital for a long time so he can get better."

"Will it be a long, long time?"

"I don't know, honey. But I'll stay with you, okay? We'll do things together and the time will go fast, I promise."

At noon, Adam was on Kelly's doorstep, ringing the bell. Eleanor stood behind him.

"We've come for Alex," Adam said. "He belongs with us."

Eleanor said nothing. Kelly noticed her hair was permed. She wore a matronly dress under her open coat and carried a patent-leather purse Kelly would bet had come from a bin at the Sally Ann that very morning. Her cheeks were powdered, her lipstick demure. She looked the very picture of a respectable grandmother.

"He's staying with me," Kelly answered.

"Look, we didn't want it to come to this," Adam said. The skin graft above his upper lip had shrunk slightly, giving him a perpetual snarl. "But we've got papers. We got a legal right to take him."

"What papers?"

Adam thrust a legal document into view. "Custody order. We went to court this morning and got an order. An emergency order. You got to give him to us."

"We're blood," Eleanor ventured. Adam silenced her with

a glare. He had no doubt warned her beforehand to keep her mouth shut.

"He wants to stay here," Kelly said. "So I'm letting him stay here."

"You don't have anything to say about it," Adam said. "Take a look over there." He pointed to the street, where two uniformed officers were emerging from a black-and-white police car. "We brought us a backup. Told the judge you were giving us trouble."

"Oh no," Kelly said.

"You're lucky we don't have you charged with kidnapping."

As the officers approached, Adam backed down the steps. He would leave it to them. Eleanor remained silent.

The officers read the custody order to Kelly, as Alex listened with wide eyes, not understanding.

Then they took him away.

KELLY LAY IN BED, staring at the ceiling.

Temporary order of custody. It was a travesty. But it was perfectly legal.

She felt among the papers in her drawer and lifted one out at random. Proof of her marriage. It was useless. With James gone, her relationship to Alex was slender, at best. She hadn't even taken the Grayton name when she married.

She needed a lawyer. She needed some piece of paper on her side.

She picked up James's birth certificate and lay there holding it above her head, reading. Legal proof of the blood ties that bound James to Adam and Eleanor, ties that now bound Alex. She felt tears sting her eyes and a sob rise in her throat.

Then she read it over again.

Chapter Nine

On her way to the hospital, Kelly drove past the bungalow and saw that the curtains were drawn. Adam's truck was parked in the driveway. No signs of life.

She stopped her car and gazed at the toolshed with its inscrutable little burlap-covered window. She tried not to imagine Alex in there, among the rusted tools and spiderwebs. But she couldn't help it. In her mind's eye, Alex's face merged with the face of James. She saw her own young self walking with Darl, both of them carefree, away from the house, leaving James behind. Abandoning him. Guilt flooded through her.

"What do you think you're doing here?" Adam was standing on the front lawn, a snow shovel in hand, glaring at her.

Kelly let her own accusing stare serve as her answer.

Adam stepped closer, brandishing the shovel. "We're watching you," he said. "You keep your interfering nose out of my business. I see your car around here again I'll call the cops. I'll get a restraining order against you."

She knew better than to engage in a pointless argument with him. Besides, she had a plan. She drove away quickly, scanning the house and yard for any sign of Alex, but she could not see him.

ANGEL WAS SEATED by Darl's bedside, her slumped posture evidence of her increasing despair. Her coat and purse lay in a little defeated heap at her feet. She looked thinner and paler than ever.

"Ange?" Kelly whispered.

"Shhh." Angel jumped up and motioned Kelly into the corridor. "He's sleeping."

"Did he wake up?"

"They said he sort of came to in the middle of the night, but—" Angel stopped. She was clearly exhausted, dark circles shimmering under her eyes.

"You haven't been here all night, have you?" Kelly's concern was genuine, but she was concealing her anger. She had things to do, important things, and she couldn't handle Angel falling apart right now.

"No. They wouldn't let me stay in his room last night, and Paul made me go home. We came back first thing this morning."

"Is Paul still here?"

"I think so. He went out for some sandwiches, but I don't know what's taking him so long."

Well, at least Paul would get Angel to eat. Kelly pulled some coins out of her pocket. "Why don't you get us some coffee? You look bushed, Ange. I'll stay here with Darl."

Angel complied wearily, and Kelly stepped into the room. Immediately she picked up her sister's purse and rummaged through it, finding the papers she needed in Angel's wallet. She hesitated, then slid the wallet into her own purse.

She approached the bed for one last look at Darl. He lay on his back, his bandaged, misshapen face an unreadable mask of contusions. She touched his hand and was frightened by the utter lack of response. His hand lay limply in hers, warm but otherwise seemingly dead. The awful knowledge that he might not survive suddenly paralyzed her will. How could she leave without speaking to him?

If he died, what would happen to Alex?

The image of the dark interior of the toolshed rose once again into her mind. Abruptly, she turned on her heels and hurried out of the hospital.

KELLY ASSUMED PAUL was still at the hospital, but she rapped loudly on the door, just to make certain. When nobody answered, she let herself in. The house was silent, except for a faint hum of music, as if from a radio turned low.

She headed directly for Allan's old room and lifted the lid on the cedar chest where, she knew, Angel still kept all of Allan's baby things. She searched delicately through the tiny clothes and cards of congratulation on his birth. Allan's old pacifier was there, packed in tissue paper, a sad little parcel. Angel had held on to everything.

Just as Kelly found what she was looking for, she heard a thump from the basement. She froze. Paul must be home. She held her breath. If Paul saw the disarray she'd created, he would demand an explanation. She stepped into the hall.

"Paul?" she called. "It's me. Just picking up some stuff for Angel."

But Paul didn't answer.

Kelly made her way down the stairs to the basement. She thought of the gun Paul kept for protection. "It's me," she called more loudly. "It's only Kelly."

Still no answer.

She reached the last stair and saw Paul sitting in a dilapidated armchair among his speakers and amps. His back was turned to her.

"Paul?"

He did not turn. Except for a slight, rhythmic movement of the ponytail at the back of his head, he was motionless. Then Kelly saw the earphones. Paul was engrossed in his music, completely unaware of her presence. A stroke of luck. She hurried back upstairs and replaced everything neatly. But before she could leave, she heard his footsteps ascend.

He had taken off the earphones, and now Kelly could hear the music clearly. With a pang, she recognized her husband's voice. Paul was listening to James playing "Long Black Veil" on the guitar and singing. In the background she could hear other voices, people laughing. Paul must have recorded the tune at some party, long ago.

She heard Paul scrabbling through a box of tapes in the kitchen, then a clatter as he dumped them out on the table, searching for something. She kept quiet, listening. She heard James strum the final chords of the song. His friends cheered and clapped.

"Shit!" Paul's outburst made her jump. If he came in here now . . . But he didn't. She heard him head back down to the basement. Just before he closed the door behind him, she heard James calling, "Kelly! Where's Kelly?"

SHE DROVE TO A CAR LOT where she traded in her station wagon. Using Angel's license, she bought a ten-year-old Mustang with bucket seats. It looked in worse shape than her old car, but it could move. It accelerated beautifully.

Back at home, she took a pair of scissors into the bathroom and leaned close to the mirror. She gathered all her black hair, Maggie's lover's coal-black hair, and began to cut. It was too thick to chop through all at once, so she had to separate it into strands. It fell onto the floor in thick, glossy clumps. She remembered how James used to stroke it and wind it around his fingers and hold it against his face. She studied her reflection. Since she could remember, she'd been hiding behind all that hair. Now she would have to do without it.

She tried Leon's office, but once again the formidable Mrs. Krentz insisted on referring her to another doctor. Kelly left a third message for Leon and hung up. She would have to do this alone, at least for now.

She lay down on her bed, wide awake, and waited for dawn.

DESPITE THE BITTER MORNING air, Kelly was sweating in the layers of clothing she wore beneath her parka, trying to disguise her shape. The dark, heavy makeup on her face protected her from the sting of the wind. On her shoulder, she wore a canvas bag, labeled WINNIPEG FREE PRESS. She held a rolled newspaper in one mittened hand. She had parked the Mustang, unlocked, keys in the ignition, directly in front of Adam's house.

As soon as she saw the door to the bungalow open, she began to walk, limping slightly, awkward in her padded clothes. If she timed this correctly, she would reach the mailbox just as Adam, gripping Alex firmly by the arm, approached the driveway.

Adam merely glanced at her, as he fumbled for his keys. She walked right up the driveway, head down, as if merely bored with her paper route. As she passed Alex, she tried to read his expression, but he was studying the ground.

"Morning," Adam said curtly.

She waved a hand in his direction. She took her time at the mailbox, clumsily dropping the bag of papers on the ground and bending to refold them. She was waiting for Adam to leave Alex alone at the side of the truck while he went to unlock the driver's door.

But Adam was more clever, or more cautious, than she'd thought. He didn't leave Alex alone for a second, but marched around the side of the truck, opened the passenger door and strapped him in, locking the door, before he returned to the driver's side.

Alex was firmly in his power.

She would have to try again another day, wait until Adam's guard was down.

There was nothing she could do but walk back to the curb. As she reached the Mustang, she tried to catch Alex's eye. Maybe she could give him a wink, reassure him. What she saw broke her heart. Alex was looking over his shoulder, staring right at her, a look of naked pleading on his face. He had recognized her. He knew.

Without thinking, she slid behind the wheel and put the Mustang in reverse, blocking Adam's truck. Then she sat still and waited.

Adam, who still had to warm up his engine, ignored her. But once his truck was ready to go, he leaned out his window and gestured for her to move her car. She remained motionless, staring at the dash. He began to honk his horn, warning her to move. Eleanor, hearing the commotion, appeared in the doorway.

"What's going on?" she called.

Adam honked loudly. Kelly braced herself. In a surge of irritation, Adam opened his door and stood in the driveway to investigate. Kelly slumped forward, as if unconscious.

"Is she all right?" Eleanor called.

"She's just stupid," Adam called back. "Or deaf."

Unnoticed by his grandparents, Alex had managed to open the door and slide down to the ground. Now he was approaching the back of the truck. He peered around, looking for his grandfather. He looked at Kelly. He hesitated.

Come *on*, Kelly thought. Come *on*! But Alex seemed frozen with indecision, or fear.

"There's something wrong with that girl," Eleanor called.

Adam turned to her, exasperated. "There's nothing—"

Kelly saw her chance. A slim one, but the only one.

"Alex!" she yelled. "Come here!"

Adam whipped around, saw that the truck was empty, and took a second to locate Alex, who was tearing down the driveway toward Kelly. Adam took one step forward, reaching out his hand toward his grandson.

"Get back here!" he commanded.

But Alex continued to run. Kelly leaned over the seat, unlatched the passenger door and shoved it open.

"Run!" she yelled. "Faster!" She turned on the ignition.

Adam, after a moment of surprise, started to chase after Alex. But he had been too confident in his own authority. Alex had a good lead on him.

Alex pumped his arms and legs as if running for his life. He dived into the passenger seat, headfirst, about ten feet ahead of Adam. Kelly stepped on the gas.

"Hang on," she said.

Alex's door swung wide as they pulled away. The tires squealed as she turned the corner against the light. In the rearview mirror, she saw Adam cutting through the cemetery beside the Cathedral, hoping to head her off. He skidded on the snow-covered grass, lost his balance, and tumbled below her line of sight. She slowed down briefly to close Alex's door, then turned her attention to the road. The morning traffic was backed up at the bridge, as she'd known it would be. She made a sharp left and floored it down Taché, past the hospital. South.

Chapter Ten

Angel held in her hands the note her sister had left behind and read it for what seemed like the hundredth time.

Dear Angel, I don't want you to worry about me or Alex. We are perfectly all right, but I had to leave town for a while. You can tell Darl I'm taking good care of Alex until he gets better. Trust me on this, Angel, and don't worry. I'll be in touch as soon as I can. Love, Kelly.

"Where could she be?" Angel asked Paul, again.

Paul didn't answer. He was deep in concentration, studying the window frame of Kelly's bedroom. He ran a dirty thumbnail along the outside edge of the sill. It was only slightly splintered. He pulled a hand plane out of his toolbox and began to plane the wood smooth.

"Vancouver, do you think? She could have gone to stay with her friend Karen."

"Called there," Paul said. He picked up the two-by-four he had measured earlier and fit it into place between the sill and the wooden window frame.

Angel read the note again. "'Perfectly all right,'" she repeated. "Jesus."

"She's probably fine," Paul told her. "Probably smart to get away. Here, hold this end, will you? Hold it tight."

Angel moved over to the window, still holding the note, and placed one of her slim hands on the block of wood. "Maybe she went to Toronto? Or ... you don't think ... New York? You don't think she went to stay with Maggie?"

Paul, who was holding five nails between his teeth, merely grunted. It was obvious he did not think Kelly was in New York.

As he hammered in the nails, Angel continued to muse. "'Trust me on this,'" she read aloud. "What does *that* mean?"

"It means you should trust her," Paul said, shortly. "Why don't you?"

"I do. I do, but I want to talk to her. Maybe she's in Minneapolis? With her friend Lila?"

"I told you Sam called Minneapolis. Lila hasn't heard from her. I called Vancouver and I called Toronto. Called every place I could think of. Even called your mother in New York. No one's heard from her." He drove in the last nail and gave the window frame a shake. It held firm. It was nailed tight.

"Your sister is smart," Paul said. "I'm sure she has her reasons. Don't worry about her, babe." He put his tools back in the box and carried it into the kitchen. "Look, why don't you go out and get us some lunch, okay? You haven't eaten a thing. I want to stay and take a look at this kitchen window, make sure it's secure." He handed her a crumpled wad of bills. "And get some tobacco."

Paul watched her drive away, but when she was gone, he did not attend to the kitchen window. He entered the back room and opened Kelly's locked desk drawer with a bent coat hanger. He shuffled through the files, reading her mail and her telephone bills. Somewhere in here there had to be a clue to her whereabouts.

KELLY LEFT ALEX IN THE CAR outside a gas station in Grand Forks, North Dakota. She dialed the number Lila had given her, praying.

"Kelly, Christ, where are you?"

"Lila, I can't tell you right now. I need you to help me, though. I'm doing something crazy."

"This better be good," Lila said. "You're two days late."

Kelly had thought out her story carefully before she phoned. She told Lila the truth about the assault on Darl and Adam's custody order, but she kept to herself her strange suspicions about Darl's assailant, and the peculiar events that had been going on in her own house. She had not forgotten the way Leon dismissed her concerns. He had as much as said she was imagining things again. She couldn't risk losing Lila's confidence as well. She needed Lila to trust her judgment. Most importantly, she needed her to understand about Adam.

Like everyone else, Lila had always assumed that most of James's problems stemmed from his own unbalanced mind. Kelly wished she had never promised James she would keep the worst of his stories a secret from friends and family. She tried now to impress on Lila how dangerous Adam really might be. Lila listened in stunned silence.

She explained about the stolen birth certificates, the high-speed drive to the border, where Kelly had passed herself off as Angela Knowles, American citizen, wife of Paul Knowles, legitimate mother of the little boy sitting happily beside her, Allan James Knowles, five years old. They had crossed over into the States less than an hour after leaving Adam behind in the cemetery. For the past three days, she had wandered from motel to motel, contacting nobody, except to phone St. Boniface Hospital for anonymous inquiries into Darl's condition. The answer remained the same: serious. No change. Now Kelly was running out of money and ideas.

Lila listened, saying only, "God. Oh my God. What have you done?"

"I did what I had to do."

"But if they have legal custody, you *can't* do it. You've got to take him home."

"We can't go back," Kelly emphasized, trying to make Lila see. "It's not safe." If Lila had heard James's stories herself, she wouldn't be questioning Kelly's actions right now. If more people had heard them, Kelly thought bitterly, this course of action wouldn't be necessary. Adam would be in jail, where he belonged.

"Then you have to go to the authorities," Lila insisted.

"I can't," Kelly argued. "I'm the one who broke the law, stealing a kid from his legal guardian."

"You have to, Kelly. If you turn around, right now, and take Alex back, they might go easy on you. You might even be able to get custody."

"Too risky," Kelly said. "It would take too long." She had already thought about this at length. If she went through legal channels, it would mean surrendering Alex to Adam first. Then a long court battle. Very long. With Leon's help she might win, but it would take time. If even half of James's stories about Adam were true, that time might cost Alex his sanity. It might cost him his life.

"Maybe if you call Adam, reason with him—"

"No!"

"Then you have to come here," Lila said decisively. "At least for now. Look, Adam won't know where you are. They'll never guess you even left the country. You'll be safe till we figure out what to do."

"Or until Darl gets better."

"Yes. Kelly, why don't you come? Come tomorrow. You can work with me, just as we planned. I've already rented a house for you. I'll help you look after Alex."

Kelly looked at Alex. He was sitting with his head down, hunched over. At first, the car trip had been an adventure. Now it was becoming an ordeal. He was sick of motel rooms and coffee shops and the endless, aimless driving. Her talk of a vacation had satisfied him at first. But now he was weary. He needed a home. If Kelly was going to keep him, she'd need to make a real home for him. He waved at her, without much enthusiasm. She waved back, trying to smile.

"You can't do this alone," Lila was saying. And she was right.

"WHAT IN THE WORLD did you do to your hair?" This was the first thing Lila said when she opened the door.

Kelly smiled wryly. "In disguise." She glanced uncertainly at the young man hovering curiously in the hallway.

"This is Jesse San," Lila said. "You'll be getting to know each other well. He's the assistant to the director."

"The assistant director?" Jesse seemed too young for the job. High-top sneakers and a Pink Floyd sweatshirt.

"No, I'm the director's assistant. There's a difference."

He shook her hand. "Pleased to meet you. Hello there, Alex."

Jesse took their bags upstairs while Lila led them into the tiny living room. As soon as Lila sat down, Alex climbed into her lap.

"And how are you, my big boy?" Lila asked him. "You came so far to see me."

Alex grinned and snuggled close to Lila. He was sleepy and didn't mind being babied. He was no doubt glad to see a familiar face, Kelly thought.

Lila produced a bottle of red wine and a corkscrew from a glass cupboard under the coffee table.

"I've been very busy since you called. I've made a lot of arrangements, so bear with me." She opened the wine, balancing Alex precariously on her knee, poured, and settled down to tell Kelly her plans.

As Lila's assistant, Kelly would have only part-time work,

but Lila had made a deal with the head of wardrobe at the Arcana, who was looking for a new assistant. On Lila's recommendation, she'd agreed to hire Kelly sight unseen—at least for the full run of *Hamlet*. "Dorothy agreed you'd be *my* assistant, first. I have dibs on you. But you can work afternoons as the wardrobe assistant. You're way overqualified, but you're going to need the money."

"What do those wardrobe assistants do exactly?" Kelly asked.

"Oh, you know, sort of everything."

"Everything," Kelly repeated. She wasn't too pleased to hear this, but she appreciated Lila's help. She was going to need steady work.

"I'll take you over to your house first thing in the morning. It belongs to a professor. A friend of Taylor's. You're lucky he agreed to hold it for you." She shot Kelly a reproachful look. "He's leaving tomorrow for a sabbatical in England. I promised him you'd sign the lease yesterday." Lila shifted Alex's little body from her lap onto the couch. He had fallen asleep, and she covered him up with a blanket. "And we'll need to find a school for Alex. I asked Taylor, and he gave me the address where his kids go. It's supposed to be good." She frowned. "I told him you have a son," she said. "I hope that's okay. I thought it would be safer to tell everyone that. Fewer questions."

"I guess so." The full impact of what she had done was beginning to register. "But Taylor already knows my name!"

"Yes," Lila agreed. "You'll have to use your real name on the set." Seeing Kelly's stricken face, Lila reached forward and drew her into a hug. "Everything will work out. Don't worry."

Kelly tried to let her body relax for the first time in days, in weeks. When she looked up, Jesse was standing in the doorway, grinning. Lila had a telephone call, he said.

"THAT WAS SAM," Lila reported when she returned. "He went to see Darl this afternoon. Apparently he's checked himself out, gone home. You didn't tell me his leg was broken."

"His leg?"

"It must be bad. Sam says he's got a cast from his hip to his ankle."

"Oh God," said Kelly. "No. I didn't stick around long enough to find out. But he must be better, if he's home."

Lila shook her head. "It sounds pretty bad, Kell. Sam said he barely seems conscious. He's talking some, but not making much sense." She grimaced as she sat down. "Sam thinks he should still be in hospital."

"Did Darl ask about me? About Alex?"

"He told Sam you're babysitting for him, and at first Sam assumed you had Alex at your place, but when Sam tried to reach you . . ."

"Oh no," said Kelly. "What are you going to tell Sam?"

Lila sighed. "Your sister, Angela, told him you've taken Alex away for a while and not to worry. But he was still pretty concerned."

"You told him I was here?"

Lila bit her lip. "I'm already involved," she said. "I don't want Sam to be, you know, mixed up in this too." She would not look at Kelly. "In case . . ."

"In case what?"

"In case you get arrested. I'm sorry, Kelly, but it's possible. I don't want Sam to be an accessory to kidnapping."

"Yes. Of course. You're right." Kelly had crossed the border with Alex. Technically, she supposed, she was an international criminal now. Things could become very ugly. She held on to the hope that Darl would recover before she got caught. She could deal with the consequences later, if she had to. For now she was only glad to see Alex sleeping peacefully, hundreds of miles away from Adam.

THE PROFESSOR'S HOUSE was beautiful. Small but elegant, furnished for comfort. The downstairs was all one room, an open floor plan with a stone fireplace at the center, separating the kitchen from the living room and broad front hallway. The professor took care to caution her about the piano, an ancient upright that must never, never be left open when not in use.

The showpiece of the house was a wide stained-glass window, six feet high, made by the professor's wife. A wedding present, he explained. Very valuable. It was set into the wall on the landing, halfway up the stairs. In rich ruby reds and royal blues, it depicted a man and a woman. The man was standing with his back to the woman, as if walking away from her. But he was turning to look back over his shoulder, an odd expression on his face, both tenderness and horror. The woman cringed, holding up her hands as if to ward him off. Kelly was fascinated by their faces, and by the border that surrounded them, black flowers and vines creeping up all the way to the ceiling. Beside the window, the landing door led out to a small porch overlooking the side yard.

Upstairs, there were two bedrooms, one of them enormous, lined from floor to ceiling with books.

"You will take good care of the books, won't you?" the professor prodded.

"Oh yes," Kelly said. The house was perfect.

He agreed to a low rent, as Lila had predicted. What he really wanted was someone who would take care of the place and watch the piano while he was away. Kelly signed a few papers in Angel's name, and he handed over the keys. He was gone before she finished carrying her bags in from the car.

Alex was excited and eager to unpack. He arranged the pitifully small collection of things she had hurriedly grabbed from his room at home, putting his storybooks and trucks on the wide wooden sill beneath the dormer window in his new room. He hung his few small articles of clothing in the closet.

"There," he said proudly.

It was kind of pathetic.

IN THE MIDDLE OF THE NIGHT, Kelly sat alone in front of the tall stone fireplace which she didn't know how to light, and poured a glass of brandy from a bottle she found in the kitchen. Alex was safe from Adam, and she was safe from whoever it was who liked to play those cruel tricks back in Winnipeg. Whoever had attacked Darl. She felt a stab of guilt that she had not warned Darl about those tricks. But there was no evidence they were related to the assault on Darl. Or to the appearance of James in her dreams, in her "haunted" house back home. Perhaps Leon was right, she thought, about one thing. Perhaps she did need to get out of that house which held so many memories. She looked about the professor's living room with satisfaction, admiring again the oddly moving tableau of the stained-glass window. She tasted the brandy and dared to smile. There was a distinct absence of James in this house. For the first time in sixteen months and twenty-six days, she almost welcomed it.

Chapter Eleven

The Arcana was an old theater, built in the booming twenties and renovated somewhat haphazardly over the years, as its fortunes rose and fell. Jesse provided a brief history as he gave Kelly a tour through the long, maze-like hallways that connected the various additions. Originally a nightclub, opened by an eccentric amateur magician, the building had been used as a men's shelter during the Depression and a Red Cross headquarters during the war until it reopened in the fifties as a dinner theater. Since then, it had gone through a number of incarnations. Right now, under the directorship of Timothy Sheer, who restored its original name, it was highly successful, one of the most prestigious theaters in the Midwest, with a growing reputation for Shakespearean productions. The Arcana's physical structure reflected its numerous identities. It was a bit like a building in a dream, Kelly thought, where doors opened upon doors, different styles of architecture abutted each other, and ceilings hung at various heights.

They toured the dressing rooms, hallways, and stage. Off the green room, there was a pleasant little corner, furnished like a home with a fridge and kitchen table, even a couch and television. The walls were painted a bright, dark blue.

"We call this the blue room," Jesse explained. "You're welcome here any time. Everybody eats lunch here and sits around, you know, on breaks."

The costume shop was in the basement, and here they stopped and rested for a minute. It was well lit, more natural light than anywhere Kelly had ever worked before. Despite the fact it was below ground level, a bank of windows lined the wall above the sewing machines. Bright sunlight slanted in from a dugout courtyard outside. Kelly looked around at the rolls of paper, bolts of muslin, pencils, rulers, measuring tape, scissors hanging on a row of hooks. She felt a small tingle of anticipation.

The head of wardrobe was a quiet, harassed-looking woman named Dorothy. She was sorting out rolls of ribbon with the help of a plump, blonde teenage girl, who smiled shyly at Kelly.

"I'm glad you're here," the girl said.

Dorothy agreed. "Yes. It will be good to have someone, finally, with some experience. Lila and I have agreed on your job description," she said. "You can help Lila as much as she wants, but you'll need to help me, too, when things get hectic. They always do, no matter how organized we are. I've been here thirteen years, and I have never seen a production that ran smoothly."

Jesse grinned. "Just what you wanted to step into, right?" he asked. "Thirteen years of chaos?" He drew the blonde girl forward gently and introduced her. "Kelly, this is Bobbie. She's our general, all-round gofer. Jack of all trades."

"And master of none," said Bobbie. She offered her hand, and Kelly shook it warmly.

"Thankfully," Dorothy said, "this play should run fairly smoothly. We have a good budget for a change. The production manager was generous. The all-star cast and all."

"The one-star cast," said Jesse. He winked. Then he checked his watch. "Look, I've got a noon meeting with

Taylor. Bobbie, maybe you could take Kelly to lunch, show her around a bit?"

"Sure, I'll take her to the hotel coffee shop, okay?"

"Fine. Meet you there when I'm done," he said. He nodded at Dorothy and spun off up the stairs, as if he were late for a briefing at the White House.

THEY ENJOYED A LIGHT LUNCH at the Fallon Hotel, just a block from the theater.

"Timothy Sheer always puts up his actors here," Bobbie explained. "It's so close and all. And management is discreet."

"Discreet?"

"Well, sometimes, if the actors are well known, they tend to get swamped by fans. The Fallon makes an effort to protect their privacy. We have to keep the talent happy, you know."

Kelly heard a note of pride in the young girl's voice, and she smiled. "You like your job, don't you?" she asked.

"Every graduate in my whole drama class wanted this job," Bobbie confided. "I can't believe I got it. They're all so jealous they could just kill me."

Kelly was amused. "Is this a hard job to get?"

"I don't know about usually. But this year it was. Every girl in the class applied. I can't believe I lucked out."

"What's so special about this year?"

Bobbie stared as if Kelly had just stepped off a spaceship from another planet. "Michael Black, of course. He arrives this weekend. He'll be staying right here in this hotel." She looked around the four corners of the coffee shop reverently. "And I'm going to meet him!"

"What's so wonderful about Michael Black?" Kelly teased.

Bobbie dropped her sandwich onto her plate and stared harder. "Are you for real?"

They were interrupted by Jesse, who came by to say he had errands to run for Taylor and couldn't stay for lunch.

"Thanks for the tour," Kelly said.

"Well," he said, "the place is ancient, but it's funky. And the people are cool. Think you'll be happy here?"

"I'll be more than happy," Kelly said.

It was true. Right now, a building full of total strangers was the best place she could possibly be.

IT DIDN'T TAKE LONG for Kelly to learn her way around her new neighborhood. With Taylor's help, she found a spot for Alex in a private school and registered him under Allan's name, telling the teacher that "Alex" was a nickname. No one seemed even slightly suspicious.

In the afternoons, when she wasn't too busy, Kelly picked Alex up early and brought him down to the theater with her. Bobbie helped to keep an eye on him.

Alex loved the theater. He especially loved to watch the set-building. The carpenters constructed two wide staircases leading up to two broad walkways, twelve and eighteen feet above the stage. Scaffolding stretched up beyond the catwalks. Sawdust and wood chips littered the boards. Taylor demanded construction begin much earlier than normal. He wanted rehearsals to take place on all levels. He wanted everyone to be "saturated" with the atmosphere, he said.

Alex begged to be allowed to climb to the top, so Bobbie and Kelly helped him up, each holding one of his hands. It was a long drop to the ground.

"What's this for?" Alex asked. "Is it a mountain?"

"It's a castle," Kelly explained. "The story is about a prince."

"And a princess?"

"No princess, no. Sorry. But there's a king and a queen and a ghost and a really big sword fight."

"Cool. You're making the ghost, right?"

"That's right." But she was not making much progress. Lila had shown Kelly all her costume sketches, so Kelly could get a feel for the way the play was going to look. Lila was doing a marvelous job, and Taylor loved it. But Kelly had no inspiration yet. Just a few sketches, no better than what a kid might do with a bed sheet on Hallowe'en, she chastised herself. Different interpretations of the play swam in her head. Was he an entirely evil ghost? No, she didn't think so, and neither did Taylor. Was he a figment of Hamlet's imagination? Not entirely, because the watchmen saw him, too. He had to be noble, Kelly thought. Noble and wronged and racked with suffering. He could wear his royal robes ... or wispy rags, torn and tormented.

"Is there a dragon?" Alex wanted to know.

"No dragon. Come on, let's get down now."

"Aw, Kelly, I want to play up here. I'm the prince!" He struck a pose, as if brandishing a sword and shield. He started to run along the walkway, but she grabbed him by the back of his shirt.

"I don't think so," she said. "Come on."

They descended the stairs, Kelly grasping him tightly.

"Whew!" said Bobbie. "Boys!"

"He's a handful," Kelly remarked. "Sometimes I can barely keep up with him."

"I don't know if I could handle a kid," Bobbie said. "Not yet, anyway. Hey, how come he calls you Kelly? I mean, how come he doesn't call you Mom or something?"

"Family tradition," Kelly said.

SATURDAY EVENING, LILA DROPPED BY to visit. They helped themselves to more of the professor's brandy while Lila filled Kelly in on the situation at work.

"Taylor is what they call a hands-on director," Lila said. "That means he's a control freak."

"I thought you loved the guy!"

"I do. I do love him. But I'm warning you, he's manic. He'll drive you crazy. Drives everyone crazy. He even drives the carpenters crazy, for goodness' sake. Consults about everything. God knows what he'll do to Michael Black."

"I hear Michael Black is flying in this weekend."

"He's going to be glad to see you," Lila said.

"Oh, come on. I'm sure he doesn't even remember me."

"I'm sure he does," Lila said. "What's the matter with you? You honestly don't remember the way he followed you around in New York?"

"I honestly don't."

"Come on! The tall, handsome one, always hanging around the costume shop when you were working. Dark hair, golden skin. I think he's Arabian or something. The one who played the villain."

"Michael Black? Didn't he play the cop? I thought he was a detective or something. He had those boring suits."

"He was the homicide detective, but he turned out to be the killer. Didn't you even ever *watch* the film?"

"No," Kelly admitted. She had virtually forgotten that *Rising Heat* even had a story to it. It wasn't her kind of movie in the first place, and besides, they had wrapped that project just when James got sick. By the time it came out, she'd been in no mood to go to the movies.

"You don't remember he asked you back to his hotel for dinner? Everyone was dying of envy."

"Well, vaguely," Kelly said, though she didn't really. New York had been a blur of invitations and conversations with beautiful strangers. But she had spent every spare minute on the telephone to James, trying to calm him down. She had worried herself sick over him. She sighed.

"Well, you must have noticed him since," Lila protested. "He's starred in everything. Didn't you ever see *Down on the Moon*?"

"What?"

"The movie! Didn't you ever see *Black Magic*?"

Kelly shook her head.

"*Last Day of July*?"

"No."

"You must have seen *A Winter in China*?"

"Lila, I haven't seen anything the last couple of years. I've been sort of reclusive, you know? Are these recent films?"

"Yeah, sorry. Very recent. Last couple of years exactly. I guess you've been . . . out of it. Sorry."

"So he's in these films? All of them?"

"He's on Hollywood's A-list. He could be making millions. But as Taylor said, he decided to return to the stage for some mysterious reason. Anyway, you'll know him the minute you see him."

"Maybe."

"You will," Lila said. "Believe me, you will."

THAT NIGHT, ALEX HAD A NIGHTMARE, his first one since they'd left Winnipeg.

Kelly was still awake, rereading *Hamlet*, when she heard his whimpers. She waited for a minute, hoping he'd fall back to sleep. But then he let out a terrible howl, and she leaped off the bed.

"Alex, honey. Wake up."

But it seemed he was awake. He was sitting up in bed, eyes wide open, screaming.

"Alex!" She shook him. "Alex, wake up."

He stared right into her face, not seeing her. And the look in his eyes chilled her blood. It was the look of a grown man who had witnessed some unspeakable atrocity.

"Sweet, come on. Talk to me. It's Kelly. Honey? Come on."

Finally, his body convulsing in a great shiver, he seemed

to throw the vision off. He saw her. For a second, a look of profound, adult sorrow crossed his face. Then he began to cry like a child, and she gathered him in her arms. His thin little shoulders shook with sobs while she held him. Finally, he cried himself to sleep, but Kelly kept holding him, unwilling to let him go.

In the morning, she greeted him cautiously. "Are you feeling better?"

"Sure," he said. "What's for breakfast? I'm hungry."

Kelly watched him carefully all day, spoiling him. In the daylight, he seemed happy and relaxed, adjusting easily to his new life. He took all the changes in stride, accepting without question the explanation she had given when they left Winnipeg: Kelly would take care of him while his daddy got better. Aside from the nightmare he seemed fine, showing no signs of homesickness. Kelly wondered whether she should talk to him more about his father, but the news from Sam wasn't exactly encouraging. He'd told Lila that Darl was still incoherent and barely able to look after himself. Kelly decided to let the matter lie. If Alex was handling things, there was no point upsetting him.

Chapter Twelve

When Kelly saw Hamlet for the first time, he was down on one knee, tying his bootlace. He walked out onto the boards early Monday morning as she sat at the back of the theater, alone in the dark, contemplating the stage. Try as she might, she could summon no inspiration. The set did not seem real to her. She imagined the ghost, forcing herself to concentrate. How would he appear from this distance? Then she heard footsteps in the wings and turned her head to see who was there. But he was already down, tugging at his laces.

Two small spotlights, high above the stage, provided the only illumination, but she recognized him immediately, not just from the movie magazines and posters, but from her very first impression of him back in New York. It was the way he held himself, the way he rose to stand, that triggered her memory. She remembered her first, simple impression of him—here was a man who *moved*—and it was still accurate. He moved swiftly, carelessly, with a strange, abrupt grace. One moment he was kneeling, concentrating, the next he was standing tall. He placed his large hands against the small of his back, raised his head and wandered, turning, about the stage.

When he mounted the stairs, two at a time, he did it without effort. Something seemed to pull him forward, upward, as though his energy were not contained within his body but surged ahead of him and drew him after.

He reached the top and walked the length of the parapet, perilously close to the edge, without looking down. He stopped and stretched, sweeping his long arms over his head. He seemed at home there, in control. He wore blue jeans, a black T-shirt, short leather boots. Kelly couldn't even see his face, only the tall shape of him, standing with legs apart, shoulders raised. But she knew he was the Prince.

He leaned forward, letting his elbows rest on the railing, and dropped his head to study the floor below. Then abruptly he lifted his face and spoke.

"Good morning."

Kelly drew in her breath. She had thought herself invisible in the darkness. But he looked right at her.

There was nothing to do but answer, though she felt foolish, having watched in silence all this time. She stood and walked toward the stage, looking up at him.

"Hi," she said. "You must be Hamlet."

He laughed. "Well, not yet. But soon." He descended several steps and then jumped the rest of the way down. "And you are Kelly Quirk."

"Yes. I'm working on the costumes." She held out her hand and he took it. She felt very quiet, very still inside. His hand was cool and steady, his eyes curious and alert.

"I'm Michael Black," he said. As if she might not know.

"WHERE ARE THE LIGHTS?" he asked, and Kelly led him backstage to the control panel. He stood beside her, flicking the switches, playing with various combinations, until the upper reaches of the staircase were illuminated with a soft yellow glow. Then he strode back onto the stage and she followed slowly behind him. The top of her head reached, she estimated, just about his shoulder blades. He was well over six feet tall.

He opened his arms toward the ceiling. "I like this space," he said. "It feels good here. Charged."

He's the one that's charged, Kelly thought. His skin was luminous, his whole body electric. But he was right. The Arcana suddenly felt like a place where things were going to happen. The set, which this morning appeared to her no more than unfinished scaffolding and fake stone, took on the air of a castle in Elsinore. When she followed Michael's gaze up to the top, she could sense the ghost of the King there, his unbearable suffering, and she shivered.

BACK IN THE COSTUME SHOP, Kelly sharpened a pencil until the point was absolutely perfect, savoring the scent of the fresh shavings. With a surge of inspiration, a pleasure she'd almost forgotten, she began to sketch the ghost of the King. Long lines, a regal bearing. Now that she had seen Hamlet, she knew that the ghost would need all the help he could get if he was to be at all imposing next to his towering, electrified son. A dark cloak, burlap, perhaps, so that the lights would catch the rough texture of the material and reveal its harshness. Layers and layers of ragged cloth, to suggest the cold. Layers of the roughest burlap, the rawest silk, so that the clothes would rustle and grate against each other, so that the body would speak.

Lost in her work, she was almost late for her meeting with Taylor. The morning had passed too quickly. But she had some promising sketches, and Taylor was pleased. As he praised her work, Kelly began to remember something—she was good at this.

Filled with energy, she left early to pick up Alex.

"Let's not go home right away," she suggested to him. "Let's celebrate."

"Is it your birthday?"

"No."

"Is it a holiday?"

"No. Let's just do something special for fun, okay?"

"Okay!"

They had dinner in a restaurant, and she let Alex eat a tiger-tiger ice-cream cone with sprinkles. Then they drove to the river and walked along the banks of the Mississippi, and Kelly told Alex about Huckleberry Finn, the boy who dreamed his way to freedom. The boy who built a raft and sailed away from home.

THE NEXT DAY, LILA AND KELLY were searching through the stock for samples they might use for Gertrude's chamber dress.

"You're getting good," Lila said, when Kelly picked out a swatch of burgundy velvet for the bodice. "That's perfect."

"Yes," Kelly said. "I'm enjoying this, believe it or not."

"There is nothing like good, hard, creative work to take your mind off your troubles. I'm so glad you came here. I knew you still had the Kelly touch." She paused and smiled at her friend. "Taylor is very impressed with you, you know."

"He seems to like my work," Kelly said modestly. There was something about Lila's smile she didn't trust.

"And," Lila said, "he seems to like you. I'll have you know you're invited to a special dinner Friday night. Mostly cast."

"Dinner?"

"Taylor's made reservations for the chosen few," Lila said. "I'm not invited, but you are. Jesse showed me the invitations."

Kelly stopped what she was doing. "That's bizarre."

"Bizarre, yes. But wonderful. Maybe Taylor likes you," Lila said slyly.

"Get out of here." Kelly threw a bronze button at her, and it hit her in the ear. Lila retaliated with a thimble.

"I can babysit," Lila said. "While you step out with the

crème de la crème, I'll stay home and watch television." She rolled her eyes and let out a mock sigh.

"Get out of here," Kelly said. "They're not going to invite me to their parties."

But when she arrived home, there was the invitation in the mailbox: stiff, expensive paper, with her name on it.

What was Taylor Grant up to?

FRIDAY AFTERNOON, TAYLOR WAS FLYING. He summoned Kelly to his office, and when she arrived, he was sitting at his desk, talking to about seven people at once, including some poor soul on the telephone.

"Kelly!" He waved her in, motioned for her to stand and wait. "We need a proper trapdoor," he was saying into the telephone. "And I want it done by tech week. No." He shuffled through files on his desk, sent papers flying onto the floor. "We open the sixth of January. Yes. Right."

Kelly saw Lila bending to pick up the papers. She winked. "Welcome to the monkey house," she said.

Debbie Thompson, the actress who was to play Ophelia, tapped Lila on the back. "If you don't mind, I just have to talk to Taylor." She pushed past Lila, flattening her against the wall. "Hey, Taylor!"

Taylor held up a finger to stall her, but she wouldn't wait. She heaved her thin haunches up on the desk and sat there, letting her impatience simmer in full view. She was a full-lipped, wide-eyed blonde, with an ambitious forehead and star attitude. She was short for an actress, wiry and seething with barely controlled petulance. She blew air from her mouth to remove her blonde locks from her eyes. She emanated an exhausted kind of beauty. Not my idea of Ophelia, Kelly thought. Taylor's job—not an easy one—would be to tone down that twentieth-century soap-opera quality about her. That modern, American aggression.

"Just a second," Taylor said to her. "I'm on the ... What? No, the sixth. The goddamned sixth, I said."

"Taylor!" A voice from somewhere in the back of the office. "Can I have a decision on that guy from Ohio? I've got to catch a plane in thirty minutes."

"Taylor, the photographer's here." Jesse pushed past the crowded doorway, dragging a man laden with cameras and equipment bags. "This is John Green, from *The Arts Today*."

Taylor covered the receiver with one hand and glanced up quickly. "Good. John, can you come to the dinner tonight? We're going to the High Five, and I want some shots of Michael there, for the local angle. We'll be wanting publicity shots in costume too—as soon as possible. Kelly, I want the team to start on the patterns for Hamlet tomorrow. So get a full set of measurements today."

"Me?"

"Sure. You don't mind, do you? The cutter's gone home already."

"Doesn't an actor like him ... I mean, isn't that stuff on file cards or something?"

"Well, usually," said Taylor. "But he bulked up a lot for that last action movie, and I'm not sure what's current. Better do it today and make sure. He's in his dressing room still, I think. You should be able to catch him."

Kelly squeezed out of the office, where Debbie was threatening to throw a tantrum, and made her way through the hallways backstage.

Michael's name was stenciled prominently on the dressing-room door, which was ajar. She knocked and he called out, "Enter!"

He lounged in a chair before the mirror, his long legs up on the dressing table. There was barely space for his feet among the masses of flowers that scented the room—roses, carnations, daisies. He was slitting open a little pink envelope with the long, sharp silver blade of a letter opener. He pulled out a pink card with scalloped edges and began to read. He didn't look up. Bobbie was there, setting out a pitcher of ice water, glasses, lemons, honey.

"Hi, Kelly," said Bobbie, and Michael looked up.

"Kelly! Come in. I've been hoping you'd show up."

Bobbie's eyes widened. She backed out of the room. "Call me if you need anything else, Mr. Black."

"Yes. Thanks!" He tossed the card onto a mass of mail on the couch. Envelopes and letters spilled onto the floor. "Sorry about this," he said. "It's a mess in here." He leaped up and cleared some books from an armchair. "Sit, sit. Tell me what's on your mind."

She sat.

"I'm supposed to measure you—your ..." He placed both hands on the arm of her chair and leaned toward her, so close she could smell the soap he'd used that morning. Kelly stared at the rolled-up sleeves of his white shirt, his gigantic, golden brown hands, the black hairs on the back of his wrist, the length of his arms. He watched her intently, but she couldn't meet his eyes. She coughed. "Sorry. I'm supposed to measure ... your head. For the hats, you know." That was smart. How was she going to get out of that one?

He jumped backward, as if delighted. "Measure my head! That is a new one! So you are the head head-measurer, I presume."

"Uh, sort of."

"Say something," he said.

"What?"

"Say something. You're Canadian, aren't you? You look Irish. But you don't sound Irish."

"Well, I grew up in Canada. But I was born in New York City. And you're right. My mother is Irish-American."

"And your father?"

"He was—he left when I was young." She didn't feel like explaining further.

"You have a wonderful accent. A wonderful voice." He paused. "And a wonderful laugh. The other day—"

"I guess I should do this," she said, cutting him off. "Sit down for a minute." She took out the measuring tape and stood behind him. "Sit up straight." She wound the tape around his ears, trying not to touch him with her bare hands, while he stayed perfectly still. "There."

"Thank you." He grinned. "So what took you to Canada? I love Canada."

"Oh, my stepfather got a job there, and then we just stayed. What about your family? Where are they from?"

"My father is Russian, and my mother is Syrian. They're both in Paris right now. My sister is at school there. We grew up—well, everywhere."

"No wife? Children?" It struck her after she said this that of course she should already know if he had a wife. She would have read it in the magazines. But this didn't seem to occur to him.

He simply shook his head. "Unfortunately, no. I haven't met the right person, I guess." He caught her eye in the mirror. "No time."

"You're pretty busy?" she asked.

But he just laughed—very suddenly burst into laughter. His expression changed like quicksilver—one moment drawn and serious and dark, the next bright as the sun. That intense energy, showing itself to her again.

Of course he'd been busy. He'd made five movies in the past two years. I can't talk to this man, she thought. This is impossible. "Listen, I should get going. My little boy—" She started to wind up the tape measure she'd been twisting between her fingers.

He watched her movements, intent on her wedding ring. "So you—you're still married?"

"Yes," she said. "I mean, no." She blushed. "I'm widowed now." Such a strange, old-fashioned phrase.

Michael's eyebrows lifted. "You mean he…? So young?"

"Yeah." This was not a story she wanted to tell. She thought of James's wild behavior in New York. Did Michael remember that? "I'll see you later," she said, edging closer to the door. "I'll see you at dinner tonight."

"Sit beside me."

"What?"

"At dinner. Sit beside me. I'll tell Taylor to arrange it. Is that all right?"

"Sure. Fine," she said. She got out of there as fast as she could. She had no clue what his measurements might be— not even his hat size.

Chapter Thirteen

Alex stood behind Kelly's chair and watched as she dried her cropped hair. "Where are you going tonight?"

"To a restaurant. With some friends from work."

"Can I come?"

"Not tonight, honey. This is just for grownups. You stay here with Lila, okay? I'll see you in the morning."

"I don't want you to go," he said. He crawled into her lap, and she hugged him. She didn't want to go, either. She knew she'd be out of place among the other guests, a lowly if valued assistant invited to tag along with the stars. But she also knew she was expected to attend. Taylor had arranged it, and heaven forbid she should interfere with his arrangements. He *is* a control freak, she thought. Lila was right, as usual. But it was a good job, all things considered. It was a fantastic job, she corrected herself, and she had no desire to jeopardize it.

Lila arrived at seven, with the dress she had promised for the occasion.

"Hi, Alex." She bent to kiss him, handing the garment bag to Kelly.

"Kelly's going out," Alex said glumly.

"I know. She's going to a party. But we'll have our own party here by ourselves, okay? I'll help Kelly get ready and then we'll play. Why don't you pick out some games for us?"

"Okay." Alex brightened a little. He headed up to his bedroom to sort through his small collection of toys.

Lila followed Kelly up to her own bedroom and watched as she got dressed. "The traditional little black dress," she said. "Very tasteful. What jewelry are you wearing?"

But Kelly's thoughts were elsewhere. "Any news from Sam?"

"Not since Monday. He's driving all over Manitoba, putting together a prairie craft show for the gallery. How about that silver necklace with the matching earrings?"

"You'd think he'd call," Kelly said. "And let us know how things are."

"Kelly," Lila reminded her, "he doesn't even know you're here. I've convinced him not to worry about you. For all he knows you're in Hawaii, living it up. And he never was that close to Darl, you know. It was James who was Sam's friend." She fished through Kelly's jewelry box. "Where is that necklace?"

"True," Kelly admitted. Sam was completely unaware of the urgency of her situation, or even that she was in one. As far as he knew, James's brother was recovering from some regrettable but perfectly ordinary crime.

"No news is good news," Lila reassured her. "I'm sure Sam would call if there was a turn for the worse." She saw Kelly's worried face in the mirror and sighed. "Look, Sam doesn't even know about the custody problem. It's not in the papers or anything. I doubt it's even a police priority. They might not know exactly where Alex is, but they know he's with you. Everyone knows he's perfectly safe. Even Adam knows that."

"True again," Kelly agreed. She glanced at herself in the mirror. "Isn't this a little low-cut?"

"It's perfect," Lila assured her. "Not too flashy, not too dull. All you need is a necklace. How about this?" She held up an amethyst necklace and matching earrings.

Kelly shook her head. "No. You were right the first time. Give me the silver one."

"It's not in the box," Lila said. "Where do you keep it?"

"I'm sure it's in there." Kelly frowned at her reflection. She still wasn't used to her haircut, having her shoulders exposed like this. She looked positively, well, naked, above the dress.

"See for yourself." Lila pointed at the jumble of jewelry spread out across the pillow.

A chill spread slowly through Kelly's body. She could see at a glance that Lila was right. She felt the color drain from her face.

"What's wrong?"

Kelly didn't answer.

"You probably left it in Winnipeg. Try the amethyst."

Kelly didn't answer. She was trying to remember her frantic packing the day she kidnapped Alex. So many details to take care of. Had she looked inside the jewelry box before she shoved it hurriedly into her suitcase?

"What's the matter?"

"It's just that James gave it to me."

"It will turn up," Lila said kindly.

The words echoed in Kelly's mind with a sinister ring.

ALONE DOWNSTAIRS, KELLY WAITED for her cab, pacing back and forth in front of the windows. She realized her hands were shaking. The missing necklace had rattled her more than she'd admitted. Had someone followed her all the way to Minneapolis?

Could he really still be alive?

She thought once again about the Type A blood. She had to know.

She dialed the number of the Riverside Clinic in Winnipeg and listened to the ringing, bracing herself for another frustrating non-conversation with Mrs. Krentz. But it was Frances who answered, and she was much more forthcoming.

"Kelly? Hi. Gee, I was so sorry to hear about Darl. How is he?"

"He's about the same," Kelly said, hoping Frances couldn't tell she was calling long distance. "I need to speak to Leon Chartrand."

"Leon's not back yet," she said. "I can take a message."

"No. No, I'll call back. When will he be in?"

"He's on holidays. He won't be back until, oh, next week. Let's see. Yes, December tenth."

"Holidays! When did he go on holidays?"

"Two weeks ago. He took leave to go up to the reserve to see his folks. I think his grandmother's sick or something."

"I left a million messages for him!" Kelly exclaimed. "Mrs. Krentz never told me he was out of town!"

"Well, you know Mrs. Krentz. She won't tell clients anything personal about the staff."

But Frances might, Kelly thought. Frances just might do her a favor. "Do you have a number for him?" she asked, her fingers crossed.

"No. There's only a note here that we're supposed to refer all his clients to doctors on call. He's not to be disturbed no matter what. Mrs. Krentz said they don't have telephones up there."

"Of course they do," Kelly said. She tried to keep her voice pleasant. "Frances, there's something I need. I just want to check something in my husband's file, and if you could—"

"You mean James?"

"Yes. If you could just look it up for me—"

"I can't do that, Kelly. Sorry. I could get fired for that. You'll have to wait for Leon to get back."

Rules and regulations. She wasn't allowed to know the contents of a file that wasn't supposed to exist.

"Kelly? You there?"

"Yeah. Okay. I understand. I'll call back on the tenth." While the taxi driver waited, she remained in the house, pounding her fist softly against the wall. The thing she hated most in the world was feeling helpless. Being blocked like this, at every turn.

She felt a sudden, keen desire for a drink.

Chapter Fourteen

From a fifth-floor window of the hotel, he watched her stepping carefully out of the taxi.

She had arrived alone.

She stopped on the sidewalk and opened her coat to smooth out the short skirt of her dress. Then she straightened up, glancing nervously up and down the sidewalk. She was definitely unsettled. She knew she didn't belong here.

And she was worried. He recognized the nervous gesture she made, flicking her hair back over her shoulders, although there was nothing there to flick any more. He deeply regretted the loss of all that beautiful, glossy black hair. Well, it would grow again. If his plan worked, he would gain back everything he had lost. Everything that had been stolen from him.

He saw her raise her head. She was looking right at him. No. She couldn't see him in the darkened window. She was merely surveying the elegant façade of the building. He thought she was biting her lip. Her eyes swept across the wide white grounds of the hotel as she stepped quickly, eager to be inside. Anxious.

Yes, his plan was definitely going to work.

THE HIGH FIVE WAS A POSH, candle-lit private dining room on the fifth floor of the White Eagle Hotel, overlooking Medicine Lake. Taylor and Jesse were there when Kelly arrived, standing by the enormous windows, watching the bartender make their martinis. A table for twelve was spread with white linen and silver, crystal wineglasses, yellow roses. Well, Kelly said to herself, it's been a long time—like, never—since you've eaten in a place like this. She tried to walk gracefully across the plush red carpet in her new high-heels, but they cut into her feet.

Taylor wore blue jeans, an impeccable white shirt and a dark, very formal jacket. Jesse wore a brown business suit, half a size too large. He looked uncomfortable.

"Look at this view," Jesse called, as Kelly made her way across the treacherous carpet. The heavy drapery was drawn aside to reveal the night sky, the city glittering at a distance. A thin crescent moon rose over the frozen lake.

"Minneapolis," said Taylor. He swept his arm out toward the scene below them. "City of Waters. Alias Elsinore."

The room filled quickly with people. Timothy Sheer, the artistic director of the Arcana, appeared with a stunning blond young man on his arm, whom he introduced simply as Rocko. Rocko made his way to the bar, where he hovered until dinner, growing steadily drunker and more charming as the evening progressed. Gloria Moorehouse, who was to play Queen Gertrude, arrived with Kevin Wong, who played Ophelia's brother, Laertes. Ophelia herself, or rather Debbie Thompson, fluttered into the room in white chiffon with dragonfly-blue sequins on the skirt, a kind of Cinderella-at-the-ball effect. Her husband, a distinguished Bostonian heart surgeon, beamed with goodwill as he shook hands all around. Everyone was delighted, glamorous. Everyone hummed with suppressed excitement. Everyone's eyes shifted constantly toward the door, waiting for Michael Black.

When he finally arrived, alone, a hush descended on the

little crowd. Taylor moved forward to greet him. Michael was polite, deferential. He stood in one spot, nodding and shaking hands, recognizing everyone in turn. Debbie Thompson balanced on tiptoe to kiss his cheek. Kelly backed against the wall, caught in a small crush of servers and bartenders, cooks and even two maids who had sneaked in somehow, craning their necks, trying to see the celebrity.

The maître d' came forward and whispered in Taylor's ear, and dinner began. Waiters called out the names written on the little cream-colored cards at each place. Kelly was summoned to the right of Michael, who sat at the head of the table, with Debbie at his left.

"Ah, there you are," he said to her, quietly. He stood to pull out her chair.

Debbie scrutinized Kelly's body, looking her up and down, from head to toe, openly and critically. "That's quite a fashion statement," she remarked coolly. "Especially for a costume designer."

"What?" Kelly looked down at her little black dress.

"No jewelry at *all*?" Debbie asked.

Kelly sat down, her hand rushing to her bare throat. In her panic over the missing necklace, she'd forgotten all about accessories. She'd left the house while Lila was still upstairs. She felt herself blush.

"Well, she has a little color, at least," Debbie said to Michael. He appeared not to hear her.

"Now, Deb, don't bite." It was Rocko, seating himself at Kelly's right. He had carried two glasses of Scotch from the bar and set them both in front of his place beside his wineglass.

Debbie ignored him and began an animated conversation with Michael, a long story about the leading man in her previous play, who suffered a stroke during intermission one night, throwing Debbie into a difficult situation.

Bursts of laughter erupted at the far end of the table,

where Taylor held court. Timothy Sheer wrote a note on a piece of paper, folded it in four, and sent it, via a waiter, to Rocko, who put it in his jacket pocket without looking up, or reading it. He was intent on catching the attention of the wine server. Kelly fiddled with her name card, admiring the script. She accepted a glass of white wine. There was a little menu beside her plate, which she pretended to study.

White Bean with Roasted Pepper Coulis
Spicy Thai Peanut Noodle Salad
Tequila Lime-Grilled Prawns
Cherry Sorbet
Grilled Trout served with a warm Mango Chutney
and a Mango Beurre Blanc
Dessert

Rocko leaned over and read it all aloud, in Kelly's ear, in a fake English accent. "My," he concluded. "Lovely."

Kelly smiled at him. "What are you going to have?" she asked.

"My dear," he said, "this is it." He waved the card in the air. "This is dinner."

"All of it?"

"Why, yes. They don't give you any *choices* here." He screwed his delicious red mouth into a comical pout. "Pity. But it's true." He reached over and plucked her napkin from the tablecloth, shook out its delicate folds with a flourish and placed it on her lap. "And this is your napkin. And this is your salad fork. And this"—he tapped her wineglass with the fork—"is the booze. So drink up!"

She raised her glass and they toasted. "We're going to get along splendidly," he announced. "I can tell."

"So there I was with this understudy," Debbie was saying, "all of twenty years old—and he lisped! He positively lisped all through act two. It was humiliating."

"Michael," Gloria called, "have you been to the Tropical Club?"

"He's not going to go to the Tropical Club," said Kevin. "We should take him to the Neptune."

"I hear it's difficult for him," Debbie's husband said quietly, "to go out in public. I heard—"

"But he'll love the Tropical Club. Michael!"

A waiter removed the soup plates. Several, Kelly noticed, were still full.

"So, anyway, I got through the night," Debbie continued. "But we didn't get an ovation. Just a sort of smattering of applause. Don't you hate that?"

Michael smiled politely, then turned to Kelly. "How are you tonight? Are you enjoying the party?"

"It's lovely," she said. She kept her eyes on the tablecloth.

"And your work? Are you enjoying your work at the theater?"

"Oh yes." She looked up then, warming to the topic, but when she saw his dark eyes shining so warmly on her, she could think of nothing intelligent to say.

"Michael!" Debbie interrupted. "Did I tell you I'm writing a screenplay?"

"No," Michael said, his eyes still on Kelly.

Debbie placed a hand on his shoulder and succeeded in turning his attention back to her. She began to give him the details of the plot.

"I love my work," Kelly said. But nobody heard her.

"GOD," SAID ROCKO TO KELLY, after the main course. "I could use a cigarette right about now." He drained his glass and reached for the wine bottle. "Do you smoke?"

"I used to."

"I'm so dreadfully weary of the cigarette police. Absolute fascists. Join me for a smoke, won't you? We'll just hop out on the terrace." He collected his wineglass, held it at eye level and wiggled his free hand from left to right, in indecision. Then he grabbed the whole bottle. "Come along."

Kelly was not sure if this was acceptable, leaving between courses. But she doubted if anyone would miss her. She followed, taking her wineglass, too.

The stars had come out. The night was cold, but calm. The wind was still. They stood leaning against the balcony railing, and Rocko draped his jacket around her shoulders. Down below, they could see several people huddled under the green awning above the winding walkway to the lakeshore. They seemed to be assembling for some performance.

"The height of pretension," Rocko remarked. "A back door with a canopy."

Kelly sipped the wine, a very dry white. The whirling constellations and the sparkling, distant city seemed to reflect each other, and for a moment she felt herself spinning far above the planet, giddy.

Rocko produced a crumpled package of Marlboros and lit up. They clinked glasses and drank.

Rocko looked up at the sky. "*This most excellent canopy*," he quoted. "*This brave o'er hanging firmament.*"

"That's *Hamlet*, isn't it?"

"Yes. Yes."

They were silent for a minute, watching the people below.

"I have a degree in English," Rocko said.

"That's good."

"Yes, it's a great help for an actor," he said ironically.

"Well, you know your Shakespeare."

He smiled forlornly. "My specialty. Unfortunately there's not much call for it. Or rather, there's not much call for me." For a moment, he seemed to drop his cocky pose. "I've been unemployed for a year."

"I'm sure things will look up for you soon," Kelly said kindly.

"It's long past the aperitif, darling."

"What *is* an aperitif, anyway?"

"You're a doll," he said. "But you're innocent, aren't you?"

"I don't know."

"He'll eat you up."

"Who?"

"Swallow you whole." He pulled the note from Timothy out of his pocket and unfolded it.

"What does it say?" she asked.

"I don't know," said Rocko. "I already know." He didn't read it, but began to refold it into the shape of an airplane. "Here you go," he cried. He aimed it at the moon and let it fly. It swooped and rose a little into the air before descending into the crowd below. A teenage girl looked up and set off running to catch it.

"We'd better go back in," she said.

"Can't miss the chocolate cheesecake."

Kelly laughed. "It's not that. I just don't want to offend anyone. I don't want to lose my job."

"Oh, he is going to chew you up," he said. "Digest you."

BACK INSIDE THE HIGH FIVE, dinner was waning, the table in disarray. Gloria and Debbie were arguing over something. The date of a Katharine Hepburn movie, it sounded like. As Rocko predicted, a slice of chocolate cheesecake decorated every plate. Nobody had touched it.

"Michael will know," Debbie was saying. "Michael, when was *Adam's Rib*?"

"Nineteen forty-nine," Michael said, with his eyes closed.

"You see?" cried Gloria. "Tracy was almost fifty years old already."

Timothy and Taylor were conferring in a corner, engrossed in some detail or other, when Timothy spotted them. "Rocko!" He hurried over. "Are you all right?"

"Timothy," Rocko intoned, formally. "I would like you to meet my good friend Kelly. Kelly, this is Timothy Sheer."

"We've met," Kelly told him.

"Not really," said Rocko. "Not intimately …"

"Yes, hello, Kelly." Timothy was angry. "Look," he said, drawing Rocko aside, "why can't you ever behave—"

She walked on past them toward her seat. But a man in a white suit cut her off in his hurry to approach Taylor. "Mr. Taylor? I'm the manager of the White Eagle. May I have a word with you, sir?"

"Yes?"

"Sir," he said. "There is quite a crowd in the lobby of the hotel. I believe they are hoping to see your guest of honor." With a thrust of his chin he indicated Michael.

"How big a crowd?" Taylor asked.

"Some two dozen women, sir. They are waiting by the front door. And there are a few out back as well."

Taylor looked out the window, clearly annoyed. "How long has this been going on?"

"They started to arrive an hour ago. Someone got word, I suppose …" He trailed off, embarrassed. "We've asked them to leave. But there's no budging them."

Jesse looked out the window. "Is there another exit?"

"Through the kitchen, but—"

"I'm not taking him through the kitchen," Taylor said. "Call security. Get them out of here!"

"Taylor, no," Jesse said. "It will get in the paper."

Kelly squeezed past them all, back to her place. She wanted to get her purse, and she was dying to take off her tight shoes. Everyone was standing now, excitedly discussing the problem of the Michael Black fans. The only one left at the table was Michael. He pushed his chair back and stretched his legs, listening patiently to the commotion, his head tilted slightly to one side, hands folded over his stomach.

When she scooped up her purse, he caught her eye for a second.

"Good night," she whispered.

"Good night," he said. "Sorry." He smiled—rather sadly, she thought, with only half his mouth. He was obviously tired. But even with his subdued demeanor, he generated more energy than all the fevered guests combined.

She left them to sort out their own problems, called a cab from the lobby, and was home before midnight. Lila was obviously disappointed. She'd given herself an avocado facial and was sprawled in front of the television with a green face, her hair wrapped in a towel.

"What are you doing home so early?" she cried.

"Got to sleep," Kelly said. She stumbled into the bedroom and locked herself into a drunken dream that ebbed and flowed all night without content, like a clean ocean tide.

BY THE TIME HE FINALLY LEFT the hotel, he was exhausted. Whether from lack of sleep or from the sheer length of his nervous anticipation, he wasn't sure. He had watched her, but had not been able to get close to her. The crowds of fans, the many guests, had made it impossible.

If he simply approached her honestly, told her his feelings, would she speak to him? She might. Perhaps she would reach out one thin white arm and stroke his cheek, gently, the way his mother used to do when she was feeling well. Perhaps she would tilt back her head and laugh, the way she had laughed tonight out on the balcony. That had angered him.

No. He could never tell her. He would stick to his plan. It was a good plan, a subtle plan, one that would bring her to him willingly. Before she guessed the truth.

Chapter Fifteen

The following week was hectic. The cutters were at work, not to be interrupted come hell or high water. Kelly was sent out for various items: new scissors, drapery tacks, bottles of wine. She welcomed the diversion.

Rehearsals were well under way, and Taylor worked everybody hard. He assigned Debbie to a voice coach, and Kevin and Michael battled it out daily with the fight choreographer. Kelly didn't see much of Michael, and when she did run into him in the halls, he was usually drenched in sweat, his shirt sticking to his chest.

Her finished ghost sketches went to the cutters on the second team, who had numerous questions that she answered between errands. George Laugherty, who would play the ghost, arrived and was, suitably, rather elusive. Kelly had to chase him down to get him to his fittings. He preferred to spend his afternoons in the Fallon Hotel bar, claiming he had very few lines and for goodness' sakes he was *dead* all the way through the play, it hardly mattered what he wore, and would they please just leave him alone!

His irreverence irritated many in the cast, but Kelly found him amusing.

The day that he first caught a glimpse of Michael in the halls, George cried aloud, "My son!" He threw the back of his hand dramatically against his forehead. "My beautiful son!"

"Don't get too attached to him," Taylor said. "It's your job to destroy him."

"To tell him the truth," exclaimed George. "Surely to tell him the truth!"

"That's right," said Taylor. "To destroy him."

Michael staggered past them, oblivious.

SAM FINALLY CALLED from Winnipeg, but when Lila asked about Darl, the news was not encouraging.

"The only good news on that front," Sam said, "is that Darl has plenty of help. He says Kelly is looking after Alex."

"Have you, um, talked to Kelly?" Lila asked.

"No. She's taken Alex out of town. She went to visit her mother, I think." Sam didn't want Lila to worry.

"Oh," said Lila, relieved. She didn't want Sam to worry. "Have you talked to Kelly's sister?"

"Yes. She's supposed to be helping Darl with housework, but she doesn't seem very—"

"Competent?"

"Not very," Sam admitted. "Darl told me there's also a home-care worker from the hospital checking in," he added quickly.

"A real nurse?"

"I assume so," Sam said. "I haven't seen her myself, but Darl said she was bringing him painkillers. He has terrible headaches. Can't stand noise. It's a good thing he doesn't have Alex around."

"Don't you think he could handle taking care of Alex?" Lila asked. If she had her wish, Kelly would be putting the little boy on an airplane and sending him back to Winnipeg immediately.

"I don't think he can even take care of himself," Sam told

her. "I still don't think he's well enough to be at home. He's putting up a brave front. Just brushes off my concerns. But he looks bad, and even with crutches, the guy can barely walk to answer his own door. And he's disoriented, I guess you'd call it. I wouldn't trust him to change a lightbulb, right now, let alone look after a kid."

Lila reported all of this to Kelly. "It really doesn't sound as if he could take Alex, yet," she said reluctantly.

"No," Kelly said. "And the custody order they showed me clearly listed Darl's injuries as the reason. 'Incapacitated,' they called him. But shouldn't he be in hospital if he's that bad?"

"Home-care," said Lila with disgust. "The modern Manitoba way. Kick them out of hospital as soon as they're breathing on their own."

"It's not safe," Kelly said.

"Don't worry," Lila quickly reassured her. "I'm sure those home-care nurses are excellent."

"Yeah." But the quality of the nursing wasn't Kelly's true concern. Darl was defenseless at home, and she feared another attack. What if someone really was out to get him? Someone who knew him? He'd be much safer in the hospital with people around.

"What about Adam?" she asked. "Any word about him?"

"No, Sam didn't mention him."

"Does Sam even know what he looks like?"

"Doubt it."

Kelly remembered the way Alex ran when Adam chased him. She was also worried about Angel. She knew her sister wouldn't be able to handle any bullying from Adam. The way things stood, Angel could tell Adam, or the police, the truth—that she didn't know where Kelly was. She could show them the note Kelly left behind. But would Adam believe her? Well, Paul could handle Adam, she thought. At least Paul had a gun.

What was she thinking?

Anyway, Adam would have to behave himself. With a possible custody battle coming, he'd have to keep his hands clean.

Lila seemed to pick up on her thoughts. "What about a lawyer, Kell? You should at least call a lawyer. Get the ball rolling in case you have to go to court."

"Not yet." She would have to talk to Leon first, beg him to testify. "Maybe it won't come to that. Darl has to recover soon."

"Maybe," said Lila. She sounded doubtful. She had heard the concern in Sam's voice; Kelly had not. "Sam says your house is okay, anyway. Your sister's been watering the plants. And Paul did some repairs, made the place secure."

"That's good." She pictured Paul in her house, going through her things, James's things—or what was left of them. She thought of the telephone call on Hallowe'en that seemed somehow to have started all of this. Who would do such a thing? And why? She recalled her vision of James, standing in the yard, wearing his blue, patched shirt.

She felt sick when she thought of Darl's injuries, his vulnerability. Was she partly to blame? She longed to be there for him, the way he'd always been there for her. But for now, she had little choice. She was helping out the only way she could—by protecting Alex.

"I feel guilty," Lila said. "I never lied to Sam before."

BUT SAM, IN FACT, HAD NOT BEEN entirely truthful with Lila, either. Darl was much worse off than Sam had admitted, and, worse, Kelly was nowhere to be seen.

Darl's appearance was frightening. The facial swelling had receded, but the bruising was still visible. The skin around the two black eyes was fading to a sickly yellow. Darl's shaven, stitched-up head made him look pitifully needy. But the physical injuries were the least of it. It was Darl's behavior that made Sam shudder. He wasn't himself at all.

Sam couldn't believe the doctors had let him go home. Anyone who knew him could tell he was badly brain-damaged. The first time Sam went to visit, Darl had stared at him without the slightest flicker of recognition.

"Darl, it's Sammy," Angel had prompted, and Darl had managed a weak grin.

"Hey, Sammy," he'd said. "How's it going?"

Sam had stayed to chat, but not for long. Darl's speech was slurred, he made strange mistakes of logic, and he seemed at times to lapse into unconsciousness, even when his eyes were open. He had difficulty remembering even the most basic things. Of the brutal attack that had left him so disabled, he had no recollection at all.

But he made a valiant effort to appear normal, even cheerful. "Hope you don't catch this flu," he said, as Sam was leaving. "It's a killer."

"Right," Sam said. He couldn't tell whether Darl was joking or not. And he couldn't get out of there fast enough. His skin crawled when he thought about it later. Darl's eyes were like two flat green disks, his expression blank. Words came out of his mouth, but his voice was hollow, empty of personality. And "*Sammy*"? Darl had never called him that in his life. He couldn't shake the feeling that Darl had no idea who he was.

"Where is Kelly?" Sam asked Angel when they were out of Darl's hearing. "Shouldn't she be here, helping out?"

"She left town," Angel said. "With Alex."

"But why?"

"I think she's afraid. The, um, the cops told her the mugging might have been personal—an enemy or something."

"And you believe that?"

"Not really. But Kelly—"

"Kelly's paranoid," Sam said. "She's been a nervous wreck since James's suicide." He remembered the day she had confided in him, afraid her mind was playing tricks on her. And he had brushed her off. Damn it.

"Where did they go?" he asked.

"She said they're perfectly safe. She said she'd be in touch."

There was nothing more Sam could say. If Angel knew where her sister was, she wasn't letting on.

BY WEDNESDAY THE TEAM had Hamlet's opening costume ready for the first fitting. Barbara was the cutter on the team. Kelly had quietly arranged for Bobbie to take Michael's measurements last week, so her own reluctance went undetected by anyone, except perhaps Michael himself.

Lila insisted that Kelly be present at the fitting.

"No way," Kelly protested, as Lila pushed her down the hallway. "I don't need to be there."

"Are you kidding?" Lila asked. "Michael Black in his underwear? Are you crazy?"

"I don't need to be there," Kelly repeated.

"Yes, you do," Lila said firmly. "I need your assistance. You have to take notes. And I'm your boss, remember?"

So Kelly hid behind Lila in the fitting room, trying not to look, as Michael peeled off his T-shirt and jeans. But she saw him anyway. A torso as long as some men are tall, it seemed. A long expanse of warm, unblemished, cinnamon skin, and muscles that moved easily, comfortably, as though they had never known injury or hesitation.

Barbara stepped up on a stool to dress him, while he stood with his arms outstretched. His expression was one of complete detachment. He was used to this, Kelly guessed. Undressing in front of three women, anyone.

He became tangled for a moment in the complicated doublet, and Lila tugged confidently at the garment, manipulating his arms as if he were a huge toy doll. When he was dressed, finally, she asked him to turn around, and he turned, willingly. He stretched and bent at the waist, testing the fit. He did not bother to look in the mirror. That was Lila's department. He only wanted to make sure he could move.

Lila conferred with Barbara at length. Michael and Kelly waited. Kelly had nothing to add, nothing to say. She was acutely aware of the impersonal nature of the situation. He was a beautiful object they were decorating. She was simply a witness, recording the process. Every time she glanced up at him, he seemed to be watching her. She looked at the floor. Finally, Lila and Barbara reached some kind of agreement. They began to remove his clothes again. Kelly's feelings of awkwardness increased. She was no longer needed—if she ever had been—so she slipped out of the room. She glanced at Michael as she left, and saw a small smile cross his lips, so faint she wasn't certain whether it was really there.

GEORGE LAUGHERTY WAS A BIG MAN. Not as tall as Michael, but tall enough, and much broader, more thickset, though considerably older. He carried himself like a king, even when he was merely sitting down to eat waffles and eggs in the dining room of the hotel. He would stand up well next to the Prince on stage, Kelly decided happily. No need to worry that Michael would diminish his presence.

Lila and Kelly met with him over breakfast on a Monday morning to show him the sketches and generally get to know him. He was an avid talker, a storyteller, and everybody loved to listen to his voice. As he told of the great adventures of his youth, Kelly was sitting beside him, watching his face and his broad gestures in the mirrored wall across the table. He was watching himself, too, she noticed, and frequently he caught her eye in the glass and grinned. He was rehearsing, she realized. He was performing not only for them, but for himself, perfecting his act.

"Tell us about Dublin," Lila urged. But they were interrupted by the arrival of Debbie Thompson, who skipped up to the table, trailing one thin arm like a tow rope, tugging Michael along behind her.

"Morning, George," she called. She flashed short smiles at Lila and Kelly, then ignored them. "Mind if we join you?" She bent toward the mirror and rearranged her hair, frowned at her image, feigning disgust.

George stood up and bowed to Debbie. He shook Michael's hand. "Michael, have you met our designers?"

"Yes," said Michael. He smiled politely. He pulled out an empty chair for Debbie, who sat down and promptly began to fish in her purse for cigarettes. Absent-mindedly, she patted the chair beside her. "Michael, sit."

"No thanks," he said. "I'm going to get an early start today." He consulted his wristwatch.

"You have to eat," Debbie protested.

"No, I don't," he said mildly. "I'll see you all later." He turned and walked away.

Debbie propped a menu in front of her face, blowing a thin stream of smoke over the top, in Kelly's direction. "He really should eat something," she remarked casually. "He barely got a wink of sleep last night." She lowered the menu and looked directly at Kelly. "But there's no telling him anything. He is *so* headstrong." She fluttered her lashes, and Kelly felt her own face turning warm.

"Stubborn, is he?" George asked.

"Has to have his way," Debbie said, with a coy smile.

So, Kelly thought, that's the way it is.

In the mirror, George Laugherty rolled his eyes.

KELLY CALLED THE CLINIC the morning of December 10 and was put on hold. Then she was cut off. Twice. It almost seemed there was a conspiracy at the clinic to keep her from talking to Leon. She had a sudden, creepy suspicion that Leon was really there in his office all along, avoiding her calls. But no. *He* had called *her* in the first place. He had left an urgent-sounding message. She had to keep trying.

When she finally got through, Mrs. Krentz agreed to take a message, but Kelly was reluctant to divulge her location. "I'll call back," she said, and hung up.

She called back several times, with no results. She was ringing up quite a phone bill trying to reach Leon. Mrs. Krentz became nearly hostile, hinting that Kelly's constant messages were verging on criminal harassment.

On the eleventh, she simply asked to speak with Frances.

Frances lowered her voice when she came on the line. "Kelly? I shouldn't be telling you this, but Leon's not back yet."

"He's still on holidays?"

"He was supposed to be back yesterday, but he never showed up. Mrs. Krentz says, you know, they lose track of time out there, on the reserve."

"Leon? Lose track of time?" Leon was one of the most punctual people Kelly knew. "I doubt that."

"I know. I doubted it too. And then today some collection agency came in, looking for him, 'cause his car's been impounded."

"Didn't he drive it out to the reserve?"

"Well, I thought so, but they found his car—"

"The station wagon?"

"The wagon. They found it at the airport. In the long-term lot. The ticket expired."

"The airport?" Great. Where the hell did he go?

KELLY DID NOT HAVE TIME to wonder. It was time for George's first fitting. Barbara squatted at his heels, pinning up the ragged hem of his cloak. George was enjoying the attention. But Kelly could see almost immediately that the costume wasn't going to work the way she planned it. The chains were too heavy. George wouldn't be able to move properly.

"Walk across to the hallway," she said. "Now down the hall." They watched him. "Okay, now turn around, come back toward us."

"No," said Lila. "It won't do."

"No," Kelly agreed. "He should be more fluid. Lighter."

"More ghostlike," said Barbara.

George stood patiently, arms folded uncomfortably across his chest. "I could get used to it," he said. "I could practice."

"Sure—you could wear them to the Neptune Dance Club," Lila joked. "I *don't* think so." She reached up to remove the cloak and then unfastened the chains around his chest. She handed the heavy links to Kelly. "What if we make the links smaller?"

Kelly shook her head. "I don't want them to look like jewelry."

"What if we make them out of something lighter? I don't know, like, aluminum?"

"No," Kelly said. "It wouldn't *sound* right." She was pacing. "Maybe just part of a chain—a broken one. At the wrist?"

Lila was putting the cloak back on George. "At least this looks good. It falls better now."

"Yeah." Kelly walked around behind the actor. "Lift your arms. Move around."

George stood straight and raised his arms above his head. The cape moved with him.

"I don't know," Kelly mused. "There's kind of a Dracula effect."

But Taylor was standing in the doorway. "I like it," he said. He entered the room. "After all, this is Hamlet's fate, standing here."

"Fate as a vampire?"

"Why not?" Taylor asked. They all stood looking at George. Kelly squinted her eyes, trying to imagine him from a distance, as a silhouette. A visitor from the other side, come to tell of evil. *Love, warning, revenge.*

"That's enough for today," she told them. "We'll deal with the chains later. We'll let you go now, George." She said a quick good-bye and walked straight out of the building, down the street to the hotel lounge.

Over a double Scotch, she contemplated the true nature of ghosts. How vividly James had appeared to her, first in her dreams, and then later when she was wide awake. A watery image, growing steadily more solid, until it seemed she could almost touch him. Why?

Love? Yes. Her love for him, drawing him closer, binding him to her.

And warning? Yes, that too, perhaps. Perhaps he was warning her of what was to come, the lurking danger she had failed to see.

And revenge? She saw again, in her mind's eye, the serious face of the police officer. "Beating like that . . . it looks almost personal." She remembered the look on Leon's face when she suggested James might be alive. *You want to believe it*, he said.

But Leon had deserted her. She would have to keep her imagination in check without his help. She had to be sensible, realistic, for Alex's sake. For her own sake.

She could use another drink, but it was time to pick up Alex from school. Brave little Alex, all the family she had left, at the moment. He got her through the evenings. Surrounded by high-energy personalities all day, she didn't have time to brood. But at night, in the quiet of the house, after Alex was asleep, loneliness spread out and enveloped her like a thick, bitter fog.

Chapter Sixteen

On her way out of the hotel, Kelly spotted Rocko holding a bag from the liquor store.

"Ah, my dinner companion!" he cried.

"Hi, Rocko."

"How goes life in the dream factory?"

"Hectic."

"Yes, I suppose so. Long hours?"

"Long enough." She glanced at her watch. The school would close in twenty minutes.

"The sacrifices we make for art!" he exclaimed. "I suppose it cuts severely into your whirlwind social life?"

"Hardly."

"I, for one, would not give up my social life for anything. Why, just now I am about to attend a banquet for one. Cheap Chilean wine and"—he held aloft a cellophane-wrapped sandwich—"a gourmet meal."

"Yuck."

"You're just jealous," he said. "Well, I must be off."

"Hey, Rocko ..."

He turned around, expectant.

"Why don't you come over for dinner?" she said.

"I thought you'd never ask."

ROCKO WANDERED THROUGH the house, carrying the wine, still in its paper sack. He strolled around the fireplace, admiring the stone. He lifted the lid of the piano and played a few notes. He climbed the steps to the porch door and touched the stained-glass window.

"Gorgeous," he said. "This is a real work of art."

"Isn't it great? I love the look on her face." Kelly stood below him and pointed to the cringing woman. "It's like love and fear, all at once. It fascinates me."

"Eurydice," said Rocko.

"What?"

"That's Eurydice," he said. "And Orpheus. See? He's turning around to look at her, to make sure she's still there, behind him. He's dooming her."

"I don't know that story."

"Don't you? It's classical myth. After she's bitten by a snake, Eurydice dies and falls down into Hades. Her grieving husband, Orpheus, descends to rescue her. The king of Hades lets her go, but he warns Orpheus not to turn and look at her as they climb back up or she'll be lost to him forever."

"And he can't resist?"

"He can't resist. She's doomed. And, look, they both know it. This is the moment."

She studied the face of the man again and she could see it there, his desire and his regret, mingled and frozen in glass. The scene took on another dimension for her.

"Thanks," she said softly to Rocko.

He came back down the stairs and took the wine out of the paper bag, inserted a corkscrew. "I have a degree in English," he said.

"Yes, I know."

After a quickly prepared meal of linguini and clam sauce, Kelly and Rocko sat on the rug in front of the cold fireplace, drinking wine. Alex had a mug of hot chocolate. He lay on his stomach, crayons and paint spread out on newspapers around him on the floor, finishing the picture of a mermaid he'd begun at school that morning.

"Have you ever seen a real one?" Rocko asked Alex, pointing to the picture.

"No," Alex said regretfully. "But I have a book of *The Little Mermaid.*"

Rocko looked at Kelly. "Isn't that rather a tragic tale for such a wee lad?" he asked. "Rather gruesome?"

"It's not the same as the one I read as a kid," Kelly said. "It's a modern version with a happy ending. She gets to marry the prince."

"They made it into a romance? You're kidding, because in the original—"

"I know," she said. "Shhh."

"Oh." Rocko addressed Alex again. "Do you think there really are mermaids in the ocean?"

Alex nodded. "Way far out," he said, "where it's really deep."

"Smart boy," Rocko said. He stretched out across the floor and examined the picture. Deep shades of green and gold, fish swimming through the mermaid's yellow hair, a tangle of seaweed and coral, all in crayon. Alex was putting the finishing touch on now. A pale-blue watercolor wash over the entire surface.

"Wow," said Rocko. "*Incroyable.*"

Kelly looked too. "That's wonderful, Alex. It really looks like it's all under water."

"It *is* under water right now." Alex was serious. "I don't know what it will look like when it's dry, though."

"Well, you have to experiment," Kelly told him. "That's the only way to find out what works."

Alex covered the last corner of the paper with paint, and Kelly took the picture out to the kitchen to hang it up with clothespins. She put a wad of cotton under each pin, a trick James had taught her, so that the paint wouldn't smudge too badly. This was the sixth in a series of undersea pictures Alex had been working on—and "work" was the right word. He approached his art with an intensity unusual in a child—or even in an adult. It ran in the family, Kelly thought.

She studied the pictures: dozens of green, scaly creatures floating in a murky sea. Were they a little sinister? Was this the stuff of his nightmares? But the colors were beautiful, and most of the time Alex was perfectly happy. When he was dancing or singing or just making up nonsense rhymes, he fairly floated above the ground with sheer silliness.

Like now, for instance, she could hear him laughing with Rocko, his voice high and childish and free. She stepped into the living room to see Rocko demonstrating the art of removing his thumb from his hand. An old trick, but Alex was rolling over on the floor, giggling. He threw a pillow at Rocko.

Rocko stood up. "Hey, hey. No violence now."

"What are you doing?" Kelly asked.

"I seem to be falling apart," Rocko said. He showed her his thumbless hand.

"It's right here!" Alex squealed, grabbing at Rocko's fist.

"Hey, ouch!" Rocko said. "Well, what do you know? You found it. I am eternally grateful."

Alex, still giggling, began to beat him with the pillow.

"Time for bed," Kelly said. But she was laughing too.

FINALLY, ALEX SETTLED DOWN, though he was too wound up to sleep. Kelly let him look at a comic book, providing he promised to turn out the light when he was finished.

Rocko was pouring the last of the wine into glasses when she came back downstairs.

"Amazing kid," he said.

Kelly fiddled with the radio dial and found the jazz station. John Coltrane blowing "My Favorite Things." Then she sat down and the two friends toasted each other silently.

"Nice to have you here," she said. "This room gets pretty empty at night."

He looked around. "Beautiful room, though. You should see my place. A dump." He sighed. "No matter. I'm getting evicted, end of the month."

"You can't pay the rent? What will you do?"

"The Lord will provide," he said. He finished his wine.

"There's another bottle under the sink," she told him.

"You see?" He rose to retrieve it.

ROCKO SEEMED TO KNOW everything about everybody, and what he didn't know, Kelly suspected, he invented. He gossiped in lecture form, holding forth in long monologues, waving his hands in intricate, polished gestures, brushing his blond hair back from his forehead. He gave her the background on all of the local cast, then started in on Michael Black.

"A genuine aristocrat," he declared. "One of the truly beautiful people. Spent his childhood floating through the upper echelons of European society. He's come down in the world, now."

"Down?"

"Yes, you know Hollywood is frowned upon by the *truly* beautiful people. His family's a bit ashamed of him, I think. I heard he invited his parents to the premiere of his last movie and his mother claimed she had a migraine. Just an excuse. They wouldn't come. They exist on a higher plane, the world of true culture."

"But he doesn't put on airs," Kelly said. "He's been very nice."

"I swear," Rocko said, "the boy will eat you alive. You won't know what hit you."

"Don't be ridiculous," she said. "I don't even know him."

"It will happen anyway. Things are in the works. Steps are being taken."

"What kind of steps?"

"Mmmm . . . can't say a word. Sorry."

"I don't care, anyway," she said.

"You're not interested."

"Not in the least."

"You are aloof."

"In the clouds."

Rocko stood up and stretched. "Might as well go home, then," he said. "If my services are not needed."

"You can't say a word anyway, remember?"

He took his coat from the closet and put it on with a flourish. He had ingested a bottle and a half of wine, but he didn't even weave. He came back to her, adjusting his sleeves. "You're absolutely *sure* you're not interested?"

"Positive. Besides," she said, "he's sleeping with what's-her-name."

"What's-her-name who?"

"You know. Ophelia."

Rocko laughed. "He is not!"

"He was with her Sunday night."

"What gives you that idea?"

"She said as much," Kelly informed him, "on Monday morning."

"She's full of shit, darling."

"Well, she truly did give me to believe . . ."

Rocko shook his head. He drained the last of the wine into his glass. "Michael was with *us* all weekend. Tim and me and Taylor's entire family. Up at Timothy's cabin—his lodge, you know. Camp Incommunicado. His version of roughing it. No fax and no telephone. Just a big-screen TV and a hot tub. We all went cross-country skiing and had a regular slumber party. We didn't get back to the city til Monday morning. Seven A.M."

"You're kidding."

"I kid you not. Ask Taylor."

Kelly smiled.

"Ah," said Rocko. "This pleases you?"

She shrugged. "Not that I care," she said. "Just—Debbie gets on my nerves."

"You are not alone," he said. He took another drink.

On Friday, Lila picked up Alex so that Kelly could work late. At five o'clock, she was sitting in the theater, watching the rehearsal of the final, tragic scene, waiting for Taylor to take a break so he could approve her final sketches. She could not, of course, interrupt him.

Gloria practiced Gertrude's death again and again. She was dressed in a pink sweatsuit, and Kelly was not convinced by the scene, but Taylor seemed satisfied. He put them all through their paces. Kevin rehearsed Laertes' death, then Gloria took another turn. Hamlet had to murder Claudius and then die himself. The actors were weary. Who would have thought that dying could be such hard work?

Kevin and Michael wore T-shirts soaked in sweat. They had already spent the entire morning in fight rehearsal. Taylor was pushing them too hard, Kelly thought, as she watched Michael tear up the long staircase at top speed for the twentieth time. Surely Taylor would have to let them stop any minute now. But he demanded the final few minutes over and over again, and they performed. Hamlet crawled toward the throne that would never be his. He spoke to Horatio. He closed his eyes and stopped breathing.

Kelly could tell that Michael was resting during these brief moments. He lay there, completely still, restoring his energy. When Taylor called to him, he waited a few seconds before responding, stealing some time. Then he got up and did it again. Finally, Taylor called it quits. Kelly watched Michael rise, carrying his sword. All the dead actors stood, as though for Judgment Day, and trooped out after him through the wings, silent. Kelly followed.

Taylor was standing in the corridor, talking to Michael, who was leaning heavily against the wall, head down, one lock of straight black hair shadowing his face. Taylor had his hand on Michael's arm, shaking him slowly to emphasize each point he was making as he spoke insistently.

"Knowledge," Taylor was saying. "Self-knowledge."

Michael nodded, without raising his head. By the curve of his shoulders, Kelly could tell he was exhausted.

"The moment of death is the moment of revelation. You can't die in darkness. You have to *see*."

Michael continued to nod. He slid along the wall and practically fell into his dressing room.

"Taylor," she called, "can you take a look at these?"

Taylor turned around, frowning. He skimmed the sketches, muttered "Fine, fine," patted Kelly on the shoulder, and headed out to the parking lot.

Kelly was ready to leave, too, when Michael called to her. "Kelly, wait." He stood at the entrance to his dressing room, his head grazing the top of the door frame. "Could you wait a second?" His eyes were slightly glazed, the lids heavy.

Kelly waited.

In a minute, he emerged, slightly drier, a towel around his neck. "Thanks," he said. He seemed shy, but already she could see the strength flowing back through his body. He was standing straight again. "I never get a chance to see you," he said. "I wanted to talk to you the other night, at the High Five."

"Well, you were—you're busy." She felt her face turning red, the curse of the Irish.

He smiled. His face lit up easily. Small crinkles appeared at the corners of the brown eyes.

"You seem to think I'm inordinately busy," he said. "Aren't you just as busy? Being head head-measurer and all?"

Now she was really blushing; heat raced up into her face. "Well," she said. "I have enough to do, I guess."

"It's Friday night," he said. "Don't you think we deserve some time off?" He grabbed another towel and began rubbing it through his short hair. "I'm going to shower, and then, do you want to get some dinner?"

For some reason, she didn't say no. She just watched as he scrubbed at his head with that absurd, awkward easiness, and heard herself say yes.

Lila was happy to keep Alex a little longer. Too happy. She was rather annoyingly smug on the telephone when Kelly told her the reason.

THEY WALKED TO A CHINESE restaurant on Chicago Street. Though Michael walked casually, Kelly had to hurry to keep up with his stride.

"I never drive," he said, surprising her. "The whole operation is too complicated in a new city. And I'm always in a new city, you know?" He paused while she caught up to him. "I drive at home, though."

"Where's home?"

He grinned. "Tripoli. Cairo. Lisbon. Astrakhan."

"Where is Astrakhan?"

"That is where the Volga pours into the Caspian Sea. A magnificent city. Not like this." He pointed up at the skyscrapers that blocked the sky. "It's where my father's family settled, years ago. Boatmen."

"Your father's a boatman?"

"No." Michael laughed. They arrived at the restaurant, and he took her elbow to guide her through the door. "My father had another love."

"The theater?"

"The theater." He held up a hand to the hostess, and she hurried to his side. "For two," he said. "A window, please."

"So where is home to you these days?" he asked, as they settled at their table.

Home. A meaningless concept at the moment. "Oh, here, I guess. I'm at home wherever." What a liar.

He wrinkled his brow. "Really?" He was no fool, she could see that. But he was polite. Not the type to pry.

She changed the subject back to him. "So, Black? That's a Russian name?"

"Nobody likes to change their name," Michael said. "But we all do in this business—almost all of us."

"You too?"

He bent his head down and was silent a moment. Then he looked up, flashing his white smile. His dark bright eyes were full of humor. He extended his hand in greeting. "Mikhail Nikolaiovich Blaczekoski," he pronounced, soberly. "Pleased to meet you."

They shook hands formally across the table.

"That's a wonderful name," she said.

"A little large for the marquee."

The food arrived, and he ate like a starving man, which Kelly supposed he was. A man who had just spent five hours sword-fighting.

"How is the fight scene going?" she asked, trying to keep up a conversation.

"It's going."

"Is it hard?"

He didn't answer. He took a sip of water.

"Do you think you can get it down in time? I mean, Taylor didn't give you much time."

He reached across the table and placed his hand on her arm. Five warm fingers, a five-volt current.

"When I'm off work, I'm off," he said. He was very serious. "And right now, I'm off, okay?"

"Okay." She couldn't help the smile that spread across her face.

For the rest of the meal, they talked about anything but work. Michael related stories of his childhood, stories of grand hotels, family holidays, the names of famous people.

"It must have been fun," she said. She thought of her own childhood, sitting on the steps outside the local bar, waiting. Angel crying. James locked in the toolshed.

"It was a bit lonely," Michael said, "especially when I got older. We moved around a lot. We lived wherever my father was playing—or where my mother was singing. I met a lot of people—too many people. I met a lot of girls. I liked girls, but I never got to know any of them well enough. Not really. But you"—he paused—"you married young."

"Very young," she agreed.

"And your son?" Michael had seen Alex once or twice in the building, though she hadn't introduced them.

"He's a going concern," she said. "Keeps me very busy. Keeps me home a lot," she said pointedly, glancing at her watch.

"Right," he said. He gestured for the check.

When he walked her back to her car, he said, "Thanks. I needed to get away, for a while, from everything."

"Well, thanks for dinner." She pulled her keys out of her pocket, feeling suddenly uneasy and very tired.

"My pleasure. Look, I wanted to ask you something."

"Yes?" She waited.

"What's wrong?" he asked. "What's bothering you?" He was leaning against the driver's door, so that she couldn't get in. He was calm, alert, completely renewed, as though he'd just woken from a pleasant sleep.

She looked away, and he reached out to touch her shoulder. "Is it something I can help with?" he asked, gently.

"I'm fine," she said.

He shook his head. "Something's always on your mind," he said. "Every time I talk to you, I feel it."

"What do you mean?"

He looked at her seriously, his gaze intent. He didn't answer, just waited for her to acknowledge that she knew what he meant. But she wouldn't.

"Nothing's wrong," she said. One of the parking-lot lights was ready to burn out. It flickered, grew dim, then flared again. She watched for a while the play of shifting shadows, then looked up at him. He hadn't moved. He was still leaning against the car, with his arms crossed, still looking at her.

"I have to go," she said.

He moved away from the car, unfolding his arms. "All right," he said. "Good night."

As she drove away, he lifted one hand in farewell, one huge palm. He didn't seem angry or sad, just very serious. She saw him press his lips together, as though thinking hard.

ALL THROUGH THE FOLLOWING week, she was very aware of Michael Black. She could sense his presence in the building, even if he was in another room. She avoided him as much as she could.

Michael was difficult to read—or rather, he appeared to be too easy to read. Could a man be that uncomplicated? That transparent?

She spent most of her lunch hours with Rocko, who had taken up residence in the hotel near the theater.

"Timothy pays for it," he told her, with a sigh of resignation. "Timothy pays for everything."

"Well, why shouldn't he?" she asked. "Somebody has to."

He sighed again. "People like me, with no talent, we should just shrivel up and teach high school once we start to lose the look. The look is everything."

"You have talent."

"The only talent I have," he said, "is rapidly degenerating. I've gained nine pounds this past year alone. You—you have a bit longer." He looked her up and down, evaluating. "You have that sort of elegant, bewildered look. That black-and-white vulnerability. The kind that ages well."

"You are really full of it."

"Have you ever done any acting?"

"Can't," she said. "Stage fright."

Rocko dismissed this problem with a wave of his hand. "Nonsense. They all have stage fright. You should see Debbie Thompson before she goes on. Last season she threw up on Timothy's shoes. It was disgusting."

Kelly smiled.

"Seriously," he said, "you should consider it. With your look, you could do, say, Tennessee Williams. Or, even better, one of those thrillers, you know, with the trembling victim."

"A zombie," she said. "*Night of the Living Dead*."

They were laughing when Jesse appeared at the table to say that Taylor wanted Kelly back at the theater.

"I've only been here twenty minutes," she complained.

Jesse leaned closer, coughed, and lowered his voice. "Michael Black is looking for you."

"Ah," said Rocko.

"Shut up, Rocko. Let me finish my lunch, Jesse. I'll be back in fifteen."

Jesse wasn't pleased to leave without her, but he did.

"That's the stuff," said Rocko. "Keep the man waiting, build up that anticipation."

"Oh, shut up. He probably wants me to polish his shoes or something."

"You are severely nuts," Rocko said. He shook his head. "Severely nuts or just plain dumb."

Kelly was surprised to see Michael sitting in his dressing room, cool and comfortable, wearing a black cotton jacket, black jeans. He was tackling his mail again, ripping the envelopes deliberately and precisely with the silver letter opener. Taylor was there, looking less harried than usual.

"Not in rehearsal today?" she asked.

"Afternoon off," Michael said. He looked at his watch. "I want you to come with me to the Roxy. They're showing Zeffirelli's *Romeo and Juliet.* We can make it if we take your car."

"A movie?"

"Michael needs a break," Taylor said. "We're getting nowhere today, anyway. Go ahead, Kelly. We can get along without you."

"Come on," said Michael. "It's a magnificent film."

As they walked out through the stage door, Debbie appeared, looking hot and unhappy. "Where are they going?" she asked Jesse.

"To a film," Jesse told her.

"A film?"

"Uh, well . . . it's Shakespeare," he said brightly.

"In the middle of the day?" Debbie appealed to Taylor. "That's not fair."

"If he wants to go to the movies with Kelly," said Taylor firmly, "he goes to the movies with Kelly. Now let's get back in there and try that scene again."

Kelly could feel Debbie's eyes burning two jealous holes in the back of her head.

It was, of course, a magnificent film. She had seen it before, but today for some reason it broke her spirit. Juliet's childish love, her wondrous, childish devotion, her bitter death. The stricken parents at the end, their terrible punishment. A gray depression settled over her.

"Shakespeare was a cruel man," she said, as they walked out, blinking, into the sun. She thought of the final act of *Hamlet*. "You almost think he hates the audience sometimes."

"Sometimes I think it's the actors he hates," Michael said. "The way Juliet has to lie there at the end, not even breathing."

"Debbie will have to do that, won't she, in the funeral scene?"

"Yes, and then Kevin and I have to jump in her grave. What a mess. The first time we did it, we all landed on top of each other." He laughed.

"Too much dying," she said. She was suddenly very tired. She stopped and sat down on the cold stone steps of an apartment block.

"Kelly?"

"Graves, worms ... Don't you get sick of it?"

"What do you mean?"

"That disgusting skull."

"What, in *Hamlet*?" He sat down beside her.

"It's all about death," she said.

"No, it's not. I don't see it that way. It's about, I don't know. . . ." He spread his arms apart and raised his hands toward the sky. "It's about character."

"Character?"

"Honor. Loyalty."

Honor, she thought. Preserving the family honor. Montague and Capulet and Adam Grayton with his code of secrecy. "That's just pride. It's all about pride and the death wish."

"No, no, no. How can you say that? It's all about love. Don't you see?" He pushed the black hair back from his forehead. His face was dark, the eyebrows wrinkled in thought, the brown eyes downcast. She waited for an explanation. He scratched at his head, concentrating, then glanced up and saw her watching him. He looked her straight in the eye.

"Hamlet doesn't *want* to die," he insisted.

"Why not?" she asked. "The world is, you know, 'weary, stale, flat.' "

"That's just a mood," Michael said. He leaped up and stood looking down at her. "Hamlet wants his life, his friends, his kingdom. He's deeply in love with Ophelia—"

"He's in love with Ophelia?"

"Yes. Of course." He looked at her as if she were incredibly dense. "Of course he loves Ophelia. Otherwise, what kind of a play would it be? There would be no play."

She sat quietly for a minute, looking up at him, thinking skeptical thoughts. Michael, high above her, stood tall in his black clothing, hands at his waist, head bent to one side, studying her, trying to figure her out. His brow creased with childlike puzzlement.

"How can you not understand that?" he asked.

From behind him, she heard a little gasp. He turned, and there were three young women, clutching one another, giggling. He smiled at them, then turned back to Kelly.

"It's a romance," he said.

The teenagers advanced, still clinging to each other. One of them stepped forward a little, peering around Michael's body to see his face. "Are you Michael Black?"

"Yes. Hello." He turned away from Kelly then and chatted with them for a bit. He signed the scraps of paper they dug out of their purses.

She watched him, recalling Rocko's remarks: that Michael belonged to some international world of high culture. She shook her head. It didn't seem true. He posed shyly for a photograph with each of his fans. He believed in character, loyalty. He thought *Hamlet* was a romance, for goodness' sake. For all his so-called sophistication, he was a total innocent.

Chapter Seventeen

He sat in the lobby of the Fallon Hotel with the newspaper open in front of him. The local press was giving the play heavy coverage, and today was no exception. A large photograph graced the front page of the entertainment section, with the caption "Michael Black escorts his leading lady, Debbie Thompson, into the venerable Arcana Theater. After a brief Christmas break, the cast will return for full dress rehearsals. *Hamlet* opens January 6."

He studied the picture. Debbie Thompson was obviously the photographer's main interest. Despite her tiny size, her image filled the frame. She was smiling directly at the camera, and her waving hand all but obscured the face of her escort. She wore a fur stole and a short skirt that revealed shapely legs and petite, delicate feet in killer stiletto heels. He lowered the newspaper and carefully ripped the picture from the page, stowing it in his inner breast pocket, alongside his traveler's checks and his airplane tickets. Debbie Thompson could be quite helpful to him, if he made the right moves. Or she could ruin things completely. Her vanity and her open ambition might be a weak spot. Perhaps he should send her flowers, with a little note. He would have to word it just right.

He raised the paper again and pretended to peruse the financial pages. The object of his intense jealousy was just now entering the lobby. He watched over the top of the newspaper, his eyes hidden behind an expensive pair of large dark glasses.

TWO DAYS LATER Michael's picture appeared again, this time on an inside page. His every move, Kelly thought, was completely public. She was lucky her own picture wasn't splashed across these pages. The day after they'd gone to the movies, she'd been mentioned in the society gossip column. Although she remained unnamed, the words still rattled her: "His companion, a dark-haired young woman dressed entirely in white, is said to be a member of the crew."

She'd been a fool to get anywhere near him.

Today, the article accompanying his picture focused on his dedication. "Mr. Black is a hard worker, according to sources at the theater. 'He's a true professional,' says Taylor Grant, who is directing *Hamlet*. 'He doesn't let the attention get to him. He just shows up and rehearses.' Mr. Black, in fact, has disappointed Minneapolis fans, who were hoping to see a lot more of the charismatic star around town."

Kelly put the newspaper down. She was sitting on the couch in her living room with an after-dinner cup of coffee. Just then, the phone rang. It was Michael.

"I want to get out of this place," he said, meaning his hotel room. "Can you meet me for a drink somewhere?"

"I don't know." She was looking at the photograph. His shirt collar was open and she could see the fine outline of his clavicle under his skin, if she looked hard enough.

"Just for an hour? I want to talk to you."

"I don't think so," she said. "Alex—"

"We can take him with us. I just want to see you for a bit."

Just what she needed. Her picture in the paper with a movie star—and a kidnapped kid.

"Not tonight, Michael. Thanks."

She hung up. A dark-haired companion. A charismatic star. Forget it, she thought.

ALTHOUGH SHAKESPEARE NEVER WROTE the scene of Ophelia's death, Taylor decided at the last minute to include it. While Gertrude described the tragic event, Debbie would act out Ophelia's madness and drowning on the stage below. This meant added hours of rehearsal, new choreography, and an entirely new costume.

Lila did not have much time to work on it. "It has to be simple," she told Kelly, as she paced the floor of the costume shop, trying to accommodate this new requirement into her plans. "I think it will have to be white. Everything white and pale."

"What about the flowers she gathers? We're not going to use real flowers?"

"No flowers. The audience will have to imagine the flowers. Taylor wants this really stark. Like a silent ballet, he said."

Kelly tried to imagine Debbie Thompson as a ballerina.

"The design will have to be super simple," Lila continued. "We have to make it so she can just slip it on over her head to save time. She'll need a wig, because her hair should be loose, really wild. I guess we could weave some flowers into the wig. What do you think?"

"I think I need a break," Kelly answered. "I can't think straight this morning."

"It's not morning any longer," Lila said. "It's past lunch time. Take an hour."

Kelly walked to the hotel, looking for Rocko. He was nowhere to be found, so she bought a sandwich and coffee and took them back to the theater. She would watch rehearsal while she ate her lunch.

She sat in the last row, well behind Taylor, who could not stay still. He was stalking back and forth as he watched. They were doing the scene where Hamlet rejects Ophelia, the scene everyone called "the nunnery part," because Hamlet tells Ophelia to "get thee to a nunnery." There was a problem with this scene, and Kelly had already heard much talk about it.

Today, she could clearly see the difficulty. Hamlet was so much taller than Ophelia that it was almost comical. Most of the play had been blocked to minimize this effect, but in this scene they had to come together, hold on to each other, push each other away.

Michael and Debbie were having trouble synchronizing their movements. At one point, they both got carried away, moved too quickly, and charged into each other. Debbie spun backward and teetered on one foot. Michael tried to catch her, but missed. She hopped, trying to keep her balance, and turned her ankle. She sat on the floor, rubbing her foot, complaining.

"It's all twisted up," she called to Taylor.

Taylor slapped his own forehead. "Jesus! Michael!"

"Sorry," Michael said. He knelt beside Debbie. "Are you hurt?"

Debbie extended her lower lip. Michael put one arm around her shoulders, the other under her legs, and prepared to pick her up.

"Watch your back!" Taylor yelled. His hands flew up over his ears. He cringed.

But Michael lifted Debbie smoothly, with little apparent effort. She wrapped her arms around his neck and sat there like a child in a swing. She looked directly at Kelly and smiled as if she had just accomplished a difficult athletic feat.

Michael bent his face toward Debbie and grinned. "Comfortable?" He carried her easily across the stage. Kelly felt a sharp lurch in her stomach as if she'd been punched.

Taylor turned away in disgust and headed for a chair. "Take ten," he yelled. "Hell, take twenty."

Kelly offered her coffee to Taylor, deciding he needed it more than she did.

"Thank God for small mercies" was his way of thanking her. He took a large, rather desperate gulp. "So how are you doing? Everything under control?"

"Everything's coming along fine," she said.

"Good. Good. Well, I wonder if you could do me a favor?"

Kelly was getting used to Taylor's "favors," which so far had included picking up a birthday cake for his wife and putting gas in his car, among other things. Not to mention taking Michael to the movies.

"I need someone to run Michael down to the lodge. Timothy's cabin, you know? It's just south of town. Not far."

"Today?"

"Tonight. This evening. You don't mind? Michael has simply got to get out of town and rest a bit. He can't sit down to a meal in his own hotel without interruption. The girls, you know." Taylor lifted his hand in a swatting motion, as if the girls were so many flies. "He needs some privacy. So Timothy's given him the cabin for the weekend. But I can't drive him myself."

Kelly nodded. This was a bizarre job.

"You don't mind," Taylor said again, only this time it was not a question. "Good. Pick him up at the hotel at seven." His tone of voice suggested that Kelly had no choice. He downed the rest of the coffee and took off.

KELLY WORKED ALL AFTERNOON making up a pattern for Ophelia's "drowning dress," as Lila called it. At four, she picked up Alex and took him back to the shop with her, so she could continue. She had to finish the pattern, get some dinner into Alex, and pick Michael up by seven. Her temples throbbed. She was determined to finish, but Alex was being a nuisance today. She settled him in a corner with some colored pencils and a huge sheet of paper. From his long silence, she assumed he was content. Wrong assumption.

He was amusing himself by sorting through the contents of Lila's bag, which he had dumped in a heap all over the drafting table.

"Alex! What are you doing?"

"Look, Kelly!" He held up a bottle of ink that he had managed to open. "It's gold. See?" He put his finger into the bottle.

"Alex! No! Oh, look what a mess you've made. These are Lila's things. Help me clean this up."

She wasted several precious minutes restoring order, and when she turned around, Alex had gotten into a scrap bag and was now sorting buttons into piles according to their color.

"Oh, this is impossible," Kelly sighed.

"What's impossible?" It was Michael. He was standing at the entrance to the costume shop, looking amused.

"Hi," said Alex, jumping up. "You're the Prince, right?"

"I'm just Michael." He shook Alex's hand.

"This is Alex," Kelly said.

"Impossible Alex?" Michael asked. "Are you giving your mother a hard time?"

Alex shook his head. Kelly quickly intercepted. "He's no trouble, really. It's just—I have so much to do." She indicated the piles of tissue paper on the table where she had been working.

"I see." Michael bent his head for a moment. "I suppose this is my fault."

"No. No, really—"

"It is," he said, looking up again. "Taylor said you could help me out today. I didn't realize—" He stopped. "What's wrong?"

"Headache." Kelly was trying to remove the kinks from her neck.

"Here." He pushed her gently into a chair and stood behind her, placing his large hands on her shoulders. "Relax." He moved his long fingers slowly along her spine and up onto her neck, feeling the muscles, finding the tension. Gently he pressed, massaging, until she could feel the tingle of release, as the tight muscles began to let go.

"Is that okay?" he asked.

"Yes." She had a vague feeling he shouldn't be doing this, but it felt so good she didn't want him to stop. His hands were enormous and strong. He cupped her entire shoulder blade with one palm and squeezed, ran his thumb along her neck until she shivered. It had been so long since anyone had touched her like this, easily, without hesitation. He slipped his fingers up under the hair on the back of her head and massaged her scalp. The headache evaporated into thin air, but still she did not stop him. She closed her eyes. His fingers moved across her head, down behind her ears, up toward her forehead. She felt his hands on her face, his fingers reaching down to stroke her eyebrows.

"Kelly cut her hair," Alex piped up.

"Yes, I know," Michael said. He ran a hand swiftly through her short locks. "She used to have hair that was longer than you."

"Did you used to know her?" Alex asked.

"A little bit," Michael said. "A long time ago." He removed his hands from her head. "Better?" he asked.

"Much. Thanks."

"She works too hard," Michael told Alex.

"She's *always* working," Alex said with a sorrowful tone.

Kelly felt as if she were floating above the ground. Every ounce of tension and worry had been drained from her body.

"You can't work all the time," Michael was saying. "I know. I've tried it. It will make you sick."

"Christmas is coming," Kelly said. "We'll get a break then."

"You need a break now," Michael said. "Why don't you come—why don't you stay up at the cabin this weekend? There's plenty of room."

"Camping?" Alex jumped up and clapped his hands.

"It's too cold for camping," Michael said. "But we can make a fire indoors."

"Yeah!"

Kelly could tell from the sound of Alex's voice that she was not going to say no.

DARL HAD HIS BAD DAYS and his worse days, and this was one of his worse days, Angel thought.

She put a fresh pot of chili in the fridge and removed the one she had brought last week. Darl hadn't even touched it. She guessed it was too hard for him to heat it up. In his state, he shouldn't even be operating an oven, anyway. She should bring something cold, instead. Something easy to fix, like . . . what? She wished someone would invent some new kind of food.

She felt guilty that she hadn't been visiting lately. Nobody had visited lately, she could tell by the state of the house. Kelly's friend Sam had come sometimes at first, but now he had gone out of town somewhere, or so he said. She suspected he was uncomfortable around sick people, as Paul was. Paul never came, and he was always discouraging Angel from coming. He always had something else he wanted her to do, like helping him catalog his tapes. And she was so easily distracted. She wasn't used to taking care of people. That was Kelly's department.

Even now Darl was calling her from his bedroom. "Kelly?"

"It's Angel," she said, appearing with a cold cloth for his

forehead. He was in pain today, running a fever. Only 101 degrees, according to the thermometer, but he seemed delirious.

"Tell Kelly to come."

"Kelly's out of town, Darl. She's working." This was Angel's stock answer. She didn't want to worry Darl by admitting she had no idea where Kelly and Alex were. And so far the answer seemed to work. He could barely concentrate on one topic long enough to pursue the subject.

Today, though, he seemed to be fixated on the idea of Kelly. She turned on the television to distract him. His eyes focused dully on the screen.

It was a trashy program, celebrity gossip. Some item about an $8-million movie contract. She bent to change the channel, but the picture of the actor in question caught her eye. There was something about him. Maybe it was just his extraordinary smile?

"The leading man refused to comment on rumors he will fly to New York soon to finalize the deal," the reporter chirped. "But fans agree they want to see Michael Black back on the big screen as soon as possible. We've missed you, Michael!" The picture showed the actor arriving at his hotel in Minneapolis. A gaggle of girls turned and pointed as his long legs unfolded and he emerged from the car. One of them jumped up and down like a child at a circus.

"Tell Kelly to come home," Darl mumbled from his bed.

"She's coming, Darl. She'll be here soon."

The program ended by scrolling its credits over a still shot of Michael Black's smiling face, the white flash of teeth incongruous under the intense, dark eyes.

Darl groaned. He remembered Michael Black, but he couldn't tell Angel what he remembered. He just lay there, repeating himself, hoping she would give Kelly the message.

Kelly and Alex stood at the window of the cabin, watching Michael chop wood. He moved vigorously, with great pleasure. He threw himself into the job with a kind of passion, his shoulders rising and falling rhythmically, without stopping. He chopped a far larger pile than necessary, and when he was finished, he picked up the ax with one hand, aimed, and embedded it securely in a tree stump.

"Aren't you exhausted?" she asked him, when he came in with his arms full of wood. He didn't seem at all tired. The work seemed to make him high. Despite the cold, his whole body radiated heat.

He laughed. "This is nothing compared to rehearsal."

"You actually . . . You amaze me, actually."

He turned his head and gave her one of those half-smiles, his eyes shining. She entertained him, apparently. "How is that?" he asked.

"The way you keep going."

"Well, I'm twice the size of you," he said. "That helps."

That wasn't what she meant, though. What amazed her was the way his spirit kept going. Day after day of rehearsals, Taylor's exacting demands, Debbie's neurotic excesses. She was curious about his stamina. How was it that he not only kept going, but kept going so politely, so wholeheartedly?

"I mean at work," she said. "How can you handle all that pressure?"

"I love my work," he said simply. "I love to work." He removed his coat and boots and began to feed the fire.

"But so many people . . . the press . . . all those girls?"

"I happen to *like* those girls." He grinned.

"Seriously, though."

"Seriously. I like them a lot."

"How can you handle so many people all the time? Don't they wear you down?"

"Not really. We've got a good cast. A good director—out of his mind, but good. Excellent, really. He's taught me a lot."

He stopped himself. He didn't elaborate on what Taylor had taught him. He would never discuss the progress of the production. Superstitious, Kelly suspected.

"But what about—"

He held up a finger. "Oh, yes. And a good crew," he added. "A pretty good crew. Cute wardrobe staff." He rolled down his sleeves and winked at Alex. Alex giggled.

"Let's not talk about work," Michael said. "A day like this—away—this is what makes it possible to keep going, to go back there. I try to escape as often as possible." He stretched out on the rug and lay on his back, folding his arms beneath his head. Alex stared at the length of him, then imitated the position. They both lay watching the sky grow darker.

AFTER A LONG EVENING, during which Alex ate far too many roasted marshmallows, Kelly made up the big bed in one of the numerous guest rooms for herself and Alex. She tucked him in, promising to join him soon, and returned to Michael.

He was opening a bottle of wine. "How are you feeling?" he asked as she flopped into an armchair by the fire. He handed her a glass of chardonnay.

"Tired." As she accepted the glass, she felt his hand trail lightly across her wrist. She shuddered as an electric current seemed to run up her arm into her chest. He smiled broadly, watching. He's playing with me, she thought. He's flirting with me openly. She sipped the wine, trying to avoid his eyes.

He sat on the floor near her chair. "It's so good to see you again," he said. "I knew I'd see you again one day."

"What are you talking about?"

"You were so sweet in New York," he said. "When you first came on the set. You were so shy. You would never talk to me."

"I don't really remember—"

"Yes, you do. I was always following you around. I kept asking you out but you refused every time. I thought if I persevered . . ." He sighed. "Then, when I found out you were married, I was crushed."

She looked up then. She stared at him. Michael Black, self-assured sex symbol, fantasy of a thousand women, *crushed*? "Oh, come on," she said. What a line, she thought.

"Really. When your husband showed up, I was devastated. And he treated you terribly. As if he owned you. We had to throw him off the set. I wanted to punch him."

"Don't," Kelly said. She held up a hand in warning. "Don't talk about him like that. He was . . . he wasn't well."

They both fell silent for a long time, listening to the faint whistling of the wind through the woods outside the cabin. Kelly sat in the armchair, watching the flickering shadows created by the flames. Michael remained on the floor. After a while he lay on his back, very still, as though he were asleep. But when the fire began to die, he stood up in one smooth sudden motion and knelt to feed in more wood. He remained there, in front of her. He rested an elbow on her knee and took her hand. His eyes were serious, questioning, and as always, she glanced away. She had the feeling that if she held his gaze, she'd be overwhelmed, swallowed up. She would vanish into him, the way her hand vanished when he held it. She twisted in her chair, turning her back to him.

"What is it?" Michael asked. "What's wrong?"

She felt her body wanting to move toward him, but she resisted. How could she explain what was wrong?

"When my husband died . . ."

He nodded his head, slowly, steadily, as if confirming a strong suspicion. "Yes," he said quietly. "Of course."

For an immeasurably brief moment, Kelly felt the presence of James in the room. Then he was gone.

Michael looked up, as though he had sensed it, too. "Who was your husband?" he asked, softly.

"His name was James." She stood up and walked to the window, but there was nothing to see. The moon and the stars were obscured by clouds, and no lights shone through the thick woods—just a faint glow from their own lamp, and a darkness that seemed to spread out before her forever, horizonless.

"Tell me about him." Michael waited, his arms still folded, but relaxed. Clearly, he was ready to wait for a long time.

"He was . . . he played the guitar." Her voice caught a little. "I'm sorry," she said. "I haven't spoken about him for so long." She could not go on.

"You don't talk about him to Alex?"

She turned her head and saw his face close behind her. He was frowning. Obviously he disapproved.

"No . . . I . . ."

He reached out and placed a hand on her shoulder. "Kelly? How did he die? So young?"

From despair, Kelly wanted to say. Hopelessness. He died of shame. But how could she explain such a thing to Michael, beautiful son of the rich and famous, secure in his charmed life? A man who believed that a holiday could solve everything? A man who believed that Hamlet's famous melancholia was just a mood?

"Could we just . . . not . . . talk?" she asked.

"All right. Okay. It's all right."

He pulled her toward him, and she let herself lean back into him, slightly. There was something comforting about the sheer size of him, even though she knew he couldn't help her.

Chapter Eighteen

Kelly slept late, lulled by the quiet rustle of the wind in the trees that sounded through her dreams like the lapping of waves. When she woke, Alex was still curled beside her, fast asleep, and she heard voices in the kitchen. Curious, she slipped out of bed and began to dress.

Rocko had arrived early in the morning and was sharing a pot of tea with Michael. "He wants to send me back to school," Rocko was complaining. "He thinks I should *do* something with my life."

"Well, why not?" Michael asked.

"He's always sending me little love notes, telling me to sober up. He's like a bloody—" He stopped when he saw Kelly emerge from the bedroom, her overnight bag in hand.

"Oh," Rocko said. He took a third teacup down from the cupboard. He lifted his eyebrows. "Well. At least *somebody's* happy."

AFTER BREAKFAST, MICHAEL TOOK ALEX outside to play in the snow, and Rocko helped Kelly wash dishes.

"So?" he said. "Confess."

"There is nothing to confess, Rocko."

"Oh, don't tell me you're one of those annoying *private* people!"

"As a matter of fact, I am," she said. "But there is nothing to tell, anyway. He just—Michael just needed to get away from the city for a while, and he needed a ride, so—"

"Clever," said Rocko.

"What do you mean, clever?"

Rocko shook his handsome head. He hoisted himself up and sat on the counter beside her. "You really are an innocent, aren't you? Is that a Canadian thing?"

She splashed him with dishwater, and he ducked.

"Whoa! Okay. You really don't know what's going on?"

"There is nothing going on," Kelly said.

He gave a giant, mock sigh. "You don't pay attention, darling. You're always rushing around after little Alex or else you're working. You have to keep your ear to the ground."

"I don't listen to gossip," Kelly told him primly.

"Well, you should. I always do. And now I'm in the inner circle, don't you know? I'm up on things. Taylor tells Tim and Tim tells me. Everyone's mighty interested."

"Interested in what?"

In reply, Rocko quoted from *Hamlet*: "*Madness in great ones must not unwatched go*."

"Madness?"

"Love, madness, what's the difference? The point is he never, and I mean never, talks about women, never takes them out in public. Not since that girl in L.A. He keeps to himself, normally. Normally he doesn't take little wardrobe mistresses out to the movies, or whisk them off for the weekend. But now ... Don't look so shocked. He's been on about you since he got here."

"What do you mean?" Out the window, Kelly could see Alex pelting Michael with snowballs.

"Asking Taylor about you, darling. Mentioning your name.

The usual mundane symptoms. You do know he arranged that whole night at the High Five just so he could see you?"

"No," she said. She saw Michael pick Alex up by both hands and swing him around in circles. The sound of Alex's laughter reached her through the window.

"Oh, yes," Rocko said. "Absolutely."

DESPITE ROCKO'S CONTENTION that Kelly and Michael were the talk of the town, nobody seemed to know they had spent the weekend together. On Monday morning, in fact, it was patently obvious that Debbie Thompson had no idea. When Kelly stepped into her dressing room to arrange a time for a fitting, Debbie made sure to show her the huge bouquet of red roses that had been delivered that morning.

"Charming little card, isn't it?" she remarked, shoving the card under Kelly's nose.

Kelly read it: "To my leading lady. The limelight becomes you."

"From Michael?"

Debbie smiled. "He's very appreciative."

"Of what?"

"Well, just between you and me, we had quite the weekend." Debbie winked slyly.

"Really?" Kelly asked, amused. "Wasn't he, um, didn't he go up to Timothy's cabin for the weekend?"

"Yes. It was lovely."

Kelly bit her tongue on her way out the door. So Debbie *was* full of shit, just as Rocko had said. The roses must be Michael's way of apologizing for knocking Debbie down during rehearsal Friday afternoon. What a neurotic little . . . ! Maybe everything Rocko said was true. Maybe the rumors had reached Debbie Thompson's ears, and her lies were a campaign to scare Kelly off.

Oh, well, she had more serious things to worry about.

WHEN SHE WAS ALONE in the blue room later that morning, Kelly tried the Riverside Clinic once again, hoping against hope that Leon had finally returned. He was her last chance. Without the files that documented Adam's abuse of James, she would never have a hope of getting custody away from Alex's grandparents. They were "blood," as Eleanor had so disgustingly put it, and they weren't guilty of kidnapping.

Kidnapping. A federal offense. She might have ruined forever her chances of getting legal custody. This possibility hadn't occurred to her when she'd taken Alex on that fateful, impulsive day. Darl was improving, physically, according to sporadic reports from Sam. But if his brain damage should be permanent . . . Oh God, she prayed, let Leon be back.

The telephone rang for a long time, and Kelly was put on hold. She listened to the wordless music, a watered-down version of the Beatles' "Maxwell's Silver Hammer." What a choice for a psychiatric clinic. She wondered if they played the same tape on the crisis line.

She felt like dialing the crisis line.

As soon as Frances recognized Kelly's voice, she put her on hold again. Kelly waited impatiently. Maybe she was right about that conspiracy theory. Her shoulders ached with tension.

Frances's voice was low and sad when she came on again.

"Kelly? Have you heard?"

"Heard what?"

"Are you sitting down?"

A bolt of fear shot through Kelly's body. Darl! Something had happened to Darl!

"What is it?" she asked, her legs trembling.

"Are you sitting down?"

"Yes." Kelly sank into a chair. "Tell me."

"It's Leon. They found his body yesterday." Frances's voice was strained and muffled, as if she'd been crying all day and she was trying not to break down again.

PAUL TOOK THE NEWSPAPER away from Angel and handed her a stiff drink of whiskey.

"It's a coincidence," he said.

Angel removed her fingers from her mouth and swallowed half the contents of the glass. Then she began to bite her nails again.

"There's a epidemic of these crimes all over the country," Paul said. "There's one every fifteen minutes, nationwide." He was making this statistic up, but he figured it was close enough.

"No," Angel said. "It's something personal. He worked at the clinic, too. He was James's doctor, remember? Even the cops mention it. Here, see?" She tugged the newspaper away from Paul. "Let me finish reading this. See? 'Dr. Chartrand is the second member of Riverside Clinic staff to be the victim of a car-jacking—' "

Paul once again took control of the newspaper. "Let me see this." He read through the article while Angel polished off her drink, poured another, and began to roll a joint.

Chartrand's stolen car had been found at the airport, Paul learned. But his disappearance had gone unnoticed for some time. He had never arrived for a promised visit to his parents' home on the Brokenhead reserve, but they'd assumed he'd been too busy to come. His work had kept him away before, they told police.

Because of the location of the body, police believed he had been attacked on his way to the reserve. Though it was difficult to tell precisely, the body had quite possibly been lying under the frigid snow for weeks.

"It's personal, like that cop said." Angel lit up and inhaled deeply.

"It's not personal. It's just . . . crime is everywhere. You know yourself. Your own wallet was stolen."

"What if they're after Kelly, too?"

"No one is after Kelly, babe. Will you stop worrying? If it *is* personal, it's probably some patient from the clinic. You know the kind of nuts they get in there." He thought of James. "Shh. Let me read this."

There was a long passage eulogizing Dr. Chartrand and his exemplary work with disturbed patients and his research into post-traumatic stress disorder. But Paul had no time to think about that. He skimmed over the background information quickly. He was looking for another mention of the location. There. Yes.

It was the same highway. The exact location was not named. But it was Highway 59.

Paul poured Angel another drink and left her sitting at the kitchen table in a stupor. "I'll be back by noon," he called, as he double-locked the doors. He took the newspaper with him.

KELLY LAY ON THE COUCH in her living room, a tear-soaked handkerchief balled up in her fist. Lila was trying to help her think of a way out of the trap that had closed around her.

"If only there was someone else," Lila lamented. "A relative. Doesn't Darl have any other family?"

"Only James," Kelly said.

"If James were alive," Lila said angrily, "we wouldn't have this problem."

"Do you have any *idea*," Kelly said between her teeth, "how many *times* I have said that to myself?"

"Sorry." Lila was silent a moment. "But there has to be somebody. What about Alex's mother?"

"Diane?" As far as Kelly knew, Diane had not seen Alex since he was three. The last she heard, Diane had settled down somewhere in Brooklyn with her lover. The infamous wrestler. The couple showed up at Maggie's place a few times, years ago. But when Diane refused to return to her husband and child, Maggie vowed never to speak to her again. Maggie couldn't have been more livid over the betrayal if Darl had been her own son.

"I have no idea where Diane is," Kelly admitted. "And I doubt she'd be any help. She never wanted to be a mother in the first place, so I can't see—"

"But legally," Lila urged. "Legally she'd be perfect. They never divorced, did they? There's no custody agreement or anything?"

"No, but—"

"She'd be perfect," Lila said. "All she'd have to do is sign a few papers and Alex would be yours. She couldn't object to that. Surely she'd do that much."

Kelly thought this over. It made sense. Diane might be a bad mother and an unfaithful wife, but she wasn't entirely heartless. She'd probably do it, once she heard the circumstances. Kelly remembered that Diane had been the only relative to take James's stories seriously. She had believed James. She had actually cried for James. Even if she didn't want to take care of Alex herself, she'd want to protect him from Adam. She would surely agree to make Kelly legal guardian, at least temporarily.

"It's possible," Kelly said, slowly, thinking. "It's a good idea. But I wouldn't know where to begin looking for her. It's been years."

"Doesn't your mother know her?"

"Did," Kelly said. "But Maggie hates her now, since she left Darl. If you betray my mother, beware. She'll cut you dead."

"But Maggie might know where she is."

Kelly doubted it.

But when she called directory assistance for New York City, she began to think there was no other way to proceed. Diane was not listed under her maiden or her married name, and Kelly couldn't, for the life of her, remember the name of Diane's lover. Her friends barely ever referred to him, and when they did, they used his wrestling name. The Black Hood. The Black-Hooded Crusher? She couldn't remember. She had no other recourse but to call her mother.

"THAT LITTLE BITCH?" Maggie asked. "No. Haven't seen her for years. How's Darl? Is he finally going to get a proper divorce?"

"Maybe," Kelly said. "You don't have any idea where she is? You haven't seen, uh . . ." She hesitated, unsure of the name. "You haven't seen her boyfriend, have you?"

Maggie let out a string of obscenities. Kelly waited.

"Well, if you have any idea where she might be—"

"Why don't you come down to see me?" Maggie interrupted. "You never came down last Christmas. Left me all alone down here, the both of you. You'd think I didn't have a daughter, let alone two."

"Ma. I wasn't feeling too good last Christmas, you know that."

"Well, you haven't so much as called since then." She paused, and Kelly could hear her dragging on a cigarette. "You all right now?"

"I'm fine."

"Well, why don't you come for Christmas, then? Bring Darl down."

Kelly lifted the receiver away from her mouth and sighed.

"I'm too busy, Ma. Look, I have to go now. If you hear from Diane, or if you remember anything—"

"She's long gone," Maggie said. "Far as I know. She didn't stay with that Charlie, either. Up and left him, too. The girl has no sense of decency."

"Charlie? Who, the wrestler?"

"Yeah, the wrestling fool. Charlie Cook."

Charlie Cook. There was a name at least. "What makes you say she left him?"

"I see him moping around sometimes. Always alone. He still drinks down at the Oyster Grill. On the corner. Remember that place?"

Kelly remembered. Unfortunately. That was the dive

where she'd gone to meet Maggie, when she was working on *Rising Heat*. She'd had to carry her mother out of there.

"So, you ever talk to him?"

"No. I just ignore him. But I've seen him, you know? Saw him there ... oh ... last summer, I think." Maggie's sense of time was not good, Kelly knew. She couldn't even keep track of her daughters' birthdays. Who knew when she'd really seen him last?

But it was a start.

THERE WERE ONLY TWO DAYS left before the crew would break for Christmas. Lila and Kelly were working frantically on finishing touches in the costume shop, getting everything ready for tech week on their return. Lila planned to go home to Winnipeg for the short holiday, and she urged Kelly to go to New York.

"If you can track down this Charlie Cook," she said, "you might be able to find Diane."

"I should," Kelly said. "It's too late to book a flight, now. It's the twenty-second already. I suppose I could drive."

"It would be worth it."

"Well, aside from the car ride, Alex might like it. New York at Christmas—" Kelly stopped suddenly. Michael was standing in the doorway, listening. "Hi," she said, nervously.

"So, you want to go to New York City?" he asked, smiling.

"If I can," Kelly said, startled by his appearance. She wasn't sure why she was so unnerved. So what if he overheard? Why shouldn't she be going to New York? It was a perfectly reasonable thing to do. The strain of all this constant secrecy was beginning to get to her.

"You're off the twenty-fourth to the twenty-seventh, right?" Michael asked. "Like everybody else?"

"I—I guess so."

He pointed at her. "Good," he said. He left the room.

"What was that all about?" Lila asked.

"I have no idea."

"Why is he always dropping in on us lately?"

"No idea," Kelly repeated. "None."

THEY WENT UPSTAIRS to the blue room, where the staff had assembled for a coffee break.

Bobbie was reading aloud from a tabloid newspaper to Jesse. "Get this," she said. "'Middle Eastern film star Michael Black is out of his element in the chilly climes of Minnesota. Sources say the reclusive actor longs for the sands of his native Iraq, or at least the beaches of California, but ever since a Los Angeles beauty reportedly broke his heart—'"

"Michael?" said Lila. "Reclusive?"

"Don't read that trash," Jesse said. "It's all lies. Taylor will have a fit if he sees this rag in here." He snatched the paper from Bobbie's hands and tossed it into the wastebasket.

"It was interesting," Bobbie said. "You should read it."

"Those rags are for nosy losers who want to know what the stars eat for breakfast."

"We already know what he eats for breakfast," said Lila.

At the same time, Bobbie and Jesse both cried, "Nothing!"

The conversation turned away from Michael Black and his mysterious Los Angeles beauty, and soon they all returned to work.

On her way home, Kelly slipped back into the blue room and reached into the basket. But the newspaper was gone. Someone had beat her to it.

MICHAEL CALLED HER that night as she was cooking dinner.

"Let's go away together," he said.

"Michael. Come on."

"The three of us. You really want to go to New York? We can have dinner in Manhattan tomorrow."

"Don't be—how could we do that?"

"They're called airplanes, you know? Big silver things, up in the clouds? I have here in my hand three tickets to La Guardia. Tomorrow afternoon."

Kelly didn't know what to say to him. "You went out and bought tickets? Why?"

"Why?" He sounded honestly surprised. "Because I wanted to."

"But people don't . . . People don't just take off and do something just like that. Just because they want to."

"Sure they do. I do."

Maybe it was really that simple. She looked at Alex, who had stopped eating to listen. There was a wary look in his eyes. He was monitoring her mood. He could use a vacation, she thought.

"Alex has never been in an airplane before," she told Michael.

Alex jumped up. "An airplane? Can we go in a real live airplane?"

Michael laughed. He could hear Alex. "We'll give him the window seat," he said. "He'll love it."

"Well, I'll think about it. I have to think about it."

Michael laughed again. "Okay," he said. "But you'd better start packing. The flight leaves at four."

AT THE THEATER NEXT DAY, Kelly did not get a chance to talk to Michael. She was hard at work on Ophelia's drowning dress. Debbie was not happy with it. It was too loose, she thought. Lila was diplomatic, trying to convince Debbie that she looked great in it, but the truth was that it did sag too much at the shoulders and bust. Debbie fidgeted while Kelly marked the white bodice with chalk.

"I don't have all day," she complained. "I have to get ready for tonight. We're all going ballroom dancing at the Neptune Dance Club."

"Who all?" Lila asked.

"Everyone."

"I see," said Lila. "Hold still. We can take this in a little bit. But not too much. It's supposed to flow, you know. And you'll have to be able to get into it quickly."

"Oh, all right," Debbie sighed. She tried on the wig for the scene and grimaced at her reflection in the mirror. "I look like a drowned rat," she said.

The blonde wig was long and uncombed. A crown of flowers dangled, lopsided, down the back of it. The flowers were Lila's creation. Large pale-pink and white petals, reminiscent of water lilies, but like nothing in nature. They were crazy petals, woven crazily through the hair by a crazy woman. A woman broken by sorrow. Debbie turned slowly in front of the mirror, and the white dress billowed softly as she moved, the layers of tattered lace and cotton spreading out around her like a ruined wedding dress.

Bobbie interrupted the fitting to deliver some mail. There were two airline tickets for Kelly, with a note from Michael, saying he'd be at the airport by four. If she was coming, she should meet him there. She guessed he didn't have time—or didn't want—to keep talking her into it. She was a little disappointed.

There was also a long white box for Debbie, another dozen red roses. And a card that read, "Save a dance for me tonight."

"Put these in water, would you, Kelly?" she asked sweetly, as she took off her dress.

"Do it yourself," Kelly said. She walked out the door.

Chapter Nineteen

The airport was packed with Christmas travelers, and Kelly kept a tight grip on Alex as she negotiated the crowd.

"Where's Michael?" Alex asked, as they stood in line at the gate. "He'll miss the plane."

"I don't think he can make it, honey," Kelly said.

She pictured Michael dancing with Debbie in his arms. To hell with you, she thought. Well, thanks for the tickets, but to hell with you.

She handed over her boarding passes. Michael had listed them as Kelly and Alex Quirk. Yet another alias for Alex. She prayed she'd be able to find Diane and talk her into seeing a lawyer. Once she had legal custody of Alex, she thought, she could go back home. See Darl for herself. In her heart, she knew Darl would get better if she could only take care of him personally. He would respond to her, she knew it. She would *will* him to get better. Angel didn't know the first thing about caring for anyone.

"There he is!" Alex shouted.

There he was. He was running toward the gate, the last passenger to board.

"Sorry," he told her, when he caught up. "Delayed."

"Mmm. Yes," said Kelly. "Had a little something to get out of?"

He looked puzzled. "It was Debbie Thompson," he said.

"Yes, I know." She pulled Alex on ahead, leaving Michael to deal with the carry-on bags. She settled Alex next to the window in the comfortable first-class seats and fastened his seat belt.

"What do you mean you know?" Michael asked when he sat down. "How could you know?"

"I saw the flowers."

"The flowers. You mean those roses?"

"Yes. She made a point of showing me. Two dozen American Beauty roses. You do know how to make an impression." She wanted to take the words back as soon as she'd uttered them. She sounded so bitter that even Alex tore himself away from the fascinating view to stare at her.

Michael laughed. "I didn't give her those. Those are probably from her husband. She made me late by dragging out rehearsal this afternoon. Taylor wouldn't let us go until she got her lines right. Rocko had to drive like a madman to get me here on time." He reached for her hand, but she pulled away.

"Kelly? Come on."

With embarrassment, she saw that he was smiling. He was enjoying this. He had the audacity to think she was jealous. She stared out the window and refused to answer him. Alex returned his attention to the view as well. Minneapolis was receding below them and passing from their sight, giving way to the snow-covered fields and icy lakes of the Midwestern plains. She was aware of Michael's eyes on her, but she ignored him.

"I never gave Debbie Thompson flowers," he said finally. "I never gave her a single, solitary rosebud. I swear it."

Alex was amazed at the sight of the clouds below him.

"It's like being in heaven," he said. He sat on his knees with his forehead glued to the windowpane.

Kelly sat beside him, her right hand resting lightly on his back, to keep him in place. Her left hand, despite her initial struggle, had been captured by Michael. He was stroking her wrist lightly with his thumb.

"I booked a suite for you next to me," he was telling her. "We can check in and then I suppose you'll want to visit your mother."

"Not tonight," Kelly said. "I told her I wouldn't be there until tomorrow." She wanted to spend as short a time as possible with Maggie. As far as Kelly was concerned, this visit was strictly a fact-finding mission.

Michael looked disappointed. "I have a meeting tonight," he said apologetically. "It's business. Sort of an audition." He took a card from the inside pocket of his suit jacket and handed it to her. It was the business card of a film producer. "I could try to be out of there by nine."

"You're going to make another movie?"

"I might. Yes. The script looks good."

Kelly was surprised. "I thought you were finished with movies."

He laughed. "Who told you that?"

"Everybody," she blurted out. "Everyone says you—" She stopped.

He looked at her. "Everyone says I what? Send roses to Debbie Thompson? Live in a tent in the middle of the desert?"

Kelly blushed. "No. I just heard. Bits and pieces. That there was—Rocko said there was a girl . . ."

"Ah." He nodded. "Rocko."

"He said there was a girl in L.A."

"There are a lot of girls in L.A.," Michael said. He leaned back and closed his eyes.

A LIMOUSINE MET THEM at the airport and took them to the hotel. In the grand lobby, everyone was dressed to the nines. Kelly was suddenly aware of her running shoes and jeans. She and Alex must look like some orphans that Michael had picked up off the street. But she was grateful for the anonymity of Manhattan. No one blinked an eye when Michael strode across the hotel lobby. There were probably people more famous than Michael staying here every day, she thought. There would be no photographers or reporters. There would be no teenage entourage.

In her room, Kelly changed into a skirt and the hated high-heels that pinched her feet. They ate dinner in the enormous atrium on the second floor of the hotel. At first it seemed there would be no interruptions, but that did not last. Before Michael had finished his appetizer, a tall, elegant woman in a classically cut suede suit approached the table. Michael's agent.

"Sorry," she said to Kelly. "I have to take him away." She smiled brightly. She seemed quite experienced at taking Michael away.

"I won't be long," Michael said. "We won't be long, will we, Sonya? I'd like to get out of there by nine."

"Nine?" Sonya took a more careful look at Kelly. "This is a serious contract, Michael."

"We won't be long," Michael repeated over his shoulder, as Sonya yanked him away. "I'll knock on your door."

AFTER DESSERT, ALEX WANDERED through the small conservatory and reported that there was a wishing pond. Could he have some pennies?

"Let's see," Kelly said. She followed Alex through the palm trees and exotic flowers. She slipped off her shoes and carried them. The air was warm and muggy. Alex pointed out a little pool in the center of the indoor garden with fat goldfish swimming in it. He leaned on the railing and took the pennies Kelly gave him.

"I have to think of a really good wish," he said.

Kelly ran her hand through his hair. Poor Alex.

"Are you thinking about your dad?" she asked.

"I'm thinking about Mrs. Chan," Alex said.

"Your teacher? Why?"

"She said I could be the magician at the Christmas show, and now it's Christmas and I'm not there."

"Oh, Alex, I'm so sorry." She knelt down beside him and put her arm around his waist.

He stared into the pool, his expression unreadable. What kind of damage was being done to him? she wondered.

"Why don't you wish for some new magic tricks for Christmas?" Among other presents, she had in her suitcase a brand-new magic kit she had bought for him in Minneapolis.

"I could," he said seriously. "But then you'd know what I wished for."

"Aw, you can tell me."

"No," said Alex. "There are some things you can't tell."

"I guess not," she said. She thought of all the things she wasn't telling Michael. The things he wasn't telling her. Lots of girls in L.A.? Was he joking? She wondered who had sent the roses to Debbie and whether Debbie really believed they were from Michael. Would Debbie be at the dance club tonight, looking for him? And why wasn't Debbie back in Boston with her husband for the holidays?

Then she turned her mind to more somber mysteries. What had happened to Leon? She and Lila had purchased a Winnipeg newspaper and read all about it. Leon's body had been badly battered and then exposed to the elements as well, so that he was disfigured "almost beyond recognition." They had used dental records to identify him. The dinner she had just eaten turned over in her stomach. It seemed as if a wicked god had laid some kind of curse on them all. James.

Angel. Allan. Darl. Leon. Alex. Kelly herself, who would likely end up in jail if she couldn't find Diane.

Was it really just extraordinarily terrible luck? Or was there some pattern to it? If she could only discern what it might be. She remembered the time that James had tried to teach her to paint a still-life. She was frustrated, because she could not make the painting look real. She had complained about her clumsiness. "Stupid hand," she had said, shaking it. "It's not your hand," James said. "You don't paint with your hands." It was the eyes, he told her. She had to learn to *see*.

Her memories were broken by the sound of a splash. Alex had thought of a wish at last.

She took him by the hand and they went up to their luxurious suite, where she tucked him into the gigantic bed. She read to him from *Sleeping Beauty*, but he was so tired he fell asleep before the prince showed up.

And Kelly fell asleep before Michael came back. If he knocked on her door, she didn't hear it.

IN THE MORNING, when they met Michael for breakfast in his room, he looked well rested and cheerful.

"How did it go?" Kelly asked.

"I'm going to be a pharaoh," he said. "Do you know what that is, Alex?"

"Sort of like a king."

"That's right. In Egypt. That's where my grandfather comes from."

"Is he a pharaoh?"

"Well, he thinks he is," Michael said. He winked at Kelly. "He's about seven feet tall and he walks around his olive gardens with a very big stick and growls at everybody and tells everybody what to do."

"That's like my grandpa," Alex said.

"What's the film about?" Kelly asked.

"Oh, you know." He winked again. "It's a romance."

"You're in a good mood," she said.

"Well, eight million dollars will do that."

"*Eight?*"

"Back in the game," Michael said.

MICHAEL INSISTED ON TAKING THEM to Maggie's apartment, though Kelly said it wasn't necessary. So they drove into the run-down Brooklyn neighborhood in a limousine. Two kids sweeping snow from their front stoop stopped working to gawk.

Michael got out of the car and started to follow Kelly.

"You don't have to come up," she said.

"I want to meet your mother."

"It's not really a good time," Kelly said. Never would be a good time. She could not even imagine Michael in the same room with Maggie. "I'll call you at the hotel." She took her bag from him and ushered Alex up the long wooden staircase to the front door. When she reached the top, she turned around. Michael was waving from the window of the car.

"Merry Christmas!" he called.

Oh yes. It was Christmas Eve.

Chapter Twenty

Maggie's hair was turning gray. She sat on a wooden kitchen chair, rolling a cigarette, eyeing her daughter suspiciously.

"What do you mean exactly," she asked, "when you say he's sick?"

"You know, sick. He was in a terrible accident." Kelly glanced at Alex, who appeared to be absorbed in a television program. "He can't take care of Alex right now."

"I been calling him," Maggie said. "He never answers the phone."

"I know. He's in bed most of the time. Headaches."

"I get headaches," Maggie said. "I answer the phone."

"Ma, please." Kelly sometimes wondered if her mother was deliberately obtuse. "I told you, this is different. His head was split right open. He can barely talk."

"So you think Diane is gonna take him?"

"I don't want her to take him, just to sign a paper so that I can take him."

"But you got him." Maggie lit the cigarette and the flame nearly singed her hair. She puffed, tried to get it burning straight.

Kelly simply shrugged. She was not about to tell Maggie that she had kidnapped Alex. For one thing, she doubted Maggie would understand. And even if she did understand, Kelly couldn't trust her to keep a secret. To be on the safe side, she didn't even mention Minneapolis, or the play. She pretended she had come straight from Winnipeg.

Maggie was sober tonight, and she had been good with Alex all day, Kelly had to admit. But she was so stubborn. So contrary. As Maggie fiddled with her cigarette, Kelly watched her closely.

Maggie's eyesight must be getting worse. It had always been poor, but in the past, vanity had kept her from wearing the thick glasses that she put on now, as the light began to fade. Yet she was still beautiful. Her eyes were as green and startling as ever, behind the lenses, unfocused and bright and deep as a green sea. Even the graying of her hair seemed only to enhance it, the flame-red color giving way to a head of soft, bright silver and gold. She was a beautiful woman, even now, a woman who had always drawn men to her easily, relentlessly, and probably still did.

But there was little use trying to seek her help.

Kelly had spent the afternoon traipsing through the neighborhood. She had ventured into many bars, including the Oyster Grill, and gotten up her nerve to ask questions of the patrons, but no one knew Charlie Cook, or no one would admit it. At dusk, she had stopped at the neighborhood grocery and purchased the makings of a Christmas dinner. Tomorrow, they would have a decent Christmas for Alex. Then she would start looking again. She'd have two whole days.

KELLY LIFTED ALEX UP so he could hang one of her winter socks from the coat hook in Maggie's narrow entry hall. Santa Claus would find it, she assured him, wondering if Alex believed in Santa Claus. This was something she should know, she realized. But she didn't want to plant any seeds of doubt by asking him.

He was a marvelously adaptable kid, really. His wistful homesickness of the night before had vanished, and he threw himself into the Christmas Eve activities excitedly, singing carols as he helped Kelly decorate cookies.

Christmas Day, Maggie behaved herself beautifully. While Kelly cooked, Maggie provided an appreciative audience for Alex's new magic tricks, letting him make as many of her objects disappear as he wished. She told him stories of her childhood, how she had come over to America in a big boat. She made Alex laugh, relating the wild antics of her brothers and sisters and their games on the streets of Brooklyn, the mischief they'd got into.

She remained completely sober until after dinner, when she rummaged through the cupboard under the sink and produced a full bottle of Scotch. Good Scotch. Where she had gotten it, and how she had managed to save it, was a mystery. She sat in the kitchen, while Alex helped Kelly to clear the table, and drank.

Kelly decided an early bedtime would be a good idea tonight.

"HAVE A DRINK," Maggie offered after Alex was asleep. "This is good stuff—fires up the blood."

"Oh, that's just what I need," Kelly said sarcastically.

Maggie looked at her sideways, through the glass. "Honey," she said. "You need a man."

Kelly shook her head. Maggie was pathetic. She'd gone through a good quarter of the bottle all by herself, and was rambling endlessly about the various men in her life. Her great romances were nothing but a series of cheap affairs, as far as Kelly could see. Maggie viewed Kelly's single status as a kind of disease that needed a cure. Kelly was a failure, in Maggie's eyes, if she didn't have a man in her life. But Kelly was in no mood to listen to advice about her love life. She tried to hurry through the dishwashing so she could go to bed.

Maggie poured a glass for her anyway. "Come on, relax."

"I prefer to remain human," Kelly said, as though she'd never touched a drop in her life.

"Oh, Jesus," said Maggie. "Here we go. Here comes the queen."

"Don't start, Ma."

Maggie leaned across the table and shook her finger at Kelly. "You were always like this. Since you were a little girl. You walk through this life like a queen. You don't touch nothing. You're too good for this world, that's what you think."

"I don't think that. That's your idea, not mine."

"You thought you were too good for us. You were too good for Darl! I told you, but you would never listen. Oh no. You had to go with the brother! You went and married that kid—that broken—that . . ." She searched for a word. "That *defeated* kid! I warned you, but you wouldn't never listen."

"You don't know anything about it."

"I know you. I known you all your life. You won't listen. You go your own way."

"I had to," Kelly accused her. "I had to go my own way 'cause you were never there."

Maggie was not buying this. She leaned away from her daughter, as far as she could, nearly tipping over her chair. "Oh, you are so hard done by," she spat out. "So terribly hard done by, aren't you? You know what I had to put up with? Two kids and a lousy little apartment in Winnipeg. St. Boniface. What a dump. Because Angel's father, may God put his eyes out, wanted to be near his family. Lot of good that did us!"

This was the first time she had mentioned Angel's name, Kelly realized, since they'd arrived. She hadn't even asked about Angel. Just Darl.

Maggie seemed to soften suddenly. Her moods could shift so quickly. She was looking at Kelly tenderly now, as though her daughter were a long way off. She spoke from way down low in her throat.

"It's a tough road you're choosing, now," she said. "Where will you end up?"

Kelly wanted to tell her mother how frightened she was, but she couldn't. "What do you care?" she snapped. "What the hell do you care?"

"Mother of God!" Maggie cried. "You are such a martyr!"

"Ma, be quiet. He's sleeping."

"You and your quiet. You were always—" A sound rose into the room. "What's that?" she asked.

They both listened. A thin wail from the bedroom. Alex was waking up.

"You see?" Kelly whispered. "You are just too damn loud."

"Just hold your horses. I'll see to it." Maggie staggered out of her chair and aimed herself toward the bedroom.

Great. Alex was going to get up now and come running. Kelly waited, feeling fed up, resigned, but Alex didn't come. She heard Maggie talking to him, and when she peeked in at the door, Maggie was reciting a poem, an old poem, in a sing-song voice. "You promised me a thing, and you said a lie to me." Alex was lying down, with his head on the pillow, and Maggie was tucking the covers around him. Kelly retreated into the kitchen. Fine. She would let her mother deal with it, then.

I have got to get out of this mess, Kelly said to herself. But how? Find yourself a man, Maggie said. This was her best advice. As if the world revolved around men, as if they would save you, stay with you, as if they were immortal. She lifted up the glass of whiskey. Why not?

She heard Maggie's voice through the open doorway, a faint lilt. "*You promised me a thing that was hard for you,*" she was saying, almost singing. Something stirred in Kelly's memory. That voice, those words. She took a good, hard swallow. Hard for you, she thought. Hard done by. A tough road. She drank again, straight from the bottle, and Maggie was right. It fired up the blood something fierce.

Kelly wandered around the kitchen for a while, drinking. Then she carried the bottle to the doorway and looked in on them. Alex was sound asleep, or at least his eyes were closed. And her beautiful mother continued to croon beside his bed. The last thing she remembered of this night was standing there, listening to her mother's coarse and lovely voice:

You promised me a thing that is not possible.
That you would give me gloves of the skin of a fish;
That you would give me shoes of the skin of a bird;
And a suit of the dearest silk in Ireland.

Chapter Twenty-One

Despite the fact that it was only ten o'clock in the morning on the day after Christmas, the bar was doing a fair business. A tough-looking gang of young men shot pool in one corner, while in the center of the room, older, bleary-eyed patrons sipped draft beer while watching a talk show on the television.

Kelly had been trudging from bar to bar for an hour, her hangover growing steadily worse instead of better. Now she summoned what optimism she had left and approached the bartender.

"Excuse me, I'm wondering if you've seen Charlie Cook around here lately?"

The bartender shrugged. "You'll have to ask around," he said. "We respect our customers' privacy here."

"All right." She started to move toward the group of men assembled around the pool tables, but then the bartender apparently had a change of heart. He lifted his chin in the opposite direction. At the end of the bar, in a circle of blue smoke, an enormous baldheaded figure in a leather jacket sat drinking by himself.

"Thanks," she whispered. She walked down the bar and

stood behind the man's back. She cleared her throat, but he ignored her. Undeterred, she swung herself up onto the barstool next to him.

"I'm looking for Charlie Cook," she said.

"What do you want with Charlie?"

"I'm a friend of his."

"Oh yeah?" The man bent forward, aggressively planting his misshapen nose directly in her face. "I don't think so."

"Well, I'm a friend of his girlfriend." Kelly leaned back, nearly sliding off the stool. She glanced nervously at the bartender for support. But he was busy wiping glasses at the far end of the counter.

"His girlfriend? Sara?"

"No. Diane. Diane Grayton. From Canada?"

His eyes narrowed, and he pulled away from her. He planted his hamlike forearms on the bar and turned his attention to his beer. After a long swallow, he wiped his mouth with the back of his hand. Then he lifted his jacket off his shoulder and displayed a garish red tattoo above his collarbone. A pair of lips, open in a parody of passion, seemed to cling to his skin in a permanent kiss. He patted the tattoo and stared at Kelly. "This here's Diane," he said. "All I got left of her."

"Well, then, you don't know where she is?"

"I know exactly where she is."

The sentence sounded like a threat. Kelly bit her lip. She wanted nothing more than to get out of this place, away from this cretin. But she had to continue. "Who ... who are you?" she asked.

"No. The question is who are you? And what the hell do you want with Diane?"

Kelly decided to tell the truth. This was her last lead, and she was running out of time. If this man didn't know Diane, there'd be no harm done. And if he did know her, well, maybe if she told him the truth, the word would get back to Diane.

"I've got her son," she said, watching carefully for his reaction.

He lowered the beer bottle slowly from his mouth and stared at her.

"I've got her son with me, here in New York, and ... and I want to know if she'll see him."

His mouth opened in disbelief.

"Here?" he said. "You got Alex here?"

MAGGIE CONTEMPLATED THE LITTLE BOY at her kitchen table. Darl's son. Well. This was as close to a grandchild as she'd likely ever get. Alex kicked the table leg rhythmically. He was bored. He had performed every trick in his magic kit twice already this morning, and he was restless.

"Do you know how to play cat's cradle?" she asked.

He shook his head.

"You go get me that big basket there, the wicker one."

Alex obeyed, and Maggie cleared the breakfast dishes from the table. They sat beside each other, and Maggie pulled a long piece of red wool from the basket. "It's my turn to show you some tricks, now," she said.

Alex smiled. He watched, fascinated, as Maggie showed him a few simple movements. He caught on quickly, and for over an hour they sat there, looping and unlooping, as Alex learned more and more complicated patterns.

"How will we get out of this one?" Alex asked, laughing, as the wool tangled into a net so tight their fingers were nearly touching. Maggie just laughed. In an instant, she wiggled a bit, pulled the wool loose from his fingers and held the web free.

Alex was impressed. "You're not like *my* grandma," he said.

WHEN KELLY HAD CONVINCED HIM that she really had Alex, proved it with photographs, the tattooed man admitted that he was Charlie Cook.

"I shoulda been his father," he said, as he gazed at a picture of Alex in his baseball uniform.

Kelly was alarmed to see tears gathering in his eyes. She hoped he wasn't going to fall apart. She wondered how drunk he really was.

"He has a father," she said quietly.

He emitted a snort of disgust. "A father! Some fathead doctor! Wouldn't even let the kid see his own mother."

"Wait a minute," Kelly said. "That's not true."

"It's true all right. He wouldn't even let her talk to the kid. It broke her heart—"

"Look," Kelly interrupted. "I don't know what Diane's told you, but it was *her* who left Alex." All of her old anger at Diane flared up then, and she directed it at Charlie Cook. "So don't go getting sentimental about it. She wanted to leave, she left. Some people are just plain cold-hearted." That was a phrase of her mother's, she realized, even as she heard it come out of her own mouth. "He needed her and she up and left him. And the thing is, he needs her now. He's in trouble. All I want to know is whether she'll help him out. She owes him. You both owe him. And if you have a scrap of conscience in that—" She stopped herself, suddenly afraid of her own outburst.

"Guess I can't help you now," Charlie said. He sighed angrily.

Kelly took a deep breath and tried again, in a gentler tone. "Look, I'm sorry if I offended you. But this is really an emergency. And it's nothing personal. This is between me and Diane. I have to find her."

He remained silent.

"You said you know exactly where she is. All you have to do is tell me."

He fingered the tattoo tenderly. "St. Kieran's churchyard," he said morosely. "She's been dead three years."

MAGGIE'S EYEBROWS ELEVATED in surprise, as she took in the stranger at her door. He was smiling politely. Extremely handsome. No, gorgeous. He was carrying presents. And flowers. Red roses. No man had brought her roses since ...

"Is Kelly Quirk here?" he asked.

"Michael!" Alex came running from the kitchen.

"Hi, Alex. Is this your grandma?"

"This is Maggie," Alex said. "We're playing spiderwebs."

"Cat's cradle," Maggie said. She extended a hand, and Michael shook it warmly.

"I'm Michael Black," he said. "I work with Kelly."

"In Winnipeg?"

"In Minneapolis, right now," Michael said. "Is Kelly home?"

"Come in, come in." Maggie relieved him of the roses. "She's gone out just now, but I expect she'll be back soon. Would you care for some coffee?"

"Michael doesn't like coffee," Alex volunteered.

"No? Some juice, then?"

"Please," said Michael. He followed her into the kitchen and watched while she arranged the roses in a vase. He took in every detail of the room: the worn linoleum, the threadbare towels. He could tell by the dust that Maggie was wiping from its surface that the vase hadn't been used in months. He noticed the faded pattern of Maggie's housedress, a style from the sixties, he thought. The cluster of empty liquor bottles in the sink did not escape his attention, either.

"THEY FOUND HER IN A WASHROOM in the subway," Charlie was telling her. "Some maniac got her down there. She never had a chance." His voice was weary. He had given up his macho stance entirely and was openly crying now, letting the tears roll down his fat cheeks.

Kelly wanted to cry, too. The shock was too much to absorb. Diane was dead? After all this time? Murdered on the streets of New York, and Maggie never knew it.

"He slit her throat," Charlie said in quiet anger. He raised his hand and drew his finger across his own throat. "Ear to ear."

The bartender set two bottles of beer in front of them and they accepted in silence.

"But who did it?" Kelly asked, when she could speak.

"Who knows? This is a psycho town." He wiped his face with the back of his sleeve. "This ain't Canada, you know. Happens all the time here. Mostly you just read it in the news and you don't think nothing of it. But—" His voice broke.

Kelly listened to his quiet sniffling as she let her eyes roam around the room, trying to force herself to accept that this was reality. The talk-show host on the television continued to laugh. The men continued to shoot pool. The bartender filled a row of little bowls with peanuts.

Ear to ear. A gruesome picture flashed into her mind.

She had never felt so alone in her life.

NOW THIS, MAGGIE THOUGHT, *this* was a real man. There was hope for her daughter after all. She served him a glass of frozen orange juice and poured one for herself, adding a little splash of vodka. Just a touch, to chase away the hangover.

He thanked her graciously. He had manners and charm and he had muscles, too. Here was a fellow who could take care of a girl. Here was real, serious husband material.

He was nice to the little boy, too.

"This one's for you, Alex," he said, passing over a brightly wrapped box.

"Wow. I already got lots of presents."

"Well, here's another one. I hope they fit."

Alex tore off the wrapping paper and discovered inside a pair of brand-new ice skates. Maggie helped him try them on.

"Do you know how to skate?" Michael asked.

"Yeah. I can play hockey."

"Well, great. I'm going to take you skating this afternoon. As soon as Kelly gets back." He leaned over and whispered to Alex, "There's a pair in there for her, too."

"Pretty good fit," Maggie said, as she unlaced the skates and took them off Alex's feet. "You better get washed up, if you're going to go out. Go on, scoot."

"So what do you do?" she asked Michael, sitting down across from him at the table.

"I do *Hamlet* right now," he said.

"*Hamlet*? The Shakespeare play?"

"Yes." He paused. "Kelly didn't tell you?"

"She doesn't tell me nothing," Maggie said. Maybe that was a mistake. It made Kelly sound mean. "She's very modest," she added. "Very accomplished, but very modest."

"Yes, she is."

"A very pretty girl," Maggie tried.

"She certainly is."

They smiled at each other, like two conspirators.

KELLY MADE HER WAY BACK to the apartment blindly. She let herself in and saw Alex standing in the middle of the living room, putting on his jacket.

"Kelly! We're going skating!"

"No, we're not, Alex."

"Yes, we are. Michael said so."

"Michael?"

With a sinking sensation, Kelly saw that Michael was

sitting in the kitchen with Maggie. It looked like they were having a heart-to-heart.

SHE HID IN THE BATHROOM, still wearing her coat and winter boots, watching the muddy snow melt around her feet on the tiled floor. She ran some water and placed a cold cloth over her forehead and eyes. Her life was a disaster. Alex's life was a disaster. His father incapacitated. His mother murdered by some psychopathic killer. She was on the run, a fugitive. And her mother flirting with a movie star in the kitchen. It was absurd. Unbearable.

All she wanted to do was to go home. She wanted James back. No. She wanted to go back to when James was alive. Before all this craziness began. Bitterly she realized this would take her back to the year before she was born. Well, fine. Better she hadn't been born at all than to be going through this.

She could hear Michael saying that it was all right, if Kelly didn't want to go, perhaps another time....And Maggie insisting no, no, Kelly would be fine, she was tired was all, she'd be out in a minute, don't go.

Maggie came down the hall and knocked on the bathroom door. "You come out here."

"Ma, please."

"What is the matter with you? He's waiting for you."

"I'm not going anywhere. Not today."

"Are you crazy?" Maggie was fairly shouting through the door. "He's not going to wait all day. If you let this fellow get away—"

To keep her mother quiet, Kelly opened the bathroom door.

"Will you be quiet?"

Maggie affected a kind of stage whisper. "You can't tell me *this* one's not good enough for you."

It was obvious Maggie had been drinking again. There would be no shutting her up.

"Do you want to have a life or not? Don't you ever want to get married?"

"I did get married, Ma."

"Goes and kills himself," Maggie muttered loudly. "There's a good husband for you."

Too late, Kelly realized Michael was standing at the end of the hall. He had heard everything. But Maggie continued. She either didn't know or didn't care that she had an audience.

"You can do better than that Jimmy. That weak, that nothing kid. You married a lunatic—"

Alex had come into the hall, too, and was also listening to this diatribe. Kelly and Michael both saw him at the same moment.

"Well," said Michael, in an attempt to spare Alex's feelings, "I guess you're glad to see his son, though. Aren't you?" He deliberately drew Maggie's attention to Alex's presence.

"That's not Jimmy's kid," Maggie scoffed. "That's his brother's boy. Darl's boy," she said proudly.

Kelly saw Michael's jaw drop, momentarily, before he recovered. "Uh, we better go," she said. "See you, Maggie." She ushered Alex ahead of her and headed down the stairs, her cheeks burning. She could hear Michael's footsteps close behind her all the way down, but he didn't say a word.

Chapter Twenty-Two

Rockefeller Center was bright with skaters in their new Christmas sweaters. The P.A. system played "Silent Night" and Kelly stood watching all the happy, normal people gliding across the ice, their breath visible in pale, ephemeral clouds before their faces.

She and Michael had not spoken to each other in the limo. They addressed their remarks only to Alex, who chattered nonstop, unaware of the tension in the air. Now Michael was lacing Alex's skates, while Kelly was keeping her face turned away from them, trying to hold her emotions in check. But before she could even begin to sort them out, she felt Michael's hand on her shoulder.

"Your mother upset you," he said gently.

"She's such a—" She tried to control her anger.

"I thought she was very nice," he said carefully.

You would, Kelly thought.

"She's a little unhappy, maybe," he added. "A little lonely."

"She's a little loaded. God, that is the last time I ever, ever set foot in her house."

Alex overheard. "What about my presents and stuff?"

"We are not going back there, Alex."

"Don't worry," Michael said to Alex. "I'll send the driver to pick up your things." He ran a sympathetic hand across Kelly's shoulder. "What's your mother's phone number?" he asked.

She told him. She was grateful, really. She knew he'd smooth things over with her mother.

"You get your skates on," he said. "I'll take care of everything."

Kelly sat down and opened the box with the skates. She wished he really could take care of everything.

THEY SKATED ALL AFTERNOON, and despite her initial reluctance, Kelly discovered that the exercise calmed her. The motion and the music and even the happy, normal people in their happy, normal sweaters soothed her a little. It was good to see Alex enjoying himself. She would have to make every day count from now on, she thought. Give him the best possible memories, before the end came. For she fully believed, now, that the end was coming, and probably soon. Every single person on earth who knew the truth about Adam was gone, dead, except for herself. She quite seriously feared she might be next. Or she would be arrested, thrown into prison. It was possible that Adam would take possession of Alex after all, and Alex would need to be strong.

Michael bent his knees as he reached down to hold Alex's hands and spin him around in circles over the ice.

Alex laughed out loud. "Again! Do it again!"

She wanted this day, moments like this, to stay with Alex, forever. She wanted him to remember, no matter what happened. She wanted him to remember her.

BACK AT THE HOTEL, after they had all showered and changed, they had a late dinner in the atrium. This time there were no interruptions, but there was still a lot of tension. Maggie's words hovered over them: *Goes and kills himself. That's not Jimmy's kid.*

Alex, hungry from the fresh air and exercise, stuffed himself with potatoes and chicken, while Kelly and Michael ate almost nothing. Kelly kept her eyes on Alex, away from Michael's steady gaze. As soon as we're done, she thought, I'll take Alex up to our room. I'll say good night to Michael and go to bed. I can't be alone with him. I can't explain. Not tonight, not ever.

But Michael would not let her escape. When she tried to close the door of her hotel suite against him, he simply put one of his large hands out and held it open. He pushed and, with no effort at all, gained entrance to the room.

"Michael, it's late. Alex has to sleep."

"Put him to bed then. I'll wait."

He waited, though she took her time.

When she came back, he was standing in the same position, arms crossed, his body relaxed but, as always, alert. There was no evidence of his usual humor, the famous white smile. His mouth was set in a straight line, and his dark eyes held no light. Yes. She could see him as a pharaoh. Ruler of the people, passer of judgments. What was he thinking? That she had deceived him. That she was a fraud. That she was not, in fact, of his kind, but instead had grown up in squalor, was hopelessly enmeshed in scandal.

He came toward her. "Kelly."

She stepped back. He followed. For a ridiculous few seconds, she continued to retreat, until her back was against the glass door of the balcony. She could feel the cold pane through her shirt.

He reached easily across the space she put between them and grasped her wrist.

"Michael, it's late. I'm going to bed."

"No, you aren't," he said. "You're going to talk to me."

She turned her back on him and looked out over the city.

He waited a moment, still holding her wrist, as if he thought she might bolt away. Then he spoke. His voice was stern and serious, but not without kindness.

"Your mother said he killed himself. Did she mean that literally?"

"Yes."

"Suicide?"

"Yes."

"Why?"

The question hung in the air. The question of the year, Kelly thought. She had no intention of answering him. Even though she was beginning to trust him, wanted to trust him, she could not bear to tell him the ugly history of her family. The disgusting details, the entanglements—the violence, the secrets, the grief. The murders. She imagined the clear brown eyes clouding over with horror. Beautiful, clueless Michael Black, who believed you could have what you wanted. He would back away.

She didn't want to hasten the inevitable. When Michael found out who she was, and what she had done, the complicated lies she had told, he would remove himself as simply as he removed himself from a crowd when he felt his energy flagging. He would preserve himself. She knew that much about him. He would retreat into the vast and easy world he was born into, and it would welcome him with open arms.

She wasn't ready to let him go. Not yet.

Finally he saw that she was not going to speak.

"All right," he said. "Okay." He let go of her wrist and began to pace the room. "Are you afraid? Is that why you don't want to talk?"

She had nothing to say to this.

She heard the sound of his fist slapping into his palm. "Kelly, I just want you to talk to me. You are always disappearing, you are always turning away. Is it James? You are not over his death, is that it? You need to talk about him."

Still she said nothing.

"Do you feel responsible? Is that it?"

Finally, her voice came out of her body in a low, anguished cry. "I don't *know.*" She let her body slide down the glass into a crumpled heap on the floor.

He was beside her in an instant, holding her. "I'm sorry," he said. "I'm sorry, I'm sorry."

He stroked her hair. He rocked her back and forth. She could feel the beating of his heart against her ear. Gently, he forced open her clenched fingers, flattened her palm and ran his thumb along the double lifeline. He lifted her hand and pressed it against his face. She felt the warmth of his mouth on the heel of her palm. She knew she would feel it there all night.

It had been so long, she thought, since anything like this had happened to her. For she knew that something had happened. Something undeniably obvious—and impossible—had occurred. It had happened the first day she saw him on the empty stage. She watched the glittering New York City lights and she knew she was living in a fairy tale. Tomorrow they would return to reality, and in reality, she and Michael were worlds apart.

"Are you okay?"

"Yes."

But she was lying. She was always lying.

Chapter Twenty-Three

There were tunnels in the basement of the Arcana. Long, crooked hallways, with rough walls that were mere boards holding back a rubble of stone, and damp, rotting posts holding up the low ceilings. Sometimes he was afraid they would cave in and crush him as he made his way through, crouching low, his back aching.

But the tunnels provided easy access to the theater. They were connected to a number of basements on the street, including the boiler room at the Fallon Hotel. He guessed that they had been used for running booze in the days of Prohibition. Nowadays, no one seemed to know they even existed. He could come and go without attracting any unwanted attention. And he could spy on her. From the stairwell that led up to the ancient, noisy furnace that heated the Arcana, he could hear almost every word spoken in the costume shop.

He had overheard Debbie Thompson's reaction to his latest bouquet. He smiled to himself. He wondered if Debbie had missed his attentions during the Christmas holidays. Well, that little absence couldn't be helped. He'd had to leave for a few days. He was a busy man. He chuckled. But now he was back.

It was vital that he keep close tabs on Kelly. He needed to know how she was feeling about him, how much she knew.

He hoped he wasn't going to have to kill her. He didn't want it to come to that.

No. After going through so much trouble, he wanted to come out of this with everything. He wanted everything back.

KELLY HURRIED TO THE COSTUME SHOP on the morning scheduled for the dress parade, dodging her way through the clamor. Dorothy was conferring with the prop supervisor, checking off items on a list. The lighting director was late, and Taylor was bellowing at Jesse as if it were his fault. The dressers wheeled the costume racks through the labyrinthine hallways, trying to avoid collisions with the actors and makeup artists who were arriving slowly, stumbling in, rubbing their eyes and asking for coffee. It was seven o'clock in the morning.

Taylor had decreed an early start, which meant that Kelly had to bring Alex with her. She'd left him in the care of Bobbie, who would have little to do today except dispense caffeine and sugar. Kelly could have come late, with Alex as an excuse, but she was determined to be here. She was dying to see Lila. They'd been interrupted during their phone conversation yesterday. Kelly had told the terrible news about Diane, but before they could talk about Darl, Sam came home and Lila had to hang up. She knew Lila would have left Winnipeg on a five A.M. flight, and she wanted to hear how Darl was from someone who had seen him.

Lila was already at the drafting table, studying the script, making notes on a yellow pad of paper. She jumped up to hug her friend.

"Oh, Kell, you poor thing."

"What? What?" Kelly grabbed Lila's arms.

"No, no. I mean about Diane. Darl's okay. He's even a bit better. He's walking around the house—with crutches."

"Is he talking? Making sense?" Darl had to be well enough to convince a social worker he was capable before Kelly could risk returning Alex.

"Well, he was pretty quiet. But he seems to listen. I was chattering on about the play, just to make conversation, and he asked about Michael. So he must have understood me."

"He asked about Michael?"

"Just asked what he was like. I think. He—his speech isn't very clear, really."

"But he doesn't even know Michael."

Lila shrugged. "Everybody knows Michael. Anyway, Sam said there's a big improvement in his attention span, compared to a couple of weeks ago." She frowned. "I honestly don't think he'd be passing any competency tests quite yet, though. He still doesn't remember anything about the night he got mugged. I asked, but he didn't seem to know what I was talking about. He just kept asking about you, wanted to make sure you and Alex were okay."

Kelly smiled. Typical Darl.

"It's as if he doesn't even know he got beaten. A kind of concussion, I guess," Lila said. "But he's improving. I'm sure it's just a matter of time before you'll be talking to him yourself."

"Just a matter of time," Kelly repeated. She knew she should feel some relief, but she couldn't shake the sense of doom that had descended on her in New York. Hope seemed out of reach. The best she could summon was resignation.

Lila smiled. "Looks like you did the right thing after all, Kelly. You kept Alex safe, and soon he'll be back home where he belongs. Now let's get to work." She straightened her pile of notes and headed out, up the stairway.

Kelly remained a moment in the silent shop, surveying the long tables and machines that sat idle now, deserted, their work complete. The mannequins were the only human figures in the empty room. They stood naked, a little lonely perhaps, against the wall. No longer needed. She turned out the lights.

TAYLOR AND LILA STOOD in the front row, calling out directions: bend, spin, crouch, leap, turn. The actors complied, sometimes acting out short bits of their scenes, when Taylor requested it. Lila and Kelly took notes. They wanted to make sure everybody could move comfortably through the play.

Ophelia's costumes grew gradually paler as the play progressed, until she appeared in her chalk and pale-pink drowning clothes. Tattered and unearthly. Utterly fragile.

The other actors' costumes were bolder, almost shocking. As the actors moved across the stage, the shifting patterns and tones created a disturbing, somewhat surreal effect. Polonius looked properly ridiculous, in his maroon doublet and clashing cold-blue hose. The various courtiers strutted across the stage like bright peacocks, feathers in their hats. The most striking of all was Gertrude, in her fur-lined, slashed-puff sleeves, all burgundy velvet and rustling salmon silk. A gable headdress accentuated her kohled eyes, the hooded sensuality of her face.

None of it was easy on the eye. Sulfurous yellows, bilious greens, the jarring, arrogant puce and purple robes of Claudius, the false King. This was a decadent court that arrayed itself in brilliant color to disguise its disease.

Only Hamlet had little color. His costumes relied on the dramatic effects of rough textures: the corrugated weave of a black doublet that absorbed the light, the stiff creases of a dark cape that seemed to enfold him in shadow, suede boots that reached to his knees, hugging the muscles of his legs as he moved. For the graveyard scene, he wore a raw canvas shirt and thick leather jacket, heavily buckled, that created a large and jagged silhouette, marking him as a dangerous outsider beside the other mourners in their long elegant lines. You had only to see him, Kelly thought, to understand the play—here was the avenger, his animal power in sharp, unsettling contrast to his all-too-human mind.

As for the ghost, he was magnificent and terrible. He came on last, so that they could view him with all the effects of the fog machine in the garish yellow lights. His chain mail was an illusion Kelly had created with open-weave hemp that she painted black and dry-brushed in silver. Beneath the coarse brown cape, it provided just a hint of military might. And a fragment of broken chain dangled from his manacled wrist.

Taylor and Lila were pleased. Kelly met with them in Taylor's office, where they discussed the few alterations needed. Sleeves too wide for Laertes to manage. A problematic garter on one of the ladies. Nothing that couldn't be fixed.

IT WAS LATE BY THE TIME Kelly finished writing up directions for the cutters. She had put in ten hours, at least, today, and her vision was starting to blur as she gathered her things and prepared to take Alex home. The set was dark, and most of the cast had left.

Bobbie was alone in the blue room, applying mascara with the aid of a pocket mirror.

"Where's Alex?"

"He's right here." Bobbie turned around, but Alex was not behind her. He was not in the hall, or the green room.

"Bobbie," Kelly said. "Think. When did you last see him?"

"Ten minutes—five minutes ago," she said. "He was right here!"

Kelly turned and ran immediately toward the stage. That

damned set! Bobbie raced after her down the corridor. They turned on the lights. They searched among the pulleys and wires, calling. But Alex was not there.

"Maybe he's visiting," Bobbie said. "Sometimes he goes around to the dressing rooms after rehearsal."

Kelly dashed down to Michael's room. His door was closed. She knocked once and flung the door open without waiting for an answer. He was alone, reading. He looked up, surprised.

"Have you seen Alex?"

"No. What's going on?"

"We can't find him," she said, and she sped off down the hall to continue the search. Michael followed.

Together, Michael and Bobbie helped her to search the entire main floor and the costume shop. They gathered Rocko and Dorothy along the way. Rocko went upstairs to check the offices. Timothy was still working up there. He hadn't seen Alex either, Rocko reported.

Kelly leaned against the wall, shaking hard now, tears running down her cheeks. Michael wrapped an arm around her shoulder. "Hey," he said. "I'm sure we'll find him." She saw him exchange a look with Rocko. "He's here somewhere. Calm down."

"Are the doors locked?" she asked.

"Yes, I just came in the back," Rocko said.

"Did you see anybody?" she asked him. "Any strangers around? You didn't see anyone outside? A car? Anyone?"

Rocko shook his head. He looked at Michael. The two of them obviously thought she was overreacting.

"Maybe he fell asleep somewhere," Bobbie said lamely. "The balcony?"

They all lifted their eyes to the upper level. "You take the right, I'll take the left," Michael said to Rocko. "Bobbie, you check the box seats." They charged down the aisle, and Kelly could hear their footsteps pounding up the stairs, but she knew that Alex wasn't up there. He would have heard them calling. No matter where he was, he would have heard them by now. She sank into a front-row seat, sick with fear.

"You don't suppose he could have got into the costume shop?" Dorothy asked.

"We looked there."

"Did you look in the back? Downstairs?"

"Downstairs?"

"In the basement."

"The costume shop *is* the basement," Kelly said. "Isn't it?"

"Well, no. That's the lowest level we use, but—"

"Where's the staircase?" Kelly was on her feet.

"Wait," Dorothy said. "It's dark down there; it's dangerous. I'll get Timothy. He knows his way around."

"Just tell me where it is!"

"Back behind the furnace," Dorothy called. She hurried upstairs to summon Timothy.

The furnace? The furnace was in an old room off the costume shop, a great green gas-burning monstrosity that had never concerned her. Now she edged her way around one corner of it and discovered a doorway, with no door on its hinges, completely hidden from view. It opened onto a dark hallway with rough, sloping cement walls, a cracked cement floor. Alex wouldn't come down here, she thought, as she inched her way along. Three feet into the corridor, she was engulfed in nearly total darkness. It's too scary. He'd never come back here.

If he was alone.

She slid one foot forward. She could sense the space in front of her, but she couldn't see where the stairwell began. She slid her other foot forward, holding on to the damp wall with both hands. Then she felt the first step.

She stood at the head of the stairs, blind, and called his name. No answer. She waited for her eyes to adjust to the dark, but there was little improvement. Slowly, cautiously, she descended, calling out for Alex.

She counted the steps, planning ahead for the return trip. After fourteen, she began to shake again. How deep was this basement? Sixteen, seventeen steps. Then the floor leveled out. Cold subterranean air, cold cement walls. She took one step forward and immediately felt the thick, sticky film across her mouth and nose. She gasped, and breathed it in, wiped at her face wildly with her hands. Spiderwebs. The place must be crawling with spiders. And in the distance, as though in another chamber of the basement, she heard a rustling. Rats? Or was someone there?

She stood perfectly still. This was all too familiar. The darkness, the fear, the spiderwebs. The toolshed. She shuddered.

She moved carefully, steadily, toward the rustling sound. There seemed to be too many walls, one leading into another, and she slid her way along, wondering how many rooms there could possibly be down here. Then, turning another corner, she saw a flash of light. Quickly, she jerked her head out of sight and listened. In the momentary flash, she had seen a figure against the wall. Huge. Whether a man or the shadow of a man, she was not sure.

Trembling, she peered out again, and the light shone right in her eyes. She could see nothing.

"Kelly?" Alex's voice.

"Alex? Where are you?"

"In here," he called. He lowered the light. He was holding in his hands one of the carpenters' industrial lanterns. It must have weighed five pounds. It illuminated the walls of the chamber he was standing in, but his small face remained in darkness.

"Alex, what the hell—what are you doing down here?"

"I got lost," he said shakily.

Alex turned away from her and shone the flashlight behind him. Kelly saw the figure she had glimpsed before. It was an ancient suit of armor, propped against the cement wall, one rusty arm broken off and lying between the feet. The little room was packed full of junk. As the light leaped across the walls, she saw a painted rocking chair, a doll's house, a wall hung with masks, the enormous, broken head of a wooden horse, nostrils flaring.

"I was in—I was upstairs," Alex said.

"Yes? And what happened? Why did you come down here?"

"I was . . ." He hesitated. He shone the light around the room again. Kelly saw a long, low corridor, like a tunnel, and heard the rustling again. There were definitely rats down here.

"Alex, turn around. Look at me."

He did, and then he saw the look on Kelly's face. "I'm sorry," he cried. He ran headlong into her arms and she collapsed with him onto the floor, hugging him tightly, as if she could conceal him within her body, the tears coming so freely she couldn't stop them, and then she started to laugh.

This was how Michael found her, sitting on the floor, hysterical. He took one look at them, went to the foot of the stairs, and called up the news that Alex had been found. Then he returned. "Are you all right?"

"I'm okay," Alex said. "Kelly, let me go."

She released him.

Michael reached down and ran a hand through her hair. "Stand up," he said. "The floor is cold." He took her hand, and she stood. She did not trust herself to speak.

Dorothy, Rocko and Timothy came downstairs, curious to see what was going on. They carried candles and another flashlight. The room was now quite brightly lit.

"I can't find a light switch anywhere," Timothy said. "I'm not even sure if it's wired down here."

"This is the old storeroom," Dorothy said. "We used it long ago. Oh, Prospero's chest!"

In the center of the room, a dusty old trunk stood open.

Alex had apparently been digging through it, looking for treasure. Kelly lowered her face into her hands and shook her head.

"Look at this stuff," Rocko insisted. So they looked. They pulled out a seemingly endless assortment of jewelry, scarves, and musty old books.

"It looks like a magician's trunk," Alex said.

"Indeed it is," said Dorothy. "This is ancient. I remember we found this chest down here years and years ago. It was old even then. But perfect for Prospero. A lucky find. It was in the back there, in one of those rooms. There are rooms upon rooms back there, a regular smuggler's den."

Timothy wrinkled his nose. "We should clean this mess out," he said. "Fire hazard."

Michael reached into the bottom of the trunk and pulled out a final item—a sad, crumpled pair of fairy's wings. He held them up to Dorothy. "Ariel?" he asked.

Dorothy laughed. "That's all that's left of Ariel, I guess." She took the wings. "This is one of the first things I ever made in this place." She bent down and ran her fingers along the edge of the trunk. "The paint's faded," she said.

"Yeah," said Alex. "But look, Kelly. There's stars and stuff. And a moon."

Kelly peered a little more closely, pretending to be interested. She could barely make out the design. The leather straps were broken, the clasp rusted.

"Can I have it?" Alex asked. "Can I keep it? I could put my magic stuff in it."

"You can have it, as far as I'm concerned," Timothy said. "You can all take whatever you want. Rocko, you're a sensitive man; you might find a use for that armor there."

"Cute," Rocko said.

"Alex, it's a mess. Look at it," Kelly said. "And you should never have come down here." There was only a slight tremor in her voice, but Michael and Rocko were watching her carefully.

"We could fix it up," Alex pleaded.

Michael knelt beside him and examined the chest. "I think we could. The wood is solid enough." He lifted it up with one hand and looked underneath. He looked at Alex. "Would you help me?"

Alex nodded.

"Look at this candelabra," Rocko was saying. "Hey, Kelly, this would go great on your mantelpiece."

"Take it," Timothy said. He was examining the masks on the wall. Dorothy was exclaiming over half-forgotten props and accessories.

Michael offered his hand to Kelly. "Let's get you out of here," he said.

"Yes," she said. "Let's."

UPSTAIRS, KELLY HUNTED NERVOUSLY for her purse and her keys. She couldn't seem to find anything. She couldn't focus. The afternoon's feeling of accomplishment had evaporated entirely. She felt scattered. Absent-minded. She finally found her spare set of keys in her briefcase, and gathered her things. Alex waited quietly, subdued.

Michael offered to help her take the trunk home, and Kelly accepted when she discovered how heavy it was. He carried it out to her car while she washed Alex's dusty tear-streaked face and helped him on with his coat. She took the opportunity to give him a lecture on wandering off.

"You could get hurt," Kelly said. "What would happen if you fell and hurt yourself and we didn't know where you were?"

"I didn't get hurt," he said. Child logic.

"But you *could* have."

"But you finded me." He wrapped his arms around her neck, and her anger melted.

MICHAEL AND KELLY STOWED the trunk in Alex's closet. It smelled of old books and rust and dank cement, and Kelly did not really want it at all. She put newspapers underneath it to protect the floor.

She felt obligated to provide dinner for Michael, who had probably not eaten in hours. Alex claimed he wasn't hungry. He curled up on the couch, wrapped himself in one of Kelly's sweaters and promptly fell asleep. It was way past his bedtime.

As Kelly made a salad, Michael sat at the kitchen table, leafing through the newspaper. He glanced up once in a while, always aware of her. He was concerned, she thought, about the fear she showed when Alex went missing. She should try to relax, she told herself. Alex was perfectly fine.

She peered into the living room and saw him sleeping, safe and sound. Then she laid out the salad with some biscuits and fruit, and sat down across from Michael.

He was reading an article and did not look up. She read a few words, upside down, and glanced at the accompanying photograph.

"Is that you again?" she asked.

"I'm afraid so."

"What are you up to now?"

He smiled. "Says here I'm going to play a terrorist in my next film."

"A terrorist?"

"Apparently. And I'm mad as hell at being typecast."

"Oh, Michael!" She leaned over and read for herself. "This article isn't right, is it? You're not from Iran. Are you from Iran?"

"I've never even been there," he said.

"Well then, it's not true!"

He was laughing now. "Of course it isn't," he said. He waved a hand, as if to indicate all the newspapers on the continent. "None of it's *true*."

Chapter Twenty-Four

Michael stayed far too late, ignoring Kelly's hints that it was well after midnight. When she suggested that they might wake Alex with their voices, he simply carried the sleeping boy upstairs and put him into his bed.

On his way back, he stopped on the landing halfway down the stairs and examined the stained-glass window. He touched it with his hand, running his fingers across the black flowers of the border.

"Orpheus," he said.

"Yes."

He came down the rest of the way, smiling at her curiously. "Whatever possessed you to put that in your house?"

"It's not my house," she said. "I'm renting."

"Oh. Well, still . . ."

"You don't like it?"

"It's beautiful," he said. "It's marvelous. But, you know." He seemed to expect her to know what he meant.

"What?"

"Don't look back," he said quietly.

Kelly raised her eyes to the picture. "But he does look back," she said. "He loves her."

"He kills her," Michael said. "It's a story about possession, attachment, wanting too much."

Kelly smiled. "It's not a romance?"

"No."

MICHAEL KEPT THE TAXI DRIVER waiting outside at two in the morning while he took his time saying good night to Kelly. He was telling her he didn't want to leave, but she wasn't really listening. She was looking at his eyes. She wasn't afraid to look in his eyes any more. The long black lashes, very dark pupils, full of light, even in the dim hallway. He kept shifting his gaze as he spoke, looking in her eyes, at her mouth, back into her eyes. His eyes kept on returning to her mouth. He moved a little closer. He touched her hair. He began to trace her lips with the edge of his little finger.

She stepped back. "I have to get some sleep."

He raised both his large hands, palms forward, and spoke in a gentle voice, the way a man might try to calm a startled horse.

"It's okay. I'm going now." He remained standing there. An unreadable look passed over his face. Sympathy? Then he turned to go.

"Michael." She had not intended to call out.

He turned.

She fell into his arms with an intensity that rocked him backward, off balance. "Hey!" he said. She caught a brief glimpse of his white smile. Then she pulled his head down and drew his mouth to hers, clutching his hair tightly in her fingers.

During the kiss that followed, she forgot that happy endings were impossible, that dreams didn't really come true. She forgot everything except the way that Michael's energy seemed to flow through her, giving her strength.

THAT WAS THE NIGHT James returned to her dreams. He appeared suspended in the air, far away, though she could see every detail of his battered body clearly. He was speaking to her again, in his incomprehensible phantom language, a sound like the mumbling of twenty men trapped underground. His thin body turned in space. His eyes fixed on her, accusing her of forgetting something.

Perhaps he sensed that she was slipping away from him, moving into the world of the living, leaving him behind, alone in the land of burning shadows, the way he once left her behind.

She reached out for him, but he drifted away. He was already becoming transparent. The last sound she heard sounded like a word. He said "Leave," she thought, but that didn't make sense. And then there were no more words. Just an insistent expression in his eyes, as if he was willing her to read his mind. As she tried to understand, the old pain revisited her and seemed to rip her open. She had a vision of her own body lying broken, bleeding, rent apart.

She sat up, suddenly wide awake and shaken. She had slept late. She was not rested, but she didn't even try to lie down again. She got out of bed and checked on Alex. He was still sleeping off his adventure of the day before.

She walked downstairs to the landing, barefoot. The floor was surprisingly warm. The morning sun poured through the stained-glass window, washing the staircase with red and deep-blue light. She sat down in the stream of rich, warm color and thought of Michael's mouth against her own. She shuddered. She had let another man into her life. A risk she had vowed never to take.

Was that why James had come back?

Was he jealous? Vengeful? Would he never let her be?

"It's too late," she said to the empty room.

She had called James to her in the first place, she thought. Maybe she could send him back.

PAUL PARKED HIS CAR a block away and walked to the house, carrying his tools in a tool-belt under his coat. It was at least thirty below, with a windchill of seventeen hundred, according to the radio.

He was of two minds about letting Angel leave town. On the one hand, it was good to have her out of the way for the time being. On the other hand, he wanted to keep an eye on her. He didn't want her causing any trouble. She didn't always listen to him. He had difficulty getting her to obey the simplest precautions. He only hoped she would remember his instructions.

Well, there was no car in the driveway. No home-care worker today. Or any other day, as far as Paul could tell. But that was just as well, from Paul's point of view. He glanced up and down the street, to make sure it was empty. No one was crazy enough to be taking a stroll on a day like this. He walked up the front path and around to the back. He tried the back door gently. Locked. That was no problem. He fumbled with the zipper of his parka, unable to manage it with his clumsy mitts on. He took them off and slipped on the pair of thin black leather gloves he carried in his pocket. He put them on hurriedly, feeling the skin begin to freeze. Then he unzipped his coat and drew a screwdriver out of his tool-belt. He knelt at the basement window of the laundry room, where exhaust from the dryer made an icy depression in the snow. The window popped out of its frame easily—not surprising, as he had loosened it from the inside on a previous visit, weeks ago, just in case. With one last cautious glance around, he crouched down and began to lower his legs through the narrow casement. He knew Darl probably couldn't hear him—and couldn't do much about it even if he did—but he was extremely quiet nevertheless. Paul didn't like surprises. If there was going to be a showdown, he wanted to be prepared for it.

KELLY HAD ARRANGED to have lunch with Rocko, but minor details made her late to meet him. Tech week was a nightmare of details. All sorts of problems were discovered and remedies were invented as quickly as possible. The prop department was busy finishing off swords and skulls and crowns and various other required objects. The painters had nearly finished the final coat on the set, and it was looking very realistic. Work in wardrobe should have been winding down, but every day it seemed there was some costuming crisis that required her attention.

When she finally got away, she found Rocko waiting patiently in the blue room, cleaning his fingernails with Michael's silver letter opener.

"That's disgusting," Bobbie was saying. "And dangerous. You could hurt yourself with that thing."

"You could kill yourself with it, little one," he replied. "If you were in the mood."

"Let's go," Kelly said, putting on her coat. "Sorry I'm late. Last-minute repairs."

"The thousand rips and tears that clothes are heir to," Rocko said as he followed her out.

"Oh God," said Bobbie. "Spare me."

"HOW GOES THE GREATEST SHOW on earth?" Rocko asked, once he was securely settled with a bottle of wine at hand.

Kelly laughed. "It is a bit of a circus," she admitted.

"Willy would die, if he could see it," Rocko said. "He must be positively spinning in his grave."

"I think he'd like it."

"Yes, well, he did adore foolishness. You know, while we're on that subject, I saw Debbie Thompson last night."

"You must see her all the time, since you're staying in the hotel now."

"Well, yes, but not in her nightgown."

"Lucky you," Kelly said dryly.

"Lucky me. She was standing in the corridor at two o'clock in the morning, knocking on his door."

Kelly didn't have to ask whose door. "You're kidding."

"Calling his name, rapping away, but he didn't answer." Rocko reached over and filled both their glasses. "You don't happen to know where he was?"

Kelly drank from her wineglass, then took a bite of salad. She chewed very slowly.

"I knew it," Rocko said.

"What does she want with him, anyway?" Kelly asked.

"What does she— My God, don't you think you're carrying this naïveté thing a little far?"

"You know what I mean. What did she want in the middle of the night?"

"Oh, I'm sure she had some ruse. She's had several, lately. Let's see." He ticked off his fingers as he spoke. "She needed ice, she needed help with her lines, she came over one night to thank him for some totally fictitious flowers—"

Kelly looked up. "They weren't fictitious," she said. "I saw them. Two or three times now, he's sent her red roses."

"He says not."

Kelly sat up straight and looked at Rocko seriously. "So who are they from? The card calls her 'My leading lady.' Are they from Taylor? Timothy?"

"Not likely. Though I wouldn't put it past Taylor. He believes in flattery as a motivating device. You really saw this card?"

"Yes."

"In Michael's hand?"

"I don't know," she said. "I've never seen his handwriting."

"Curious. Perhaps it's a fan."

"An anonymous fan? Pretending to be Michael? That's creepy."

"Creepier things have happened. Look at all the mail our

golden boy receives. You think all those letters are from sincere little film students, praising his great works?"

"I don't know."

"Well, they're not. That's why he reads them all himself. Don't you ever wonder about that? He doesn't do his own laundry, does he? You don't see him answering the telephone. God knows he wouldn't drive a car to save his life. But every day, there he is, slitting the envelopes open."

"Why?"

"Long story. He once had, shall we say, an obsessive relationship. Is that the term? He was seeing this girl in L.A.—"

"Ah!"

Rocko smiled. "Yes. He was quite taken with her. I met her once, at a party in Hollywood, when I was still pursuing a film career. Beautiful girl, really. Very young, though. I think she was Canadian, too, come to think of it. Hmmm."

"What happened?"

"Well, at the same time, Michael was getting these cards and letters from a persistent fan. His secretary became alarmed and started saving them. When they piled up, she showed Michael. At first he ignored it. But the tone of the letters became progressively more, well, 'creepy,' as you put it. Threatening. It was getting to him, you could tell. The fan called his girlfriend by name, mentioned her address. Michael panicked. Insisted the girl move in with him, for protection, and things went from bad to worse."

"Did she hurt Michael's girlfriend?"

Rocko paused for dramatic effect.

"She *was* Michael's girlfriend," he said. He sat back, enjoying the look of shock on Kelly's face.

"Eww," Kelly said. "That's like—"

"A movie?"

"Yes. What if she's back? Going after Debbie this time?"

"I think that might have crossed his mind," Rocko said thoughtfully. "He wasn't too happy to hear Debbie's tale. I was there. It seemed to upset him, though it's hard to tell. He swore he didn't send them. She was crestfallen, believe me. I didn't think about it too much at the time. I just assumed it was another of her little games. But you could be right. How intriguing. Perhaps ..."

But Kelly wasn't listening. She was trying to remember exactly when she had received the first of those phone calls. Hallowe'en. It couldn't have had anything to do with Michael. And nothing had happened here, in Minneapolis. Nothing that couldn't be explained. If there was a woman harassing Michael, she didn't know about Kelly. Not that there was anything much to know.

She sighed. "I've got to get back to the theater. We open tomorrow night."

"Everybody in town is aware of that fact," Rocko said. He signed the check, thus charging their meal to Timothy, and took her elbow to lead her out of the hotel. As they passed through the lobby, a trio of girls standing vigil by the elevator stared at them.

"Where's Michael Black?" one of them called out. "Is he in the restaurant?"

"You see?" Rocko said. "They are everywhere. And they're starting to recognize you."

Kelly groaned. "I have got to stay away from him," she muttered under her breath as she rushed through the revolving door.

Rocko stopped her outside the hotel. "What is with you, anyway?" He sounded actually angry. "What is going on with you two?"

She rushed ahead of him, taking long strides, making him run after her all the way down the block.

When they reached the theater, there was a surprise waiting for her. Angel was standing at the stage door, leaning up against the building, one leg bent and her boot against the wall. An old army-surplus knapsack hung from her shoulder.

She was smoking a homemade cigarette. She seemed to have gained some weight, and her hair had grown out a bit, but she still looked like a scarecrow.

"Angel!" Kelly rushed forward. "How did you get here?"

"Took a bus. Soon as Maggie called and told me where you were, I had to come. Where's Alex?"

"In school. My God." Kelly folded her arms around her sister and held on for a long time.

"Can we go in? I'm freezing my ass off."

"Of course. Gosh." Kelly turned to see Rocko smiling, holding the door open for them. She hustled Angel inside, keeping the introductions brief. She hurried past Michael and Debbie, who were conferring over something in Michael's dressing room. Michael called out to her through his open door, but Kelly just steered Angel straight past and into the blue room. The last thing she needed was for Angel to start talking to these people. Wouldn't Debbie Thompson love to get hold of the truth? Kelly could picture Debbie on the telephone to the police, acting horrified but secretly thrilled to be rid of her. She parked Angel on the couch and told her to stay put.

"I'll run down to the shop and see if I can get the rest of the day off," Kelly said.

Rocko came in and made himself at home, as usual. He pulled out the letter opener again and took up where he'd left off with his manicure.

"Rocko, don't you think you'd better return that to Michael? *Now?* He's in his dressing room."

"All in good time," he smiled. He wasn't about to budge.

Kelly raced down to the shop and told Dorothy she had to go. Family emergency. She shot back out before Dorothy could answer. She had to keep that nosy Rocko away from her sister.

ANGEL SAT CROSS-LEGGED on the piano bench, her back hunched, hugging a bottle of beer as if it were a warm mug of soup. She was watching Alex through the window, as he pulled a neighborhood friend on his sled.

"He seems okay," she commented.

Alex had greeted Angel warily, though, as if he had picked up on Kelly's uneasiness. Angel's arrival proved to Kelly that she wasn't as hidden as she ought to be. Michael must have mentioned the Arcana to Maggie, and Maggie might mention it to anybody. Ironic, Kelly thought. She hadn't told Maggie about the kidnapping because she didn't trust her to keep quiet, and now this.

Kelly knew she had to talk to Angel about it, now, and that was why she had sent Alex outside.

Angel insisted she hadn't told anyone where she was going. Paul wouldn't let her, she said. Paul kept everything secret these days. He was skulking around like a bad actor in a spy movie. He hadn't even wanted Angel to come. Said there might be trouble.

"Whatever that means," Angel concluded. "I think he just wanted me to stay home. He doesn't let me go anywhere these days." She hung her head, guiltily. "Not even to see Darl."

Kelly sighed. She was not terribly surprised to hear this. The last person she'd expect to stand up for herself was Angel.

"You can't tell anyone we're here," Kelly said. "Did you know Adam and Eleanor are trying to get custody of Alex?"

"Really? Paul said they might. They came to the door looking for you, but he wouldn't let them in to talk to me."

How did Paul get so smart? Kelly wondered. Maybe he was keeping Angel home to protect her. "The police didn't come?"

"No!"

"They might. Adam has an order for custody," Kelly

explained. "They had Darl declared incapacitated while he was in hospital. Claimed he couldn't take care of Alex—"

"Well," Angel shrugged, "he couldn't."

Kelly pressed her fingers against her forehead. She could feel a headache coming on. Angel was just like Maggie, she thought. She got more like Maggie every year. But where Maggie was deliberately stubborn, Angel was just plain slow. "Honey," she said. "Do *you* think Adam should be looking after Alex?"

"No. Of course not. Isn't that why you took him?" Angel looked puzzled for a second. Then she solved that problem by finishing off the beer. "Got another one?"

AFTER SHE HAD GIVEN ANGEL and Alex some dinner, Kelly tried to talk her sister into going back to Winnipeg. "There shouldn't be any connection between you and me. They could be watching you. That's why I didn't tell you where I was."

"I wouldn't have told," Angel pouted. "You could have trusted me."

If only, Kelly thought. She looked at the knapsack Angel had stashed in the hall. It must have been twenty years old, the olive-green canvas patched and frayed and falling apart. Kelly still couldn't quite believe her sister had come all this way on her own. She couldn't picture Angel making phone calls, purchasing tickets, getting on the right bus, finding the theater. It seemed unlikely, if not impossible. She wondered if Paul had sent her for some reason.

She stood up and began to help Alex, who was picking up his toys, piling his little collection of trucks into a shoebox. He was unusually quiet tonight. Tired from the excitement of yesterday, she guessed.

She carried the box of toys into the hall and tripped on the knapsack. The bag tipped over, spilling out Angel's toothbrush and pocket change, and trucks ricocheted around the floor. Annoyed, Kelly bent to pick it all up. What was this? On the floor near the front door, she saw something shiny. It was her silver necklace, the one James had given her, the one she thought she'd left in Winnipeg.

"What is this?" she asked, holding it up.

"Your necklace," Angel said.

"Did you bring this for me?"

Angel looked at Alex, then back at Kelly. "Me? I didn't bring it."

"Where did it come from?"

"Kelly, that's yours. James gave that to you on your twentieth birthday. I remember. It has those matching earrings."

"But I lost it," Kelly said. "It's been missing for weeks. I don't even—Alex, were you playing with this?"

He shook his head solemnly.

Angel gave Kelly a curious look. Then she shrugged. "Come on, Alex. I'll read you a story, okay?"

"I want Kelly," he said.

"You give Kelly a break tonight, sweetheart. Come on. I'll read you *The Little Mermaid*. Here it is right here."

Alex kissed Kelly on both cheeks and reluctantly went up to bed with Angel.

Kelly sat at the kitchen table, running the necklace through her fingers. James had bought her this necklace from the proceeds of the first painting he'd sold. They'd had a fight—she couldn't remember the cause of it now—and he had given her this outrageously expensive birthday present as a peace offering. She closed her eyes, and James appeared before her, penitent, twenty-one years old, fastening the clasp around her neck, love shining in his eyes. She rubbed the necklace, and the cold silver warmed to her touch. She had believed in that love, had thrown herself into its fire. But her love had not been good enough. The beautiful, scarred body had slipped from her clumsy fingers.

How had this necklace disappeared and how had it returned?

Was she losing her mind? There was a time when she might have accepted that explanation. But no longer.

She listed the people who had been in her house. Lila, of course. And Angel. Rocko and Michael. Not Michael! A twinge of doubt about him caused her to wince. *I followed you everywhere,* he had said. *When I found out you were married, I was crushed.* No. Ridiculous.

But Angel? That was equally ridiculous. Why would she bring the necklace here and then lie about it?

She watched Angel coming down the stairs. Like everyone else, Angel was fascinated by the stained-glass window. Kelly told her the story of Orpheus and his descent into the underworld, how he had been unable to resist glancing back at Eurydice.

"Hmm," said Angel. "A love story."

"That's what I said," Kelly replied.

She accepted the beer that Angel poured for her. The two sisters clinked glasses.

IN THE MORNING Kelly convinced Angel to return home. In order to arrange this, she had to keep Alex home from school and to call in late for work. Dorothy would kill her, she knew—it was opening night—but she had to drive Angel to the bus station.

As she carried Angel's bag into the depot, Kelly tried to impress on her, again, the importance of keeping her whereabouts a secret.

"Look, if it gets out—where we are—Adam might just decide to come down here. He could call the FBI for God's sake. I'm not kidding, Ange."

"I get it, already. Paul won't let me tell anyone anyway, not even Darl."

That made sense. Who knew what Darl might say, and to whom?

"Paul is tight-lipped as hell these days," Angel continued. "He said I should be real careful coming down here. He made me take the gun, even." She laughed and undid the pocket on her knapsack. "See?"

A large black pistol sat there, in plain view.

"Angel! Close that up! Jesus Christ, you came across the border with that?"

"I told you, he's crazy."

"Is it loaded?"

"I don't know," she said. "I won't touch it."

Her coach was announced, and Kelly walked her to the gate. Angel stood in line with the others, her head bowed, her jaw slack, hanging open. She knew she had displeased Kelly. She had failed again. She chewed at a thumbnail and stared at her feet. She lifted one cracked leather boot to examine the sole and lost her balance. She was becoming more and more pathetic every year, Kelly thought.

She left her sister standing in line and got in her car, taking Alex to the theater with her. Thanks to Angel, she would have him there with her all day. And that gun! She thought of the gun sitting in that damned knapsack, right in her own hallway, right under Alex's curious little nose. She was so angry she nearly ran a red light.

Chapter Twenty-Five

Kelly put Alex down for a nap in the blue room. He would need his sleep if he was going to stay up to watch the play tonight. She hoped he could keep his promise to be quiet during the performance. He wanted to see it, and besides, she was not acquainted with anyone in town who would miss opening night to babysit.

The day was spent mostly in checking costume bags, making sure everything was accounted for, clean and pressed and ready for the dressers. Kelly ran up often to check on Alex, and by dinnertime he was awake and playing. He had taken her lipstick out of her purse and was making it disappear in his magic box. As she watched him, it occurred to her that she had lost her keys out of this very purse in this very room the last time Alex had been playing in here.

"Alex," she said, "did you see my keys? Did you take my keys out of my purse the other day, when I was working on the dress parade? The day you got lost?"

"The day I got lost?" Alex seemed to freeze. "No," he said. But he stopped playing.

Kelly became suspicious. "Did you take my keys and make them disappear?" she teased him. "I'll bet you did. I bet you magicked them so even you couldn't find them. Where do you think they might be?" She began again the search she had abandoned the other night.

"I didn't take anything," Alex said. "Nothing."

Nothing? She thought of her silver necklace. Had he been playing with that, too? "Alex, what about my necklace? The one I found on the floor when Angel was at our house. Did you take that out of my jewelry box?"

Alex moved to the door. "No," he said. He turned the corner, and she saw him running toward the stage.

She went after him. The stage was empty now. The painters had gone home. The scaffolding had been dismantled. Only a lone painter's swing remained to suggest that this was not, indeed, the royal castle of Denmark.

Alex was already running up the long flight of stairs.

"Alex, come back here. I have to talk to you!"

He paused at the top of the first staircase, then began running again when he saw her coming after him. If she didn't know him better, she'd swear he was guilty.

She stopped. How well *did* she know him? Her brief career as his mother—her brief charade—flashed through her mind as she watched him climb higher and higher. She saw herself kissing him good-bye, hushing him, plunking him in front of the television so she could deal with her own problems, putting him to bed, always putting him to bed. She had dismissed her own doubts about his happiness all too easily. Even in Winnipeg she had never paid enough attention to him. Not really. Well, he certainly had her attention now. He had reached the summit and stood looking down at her. She ascended slowly. Maybe he had taken the necklace to get her attention. It was certainly possible.

And if Alex had stolen the necklace ...

A little spurt of hope flared up in her chest.

She listed in her mind the things that had gone missing from her house. Small, pretty things. Shiny objects. The little animals. Toys!

"Alex," she said, when she was close enough to speak quietly. "You need to tell me. Were you playing with my necklace? Did you take it out of my jewelry box?"

He stepped off the firm support of the castle's upper parapet and onto the narrow painter's swing that hung from the rafters. It swayed slightly under his feet.

"Be careful," she said. She approached slowly.

"If I did," he asked, "what would you do?" There was something almost sly in his voice.

"Do?"

"Would I be grounded?"

Grounded! Kelly almost laughed out loud. How could you ground a six-year-old? Alex wasn't allowed to go anywhere anyway.

"No, honey," she said, suppressing her smile. "I wouldn't punish you. Not if you told the truth."

Alex looked doubtful. He hung his head.

"I wouldn't," she assured him. "Remember when you took the things out of Lila's bag? I didn't punish you. And when you got lost in the basement? That was an accident, right? You were just curious." She reached across the space between them, placed a finger under his chin and lifted his face so he could see her. "You're a little boy, and little boys get into mischief. I'm not going to punish you for that."

He looked up at her, his dense brown eyes solemn. "I just wanted to use it to make a tow truck," he confessed.

Kelly felt giddy with relief. She wanted to grab him and hug him. "That's okay," she said. "It's no big deal. I'm just glad that you told me, honey."

"I love you, Kelly," he said.

"I love you too, sweetheart." She held out her hand for him to take. "Come on, let's get down from here."

"You're not like them," he said, as he stepped toward her.

"Them?"

"Grandpa and—" Alex let out a scream, as the swing gave

way under his feet. In horror, Kelly saw the rope unraveling from the pulley with lightning speed as the swing plunged toward the ground.

"No!" Before she could think, she threw herself onto her belly and grabbed wildly at the air, feeling Alex's little body falling past her, the soft swish of his hair as it slipped through her fingers. Then with a deep stab of gratitude, she realized she had caught his wrist. He dangled below her, sixty pounds weighing on her one arm, and she felt herself being pulled slowly toward the edge.

Alex did not speak or move a muscle. Neither of them made a sound, but both could hear the slow but certain sliding of Kelly's body across the parapet. She groped with her feet, but could find no foothold behind her. She succeeded only in losing more ground. First her shoulders, then her breasts slid over the edge. Try as she might, she could not bend her elbow to raise Alex closer to her. Nor could she reach him with her other hand.

She hung there, barely daring to breathe. She closed her eyes against the sight of the floorboards so far below. Then she opened them. She saw a movement in the wings. The light below her shifted, as though the curtain had parted almost imperceptibly.

"Help!" The effort of her cry slid her forward another inch. She gripped Alex tightly. But she had broken into a sweat, and she could feel Alex's thin wrist begin to slither in her wet hand. Had no one heard her? The light shifted again, and she saw a long arm part the curtain. Michael's arm.

"Michael!"

He looked up and then he was running. *Hurry*, she pleaded silently. *I can't hold on any*—but before she could finish the thought, he had reached the ledge below her. She saw his two large hands reach out to encircle Alex's waist. Alex began to cry.

"I've got him," Michael said.

"You got him?"

"I've got him. Let go." But she could not.

His voice was slow and deliberate. "Kelly. I'm holding him tight. You have to let go now, or you'll fall."

She let go. She scrambled back onto the castle wall and fairly flew down the stairs, tearing Alex from Michael's arms. Her legs trembled with adrenalin and she sank to the floor of the walkway, burying her face in Alex's neck.

Michael sat down beside them, his arms limp at his sides.

"You can sure move," she said, when she could talk again.

"Thank God," he breathed, apparently to himself. "Thank God for all those rehearsals." He closed his eyes and remained absolutely still except for the ragged rise and fall of his chest.

"Michael! For Christ's sake!" It was Taylor, standing below them. "What the hell are you two doing?"

They scrambled down and went their separate ways. There was much to be done before the curtain would rise in three short hours.

WHEN KELLY HAD DELIVERED all the other costume racks to the dressing rooms, she knocked on Michael's door. He did not answer.

When she stepped inside, she saw him there, stretched out in the armchair. He was holding a copy of the script in his hands, but he wasn't reading it. He was looking out the window at the sky, breathing deeply, in a state of intense relaxation. Kelly wheeled in the costume rack quietly and prepared to retreat without disturbing him. But he was perfectly aware of her after all.

"Come here," he said.

She came forward. He took her hand and held it loosely. They held each other's eyes for a long moment. They had lived through something terrifying together. There was no need to say anything. His dark eyes were friendly, and yet there was something distant about his gaze. He was already on stage, Kelly thought. He was becoming Hamlet.

"Hand me that stone, will you?" He pointed to a small flat jade stone on the dresser. She passed it to him.

"My mother gave me this," he said, "the first time I went on stage. I think I was nine years old."

She smiled. She was used to actors and their superstitions. "And I'll bet you have never gone on stage without it."

"No." He smiled back at her. "Never." His eyes drifted to the window, and she sensed that he had retreated once again into his inner life.

She slipped out the door then, silently wishing him luck.

KELLY LED ALEX BACKSTAGE after the performance. The atmosphere was very positive, everyone high with relief and a general feeling the play had been a success. Rocko came sauntering down the hall toward Kelly as she was ducking into the blue room to get their coats.

"Kelly! Michael is asking for you. I believe he has washed all the blood off his body, and he's back from the dead, ready to receive callers."

"Did you see the play?" Kelly asked.

"I saw it." Rocko did not sound impressed.

"You don't like it?"

"I would have changed a few things," he said. "For one thing, *when* is Hamlet going to get wise and choose the right sword? I mean, really, he's been making that same mistake for centuries. I swear that boy will *never* be King of Denmark. For another thing . . ."

He was interrupted by Debbie Thompson and her husband, who swept past on their way out to the cast party at the Fallon.

"Fine production, wouldn't you say?" Debbie's husband asked. He was so proud he fairly glowed.

"Very fine," Kelly agreed.

"I can't wait for the reviews," Debbie was saying. Her high-pitched, grating laughter could be heard all up and down the corridor.

"For another thing," said Rocko, "they could have drowned Ophelia much, much earlier."

MICHAEL HAD ALREADY SHOWERED and changed into jeans and a T-shirt. He was reclining, exhausted, on the couch in his dressing room. Both his head and his large, bare feet were propped up with pillows. Bobbie was stirring spoonfuls of honey into a cup of tea for him. Taylor was just leaving.

"We'll see you at the hotel, then, soon," Taylor was saying. "Magnificent. Really. Tears in my eyes. Hi, Kelly. Fabulous, Michael. Really."

Michael waved him away.

"Hi." Kelly smiled down at Michael. "You survived?"

He nodded.

"Taylor says he's not supposed to talk," Bobbie said. She pointed at her own throat. "His voice."

"Oh, what does Taylor know?" Michael asked. He turned on his side and leaned his head on his elbow. "Hi, Alex. How are you doing?"

"I saw you sword-fighting," Alex said. He grasped an imaginary sword and began to swing in a good imitation of Hamlet's thrusts and parries.

"He's all right?" Michael asked Kelly.

"Seems to have recovered," she said. "I wish I could say the same for myself."

Michael sat up. "Me too. I think your son took ten years off my life this afternoon. Possibly twenty. Ah. Well. It's time to celebrate."

Bobbie handed him his shoes and socks. Bobbie looked lovely tonight, in a turquoise, full-skirted gown. She was wearing her hair up and looked older than her eighteen years.

Michael stood up, fully dressed, ran a hand through his short hair and smiled at everyone. "Right," he said. "I think I can stand. Am I standing?"

Bobbie laughed.

"Let's go then," he said. He took Kelly's coat from her arm and held it open for her.

"Oh, we're not going with you," Kelly said. "I think your young apprentice here has had enough." Alex was still swinging his invisible sword, but he was flagging.

"You have to come," Michael said. He turned to Bobbie. "She has to come, doesn't she? We have to make an appearance, Kelly. It's expected."

"You're expected," she said. "I'm not. Come on, Alex." She slid her arms into her coat and began to dress Alex. "He's beat," she told Michael. "He's been going all day."

"Well, the party is at the hotel. He could sleep in my room."

"Alone?"

"Bobbie could stay with him. You wouldn't mind, Bobbie."

"Michael." Kelly drew him aside. "Bobbie is dying to go, can't you see that?"

"But I want you there. Just for an hour?"

"No. Why don't you take Bobbie? Walk in with her; she'll be thrilled."

Michael touched her cheek lightly with his fingers. "You should be there," he said. "Everyone will be there." He ran his hand across her cheek and tucked her hair behind her ear.

"I'll read about it in the paper," she said.

She took Alex out of there before she changed her mind.

AT HOME ALONE IN BED that night, Kelly did not regret skipping the party. She didn't want her mind cluttered with chatter and alcohol. It would ruin the feeling she had taken away with her from the play. She wanted to savor it. The drained and sweetly sorrowful effect of tragedy.

Taylor had achieved his goal. The play was harrowing. As she watched from the audience, Kelly had forgotten all the problems with the costumes, the set, the actors' egos, all the glitches they had been working around. The ghost and his suffering chilled her. He was a resident of purgatory, land of the undead, come to drag Hamlet into the same eternal agony of nothingness.

The story unfolded tonight as it had unfolded for four hundred years. From the moment Hamlet heard the ghost's hair-raising tale of murder, he knew that he was doomed. Throughout the five long acts, he moved inexorably, consciously, toward his own death. He had no choice.

Chapter Twenty-Six

A couple of flowers had come loose from Ophelia's wig during her vigorous enactment of her drowning the night before. Kelly was reattaching them down in the costume shop. She was alone. Lila's job was finished now that the play had opened. Lila would return to Winnipeg tomorrow, much to Kelly's relief. Now she would have an ally in Winnipeg, someone to report regularly, accurately, on Darl's condition. Tonight Lila was taking Alex out to the cabin for a little good-bye treat. Kelly still had not solved the babysitting problems she was going to have when Lila left. Maybe Bobbie?

Bobbie poked her head in, just as Kelly was thinking of her. "Hi. You done? Jane's waiting." Jane was the dresser for Ophelia.

"Not yet. What time is it?"

"Thirty minutes. And Taylor wants you."

Kelly sighed. Taylor always wanted her. She dropped everything and headed upstairs. "Where is he?"

"Michael's dressing room."

Taylor was standing outside Michael's room. He handed Kelly a key. "Could you just run down the street? Michael's forgotten something."

"I have a lot of—"

"He wants his stone. It's a jade worry stone with a little groove—"

"I know," she said.

"It will take you five minutes. He says it's right inside the door, on a little table."

Oh, brother, Kelly thought. It was twenty-five minutes to curtain.

"Kelly, please. He can't go on without it."

"I know," she said. "I know."

She hurried out to do his bidding, wearing only her running shoes and a thin sweater.

SHE WISHED SHE HAD WORN her coat and boots. Although the hotel was only a block away, she was freezing by the time she arrived. In the elevator, she rubbed her hands and stamped her wet feet to warm them. It was like Winnipeg out there.

She let herself into Michael's room with the key Taylor had given her. Michael's worry stone lay on the entrance table. She slipped it in her pocket and was about to leave when she noticed that the room was unusually messy.

It didn't seem like Michael to leave open bottles of liquor and dirty glasses out on the bar. He must have had visitors. A footstool was turned over, and a large stack of mail had been strewn wildly across the desk, envelopes and packages scattered onto the floor. The wastepaper basket had been knocked over, spilling crumpled paper in a heap onto the carpet. Had the party moved up here last night? Where were the maids? The ashtray was overflowing with half-smoked cigarettes. The room was stuffy with stale air. Kelly turned on the ceiling fan and bent to set the wastebasket upright. As she did so, she spotted a small cardboard carton lying underneath the desk.

On the side of the box, in plain black letters, she read the words WINNIPEG SUPPLY. Without warning, that small trickle of doubt about Michael came back to her. Winnipeg?

She couldn't resist the urge to open it and look inside.

LILA BUCKLED ALEX'S SEAT BELT carefully, then consulted the map.

"Where are we going?" Alex asked again.

"You'll see," she answered. "It'll be fun."

"Are we going to see Kelly?"

"Not today, sweetie. Kelly's busy at the theater all day today. We're going to drive out to Timothy's cabin and have a visit. It's Timothy's birthday. So we're bringing him a big chocolate cake. And you know what else? His yellow barn cat has some new kittens. Do you like chocolate cake and kittens?"

Alex nodded.

"Good." Lila smiled. "Now just let me figure out the route." She studied the rough lines Taylor had drawn on the back of a cigarette package and tried to decipher his hurriedly scrawled map. Of course she could simply call for directions if Timothy would just put in a damned phone. She cursed the eccentricities of the rich. Finally, she located the address on the map. She decided to take the Bloomington Freeway south. That would be fastest.

Lila started the car, casting a glance at the sky, which was rapidly filling with dark snow clouds.

She hoped it wouldn't develop into a blizzard.

KELLY STARED. INSIDE THE BOX, on the very top, folded neatly, was an old blue denim shirt. Slowly, unbelieving, she lifted it and spread it out before her. There was the patch of blue corduroy at the left elbow, the one she herself had sewn. There were the black stitches around the pocket, where she had reinforced the seam.

She tossed the shirt aside and began to examine the rest of the contents. There were a few other articles of clothing, his baseball cap, the soft leather pouch he used to wear attached to his belt. His pocket watch. She turned it over and read the inscription, "Love from K." There were the little animals, the giraffe, the spotted horse, the tiger. The silver cigarette case. The three Chinese coins he used to throw the *I Ching*. Then she gasped when she saw what was nestled tightly in the bottom of the box—a hard, flat package, wrapped in newspaper and white string. Even before she tore off the wrapping, she knew what it was. Yes. The drawings stolen from Sam's gallery. The nightmare pictures James had worked so feverishly over.

And in the leather pouch, she found James's ring—just a plain gold band, but she recognized it. He had always worn it on a chain around his neck.

His wedding ring.

He had been wearing it the day he died.

DEBBIE THOMPSON STOOD in front of the mirror in her dressing room, completely ready. Her makeup and first-scene costume were perfect, and she had to be very careful not to disturb the effect. She'd never been ready so early before.

"You can go, if you like," she said to Jane and Bobbie. "There's no point all of us hanging around doing nothing. I don't know why you got me dressed so early."

"Because," Jane said to Bobbie, out in the hall, "we usually allow a half-hour for hysterics and vomiting."

Debbie opened the little drawer of her dressing table and pulled out the latest missive from her unknown admirer. Until yesterday she'd still had hopes it might be Michael. But now she was convinced it was someone in another side of the business. Possibly an agent, but more likely a movie producer. She read the card again: "I will come to you tomorrow night, after the performance. Be ready to change your life." The note was accompanied, as always, with his trademark, very expensive roses in a plain white box. No florist's name or logo. She imagined him cutting the roses himself, in his own greenhouse. She leaned as close to the bouquet as she dared to savor the scent.

As she tucked the card away, she noticed in the drawer another message she'd received that afternoon. Odd. A young man with a bundle of parcels had approached her in the lobby and asked her how to find Kelly. To be polite, she'd accepted the note he'd scribbled for Kelly, but she'd be damned if she was going to go running down to the costume shop to summon her. She wasn't Kelly's secretary. And then she'd forgotten about it. Oh well. She'd already read the note, and it didn't make any sense, anyway. She stuffed it back in the drawer. It could wait.

She bent toward the roses again. Tonight he would reveal himself.

She heard the call down the hallway: "Five minutes." She smiled at her own reflection. She wasn't nervous tonight. She wasn't nervous at all, now that she was finally getting her due.

KELLY HELD HER HUSBAND'S wedding ring in the flat of her hand. She rolled it back and forth with her thumb across her palm, along the double lifeline, the lines that moved together and apart. She placed it on her left ring finger, above her own ring. Yes. A perfect match. Her finger, with its double band, looked strangely ritualistic. She felt as if she might be dreaming.

She left the cardboard box lying open on the floor and stood up. Dazed, she looked around the room. How had these things come to be here, in this room, Michael's room?

She remembered Rocko's words: "He will devour you."

Oh God.

She glanced at her watch. Eight o'clock. Michael would be on stage, stone or no stone. The show would go on. She would not be disturbed.

She rifled through the mail first, reading the return addresses, not even sure what she was looking for. It was pointless, anyway. There were letters from everywhere on the continent and several countries in Europe. Then she searched the desk drawers and the closet. She wanted an answer, a clue to this maddening mystery. She found nothing out of the ordinary. Although this was Michael's home, it was only a hotel room, after all. Impersonal. Other than a photograph of his family, Kelly found nothing to indicate that Michael had even existed before he came to Minneapolis.

Where had he been before he came to Minneapolis?

IN THE DARKNESS OF THE COUNTRY road, Lila fretted that she would miss the address. She drove slowly, peering into the limited circle illuminated by her headlights. The snow was coming down now, hard little flakes that seemed to bounce as they hit the windshield.

Alex was bored. "How much longer?"

"Alex," Lila said, "how many times do you think you've asked me that question?"

"Ummm. A million?"

"Close."

"A gazillion?"

"At least. Oh. There it is." At the side of the road, Lila could see a red mailbox, just as Taylor had described. She turned into the driveway and tried to read the name on the mailbox. It looked like "Johnson." Wrong place. She sighed heavily and consulted the map again.

"Looks as if we passed it," she said.

Alex groaned.

"But we're close," she reassured him. "This is number 100, and we want number 200. We're on the right road. I just have to back us up." She put the car in reverse and aimed toward the shoulder of the driveway, to give herself room to turn around. The car lurched backward, the back end dipped, and the car came to a dead stop.

"Rats."

"What happened?"

"I think we're in a ditch," Lila said. "I'll just get out and see. Are you okay?"

"Yeah."

She climbed out and surveyed the situation. Yes, she had backed into a snow-covered ditch. There was no way she was going to be able to push this whale of a car out by herself.

"Alex, I'm going to go get some help to move the car," she told him. "You wait here, and keep the door locked."

Alex nodded glumly.

"I'll be right back."

She left the headlights on, partly for Alex and partly for herself. It was a long, dark driveway, and as she trudged through the snow, the wind whipped at her face, stinging her cheeks with tiny needles of ice. She hoped the Johnsons were home, whoever they were. She hoped there was a Mr. Johnson. A big one.

KELLY CHARGED INTO the bedroom and headed for Michael's dresser, determined to tear the place apart if she had to, to get some answers. She made it only halfway across the room.

Then she froze.

Someone was sitting in the swivel armchair facing the balcony, looking out at the city below.

All she could see was the back of his head, a red collar and long brown hair tied back with a strip of braided leather.

She'd recognize that ponytail anywhere.

It was Paul.

DEBBIE THOMPSON CAME OFFSTAGE triumphant and invigorated. She peeled off her sweat-soaked dress and began to sponge her skin with the warm, soapy water that Jane had made ready. "It's really working," she told Jane and Bobbie. "The chemistry is really cooking tonight. Can't you just see the sparks?"

"You were magnificent," said Jane, who hadn't been watching. She had been busy with Ophelia's costumes. It wasn't like Kelly to have left her in the lurch like this. Jane had just finished mending a tear in Ophelia's next costume. And she still had a couple of flowers to reattach on the wig for Ophelia's drowning scene.

"Sit down," she told Debbie. "We need to fix your face."

But Debbie was too excited to sit down. "This is it," she was saying, as she fairly danced around her tiny dressing room. "This is the one that will launch me." She laughed and hugged herself. Then she spun around to face Bobbie and stopped suddenly. "Any messages for me? Did anyone ask for me?"

"Not tonight," Bobbie told her.

"Come on," Jane said. "Sit down."

Debbie took her place in front of the mirror. "Are you sure there was no one to see me? No one came backstage?"

"Nobody here but us chickens," Jane said. "Stay still."

"Except that one guy," Bobbie said. "This afternoon."

"Where did he go? Did he leave a message?"

"I don't think he's your guy," Bobbie said. "He was looking for Kelly. We told him she'd be here by eight, and he said he'd come back. But he never did."

"Neither did Kelly," Jane reminded her.

"Well, shit," said Debbie. "I was expecting somebody. Maybe he's in the audience. Oh, this is going to launch me, I just know it."

"For sure," said Bobbie. Behind Debbie's back, she rolled her eyes at Jane. If Debbie wanted to be launched, Bobbie would launch her, all right. Right into outer space.

HER HEART POUNDING, Kelly stepped backward, toward the door, trying not to make a sound. But then she paused. Why be quiet? Paul must have heard her already. Heard her unlocking the door, rifling through Michael's things. He knew darn well she was here. What kind of game was he playing?

Why didn't he move?

For a long minute, she remained rooted to her spot on the plush hotel room carpet.

The room was eerily silent.

Kelly tried her voice: "Paul?"

There was no response.

"Paul, is that you?"

Anger and curiosity overcame her dread, and she stepped forward, made her way across the room and placed her hand on the back of the swivel chair.

"Paul? What is going on?"

She spun the chair around and stared at him.

Paul stared back, a look of surprise on his face, eyes open wide. The front of his shirt was soaked with blood. He was clearly very dead.

Michael's silver letter opener was embedded in his heart.

THE JOHNSONS WERE NOT AT HOME. Lila knocked until her knuckles were sore before she gave up and waded all the way back to her car. The snow was getting deeper by the minute. She felt the dampness seeping into her boots. She wasn't dressed for this weather.

"We'll have to walk," she told Alex. She opened the car door and helped him climb out of the ditch. "It can't be too far."

They returned to the main road and headed west, the way they had come. Lila walked on the inside, keeping Alex on the shoulder, well out of the way of traffic.

But there was no traffic. This particular strip of road was deserted and dark. The wind-driven snow had completely obscured the blacktop, and Lila could not make out even the tire tracks left by her own car a short half-hour ago. Alex stumbled. His little legs weren't long enough to keep up to Lila's pace in the deepening drifts. She held his hand and pulled him along, mercilessly.

"I'm cold," he said.

"Come on, sweetie, keep moving."

Alex protested, complaining he could go no farther. Lila wasted no time coaxing him. She just kept hold of his hand and pulled. She would drag him if necessary. She knew what could happen to them out here. She did not intend to freeze to death by the side of some obscure country road. After all she and Kelly had gone through for Alex, there was no way she was going to let some blizzard get him.

She spotted another mailbox, right in front of her. This must be it. She could see where the driveway was by the curve of the trees. They turned down it. As they rounded a bend, she could see the cabin. Gratefully, she saw the cheerful lights in the windows. Alex seemed to get a second wind. The two of them hurried, weary, wet and cold, up to the front door.

"Ah," said Rocko, "our guests have arrived."

Behind him, Lila could see Timothy standing before a blazing fire, a glass of wine in hand.

Finally. Light and the promise of warmth.

KELLY'S FIRST IMPULSE, when she reached the hotel lobby, was to call the police. She darted into one of the wooden telephone booths and leaned against the wall, panting. She had panicked. Too frightened to wait for the elevator, she had run down the stairwell. Eleven flights. Her hands shook as she fished in her pocket for a quarter, and came up with Michael's worry stone.

If it was good luck, it wasn't exactly working.

She found some change in her other pocket, but hesitated to dial the numbers. She could make an anonymous call, then disappear. But where would she go? As soon as the body was found, the police would be everywhere, questioning everyone involved with Michael. And what could she tell them?

She knew too much. And too little.

She pictured herself arrested for kidnapping. Maybe even for murder. Alex taken away and sent back to Adam. No. There was only one thing to do: wait until Lila brought Alex back—they were due home at eleven—and then get out of town as quickly as possible. Lie low, at least until Darl recovered fully. Let the authorities sort this out without her. She was innocent, after all, she told herself. She was really, perfectly innocent. She wiped tears from her eyes.

Still shaking but breathing more easily, she made her way out through the lobby as inconspicuously as possible. The wind had picked up. Pedestrians on the sidewalk bent their heads and held their collars tightly at their necks. But Kelly walked as if impervious to the weather.

All she could see was Paul's amazed face, the dark blood on his shirt. She thought of Leon, battered beyond recognition. She thought of Diane, her throat slit from ear to ear. Darl with his swollen black eyes and stitched-up head. James, every bone in his body broken, crushed by the rocks at the bottom of the falls. Dead.

Or was he?

KELLY'S KEYS LAY ON THE TABLE in the costume shop where she had left them. She put them in the pocket of her jeans. She pulled off her wet shoes and socks and dried her feet with a towel, trembling all the while.

She made her way cautiously to the blue room. She didn't want to run into anyone. Not now. But she wanted her purse, with her fake identity cards, and she needed her coat and fur-lined boots. The stairway and hall were empty. She opened the door to the blue room slowly, to keep it from squeaking, and closed it carefully behind her, before looking up. Bad luck. Someone was there.

Someone was seated at the table, bent over a sheaf of papers. He raised his head and Kelly nearly cried out loud.

"Darl!" A tremendous sense of relief hit her like a gust of winter wind.

"Kelly." Darl's voice was soft, matter-of-fact.

"What are you—?"

"Doing here? I've been waiting for you. I've had a hell of a time trying to track you down."

"But how did you get here? Sam said you were completely laid up." She stared at his legs. He was wearing corduroy trousers. There was no sign of a cast.

"Well, Sam exaggerates."

"But why? Why would he? He said your head injuries were so bad you could barely function. But look at you!"

Darl laughed gently. "I wasn't as bad off as everyone thought," he said. He stood up and walked toward her. Except for a slight limp, he seemed perfectly fine.

"Oh, thank God," Kelly said. Darl reached out for her and she held on to him tightly. He embraced her, and she leaned against him.

"Oh, Darl. You won't believe what's been going on."

TIMOTHY PROVIDED SOME dry slippers for Lila, and they wrapped Alex in blankets and set him before the fire. Alex played happily, enthralled by the kittens, which climbed with their clumsy little legs all over his lap, while their mother watched warily.

"It's in a ditch, pretty deep," Lila was telling them.

"Well, you can stay here the night," Timothy suggested. "We'll get it out in the morning."

"I have to get Alex back tonight," Lila said. "I promised to get him back by eleven. All I need is a good push."

Rocko peered out the window. "You don't mean to say you expect me to go out there in this weather, in the dark, and actually push a car out of a ditch? With my own hands?"

"Yes," said Lila.

Timothy laughed.

Outside, the snow fell faster and faster. It was beautiful, Lila had to admit. From in here it was beautiful. Illuminated by the firelight of the cabin, the falling flakes appeared as tiny silver streaks against the dark forest.

KELLY EXPLAINED EVERYTHING to Darl, speaking as quickly and as quietly as she could. She knew that no one was likely to enter the blue room during the performance, but she didn't want to take any chances. And she definitely wanted to get out of there before all hell broke loose.

"I had to keep quiet. Couldn't go to the police because of Adam. But now, now that you're better, we can tell. We don't have to worry about your parents any more."

"No," Darl said grimly. "It's not them we have to worry about." He looked soberly at her. "You didn't hear? Take a look." He handed Kelly a newspaper clipping.

She read it quickly. It had been front-page news in Winnipeg, two days ago. Adam and Eleanor Grayton's house destroyed in a mysterious explosion and engulfed in fire, possibly arson. Mrs. Grayton was found in her bed, dead of smoke inhalation. Her husband suffered third-degree burns to his chest. He was rushed to St. Boniface Hospital, where he remained in stable condition, barring the risk of infection.

He'd survived again!

"The house," Kelly gasped. "Set on fire?"

She reread the article, searching for details. There was no mention of the previous fire, no mention of a suspect.

"Jesus," she breathed. "It's like, as if, he came back to finish the job."

Chapter Twenty-Seven

Hamlet was scaring the living daylights out of his mother on stage. The audience leaned forward in their seats, aghast, as Hamlet thrust his sword through the tapestry on Gertrude's chamber wall, killing the unfortunate eavesdropper hiding there. The unseen body dropped to the ground with a horrible thump.

"*Is it the King?*" Hamlet cried. He drew back the curtain. The audience held their breath, though they knew full well it was not the King. They had all seen this play before. They knew what was going to happen.

Gertrude backed away from her son, who had clearly gone stark raving mad. She trembled at his wild speech. He pulled her down onto her bed and ripped the locket from her neck. He held before her two pictures, one of the late King, one of her present husband: "*Look here upon this picture, and on this, The counterfeit presentment of two brothers.*"

THE SPEECH WENT ON. From the blue room, the words could not be heard distinctly. Only the rhythm of Michael's voice, rising in anger, penetrated the walls. It continued like the low rumble of faraway thunder, or a distant concert, Kelly thought. She could not understand why it had the power to distract her so. She should be getting out of here with Darl. She should be putting on the boots that Darl was holding out, urging her to get dressed. She should be listening to Darl.

But Darl wasn't making any sense. He kept talking about the fire. Something about starter fluid.

She couldn't follow his logic. "Darl, this is no time for all that. Paul is dead, don't you understand? He's lying there dead, just down the street. This very minute. Someone stabbed him. The killer could be out there. He could be in here somewhere—anywhere—right now. Probably the same person who tried to kill you!"

"Who, Chartrand? I don't think so."

"Leon? *Leon* tried to kill you?"

"Tried," Darl said. "Almost succeeded, too."

"But why?" She sat down. Her body was refusing to cooperate. Nothing made sense. Why would Leon...?

Darl wasn't really well after all, Kelly thought, her senses beginning to clear. He looked fine, but his head injury had rendered him completely delusional. "Darl, how much do you remember?" she asked gently.

"I remember everything. Chartrand's been trying to kill me for years. For years! He got James, but I wasn't going to let him get me."

Kelly felt the tears spring into her eyes. Poor Darl. "Sit down," she said. She reached out and took his hand. She had to think fast. She had to make him understand.

She spoke very softly, as if talking to a child. "Leon Chartrand was our friend, Darl. Don't you remember? He helped James. He was helping me. Somebody attacked him on the highway, the same way you were attacked. They beat him with some kind of blunt—"

"Tire iron," Darl said impatiently. "Look, you might as

well know. The night you told me he was still messing around with James's files, I offered him a ride to the reserve in my truck, and when we were halfway there, we got in a fight. I hit him with the tire iron."

"What?"

"He fought back like a son of a bitch. He took it away from me and nearly busted my skull in two." He put a hand to his head. "It still hurts like hell. But I got him. He was lying there all sort of mangled. I covered him up with snow. Then I ditched the truck—sent it headfirst to the bottom of the floodway, and I ran as far as I could till I passed out."

"You didn't run anywhere, Darl," she said patiently. "Your leg was broken."

He shook his head. "No. Soon as I got out of the hospital, I put that cast on. I thought Angel would tell you how sick I was, and you'd come home."

She just stared at him.

"You think I don't know how to put a cast on? You think I don't know what a brain injury looks like? The doctors at the hospital sure knew there was nothing wrong with my brain. They kicked me out pretty quick. But it was easy to fool Angel and Sam. When I got home I just did a little acting—and a little costume design." He smirked. "I convinced everyone I was half-dead. And it worked. Angel was beside herself." He shot an accusing glare at Kelly. "*She* cared. She would have moved in with me, if Paul had let her. I had to tell her I had a private nurse, just so she'd leave me alone. So I could get out of the house, and—"

"But, Darl—"

"Enough. Put on your boots," he said. "I've come to bring you home. You and Alex. You've kept him long enough."

"But I would have brought him home, Darl," she said very slowly, in wonder. "If I'd known you were all right."

"Yeah. If you'd known I was okay, you would have sent Alex home and taken off with that Arabian prince of yours."

"What are you saying?"

"You know it's true. Even back home you were slipping out on me. You kept secrets from me. You never told me about the phone calls from James. When his stuff went missing, you went to Chartrand! You were supposed to come to me!" He struck his chest with his fist. "You were supposed to come to my house. To me!"

Kelly rested her head in her hands. This could not be happening to her, but it was.

"You took James's things," she said quietly, without looking up. "From my house. You telephoned me. You made me think—"

"I had to. You were getting so—you were getting away from me. You were going out with men. Going back to work. You were talking to everybody. I just wanted you to stay home." He put his hand on her shoulder, hesitantly. "I just wanted things back the way they were. Just wanted you to slow down a bit. Was that so much to ask?"

Even though she had not yet grasped the full weight of everything he was telling her, she understood this. The box of James's things belonged to Darl. He had taken them from her house, sent some of them back. Played with her. Made her doubt her own mind. To draw her in, keep her under his control. Yes, this part of the story made a sick sort of sense. It had started in the fall, when she'd been getting stronger, when she hadn't needed him so much any more. And she had fallen for it. She had nearly given up her whole career, her whole life. Darl knew her well, she thought. He knew exactly which things to take. He knew she'd want to believe her husband might be coming back.

How she had longed, in her secret, stupid heart, that it were true. With a sharp pang, she realized she had still been hoping . . . even today. . . .

She stood up in one swift motion and slapped Darl across the face so hard he fell off the chair.

IN THE GREEN ROOM, where he was waiting to go on, George Laugherty thought he heard a muffled scream from somewhere back beyond the wings. It startled him out of his pre-performance ritual of meditation. He stopped listening to the play and turned his attention to the rooms behind him. He walked, clanking in his ghost costume, out into the hallway and peered up and down.

Nothing.

He walked toward the dressing rooms. Was that Debbie? Her door was closest to the stage and she had left it ajar. He could hear her clearly now. She was laughing, much too loudly, over some fool thing. She had ruined his concentration entirely. He hurried back to the green room, just as he heard Michael cry, "*A king of shreds and patches!*"

Damn. He had missed his cue.

DARL HAD BESTED HER EASILY. He was holding her close against him. "You are staying with me now," he said.

She could hear noises in the hall. Taylor's hushed, excited voice.

She tried again to scream, but he placed a hand across her mouth. He shoved her down on the couch and lay on top of her, pinning her arms beneath her back. He kept one hand over her mouth, the other around her neck. He held her lightly, but firmly, his muscles ready to tighten.

"Will they come in here?"

She shook her head.

"Don't *look* at me like that," he said in a harsh whisper. "Everything I did, I did for you. I spared you because I thought I could keep you, you know, in the family. But you wouldn't listen. You stepped outside. First you went to Chartrand and then you flew off—out of town. I thought you'd be scared, you'd need me, but then, when I came after you, what did I see? First time I came down here, what did I see? You having a fine time. You'd forgotten all about me. Then you took up with that . . . that . . . actor!"

Kelly was trying to absorb this. Darl had been here? In Minneapolis? He must have flown down . . . Leon's car at the airport. Of course. He must have stolen Leon's car from the clinic parking lot . . . no one watching over Darl but Angel.

"You had no gratitude. No understanding. I tried to keep you close, but you—" In an apparent wave of hopelessness, he loosened his grip slightly. "It all just became uncontrollable," he said in despair. "I couldn't contain it all."

She struggled out from under him. He grabbed for her, but she decided, this time, not to resist. She had no hope of winning a physical confrontation. She tried to put him off guard by sitting down beside him on the couch and holding his hand.

"Darl," she said, "calm down. I know you're angry. And I'm sorry. But I didn't know you were in town. How could I know? You came down with Paul?"

"Paul came down after me. He was right here in the theater, this afternoon, trying to get to you before I could."

"What happened? I want to know." She stroked his hand lightly.

"Nosy little Paul." Darl shook his head sadly. "When you didn't come home, he got suspicious. Broke into my house, snooped around in my basement and found the box, found the tapes I stole from him. He found the pictures, everything. He came down here to show you. Him and Chartrand, they had to show you those goddamned pictures! I should have burned them!"

"He never showed me anything," Kelly said. But Paul had tried. He had left the box hidden under Michael's desk.

"He went looking for you at your boyfriend's hotel room, but I followed him."

"You killed him," she said quietly. "He was trying to warn me, and you killed him." She remembered the mess of mail on Michael's floor. Darl must have grabbed for the letter opener in a fit of rage. What was he capable of?

Who was he?

"I told you, don't look at me like that. You said yourself he was no good for Angel."

A picture of Angel, crying, flashed through Kelly's mind. First her baby, now her husband. She would never survive this. The thought of Angel's grief enraged her. She forgot her clever plan to calm Darl down. She lashed out at him with both fists.

A mistake.

He was holding an object so close to her eye it was nothing but a metallic blur. She jerked her head back. A long thin blade, like a fish knife, was pointing straight at her throat. All she could think of was Charlie Cook's finger slicing the air. Ear to ear.

"You are coming with me. Now. Open the door and look outside."

He pushed her toward the door, keeping the knife close to her throat, gripping her elbow.

"My boots," she tried.

"Open it!"

She moved tentatively out into the hall. But when Darl started to follow, she turned and slammed the door on his arm. He let go of her, and she ran.

She made the first turn she came to, trying to throw him off. But it was a dead end. She was heading for the stage.

As she ran toward the wings, she saw the open door of Debbie's dressing room. Debbie was washing the makeup from her face, preparing for her drowning scene. The drowning costume hung on her outer door. A good hiding place. Kelly slipped behind the dress, trying not to breathe, trying to be still. She could hear Darl coming. She could hear Laertes and the King plotting Hamlet's death on stage.

Then she heard Debbie gasp: "What the hell are you doing?"

Darl had entered her dressing room.

Kelly watched through the hinges of the door. Darl stalked wildly across the floor, completely mad now, and headed for the closet. Debbie dashed out into the hall, in her underwear, and flew down the passage away from the stage.

Darl flung the closet open and began to paw through the hanging clothes, looking for his escaped prisoner.

Kelly grabbed Ophelia's drowning dress and stepped into it. It fit easily over her jeans and T-shirt. She put the wig on her head.

There was nowhere else to go. She stepped out, backward, onto the stage.

Behind her, she could feel the hot stage lights. She could hear the incredibly quiet breathing of seven hundred people, waiting for Ophelia to begin.

They were watching her, waiting for her next move. She turned to face them. She didn't have to say anything.

All she had to do was to act insane.

Right now, that didn't seem too difficult.

Chapter Twenty-Eight

Moving across the stage in a sort of trance, Kelly could hear Gertrude high above her, describing her death:

There is a willow grows aslant the brook,

That shows his hoar leaves in the glassy stream.

Kelly was barefoot, stumbling, disoriented. The whole space of the stage seemed to have shifted, grown enormous. The hot beams of the lights penetrated everything, turned everything colorless. At first, she simply stood still, head raised, watching hundreds of dust motes drift before her face through the thick white air.

Then she was dancing, slowly, grieving, feet slapping the black floor of the empty stage, spinning herself dizzy, picking imaginary flowers, the rhythm of Gertrude's words reverberating through her bones:

When down her weedy trophies and herself

Fell in the weeping brook. Her clothes spread wide;

And, mermaid-like, awhile they bore her up.

She fell. She floated through the air which eddied round her thick as water. She bent her knees, swept her arms around her body, and collapsed, sinking out of sight as the lights went dim. Everything was darkness.

AFTER OPHELIA HAD DROWNED, Kelly knew, she had to hide in an alcove upstage until her funeral. She had to lie down on the funeral pallet concealed there and wait to be carried back on, to be buried in the downstage trapdoor. There was no other exit from the stage. Then she could escape, although she was not sure where she would go. Everything was unraveling too fast.

Hamlet was talking to the skull on stage, poor Yorick. Kelly had never liked this scene, but now that she was lying here, dead, she had to admit it had a certain power. Hamlet's voice was strong, young, full of awe, as he marveled at the fate of the vigorous body, reduced to dust and loam. She suppressed the sob that rose in her chest. She had to stay completely in control.

Four attendants arrived to hoist Ophelia onto their shoulders. There was no time for them to be surprised when they saw her face; they had to follow the procession. The members of the funeral party, true professionals, seemed to take it in stride. Only Hamlet stumbled a little on his lines. When he cried out, "*What, the fair Ophelia?*" there was genuine shock in his voice.

The attendants lowered her into the grave and Gertrude scattered petals. They fell on Kelly's face, and one got into her mouth. She was trying to spit it out, fighting hysteria, when Laertes leaped into the grave. She barely managed to roll aside so that he didn't land on her.

"*Now pile your dust upon the quick and dead,*" Laertes crowed, and then he wobbled, losing his balance. Ophelia's body was supposed to be long gone by now, and he stumbled, trying not to fall on her. He cursed, under his breath. What the hell was going on?

Then Hamlet leaped into the grave, and he and Laertes began to fight. Kelly, having no practice at this, couldn't get through the exit quickly enough. Laertes stepped on her hand, hard, as she squeezed through the trapdoor.

"Ouch!" She bit her lip, but it was too late, the word was out. As she crawled through the dark tunnel, toward the light, she could only pray the audience hadn't heard her.

DEBBIE, WRAPPED IN A BATHROBE, was talking to the guards, gesturing nervously, and Taylor was striding around in circles, pulling on his hair. Kelly ducked into the washroom and stripped off the dress and the wig. She had to get out of there, get to her car, to Alex. No time to explain. She listened at the door.

"He's vanished," one of the guards said. "He's either left the theater or got himself into the audience somehow."

"Jesus," said Taylor.

Debbie was crying.

"Some kind of stalker," the other guard was saying. "One of those obsessed types. A number-one fan. I read a book on these types."

"We'll have to call the police," Taylor said. "But not yet. Wait till the play's over, clear the place out."

"How much time is left?"

Taylor glanced at his wristwatch. "Twenty minutes. The sword fight's over in twenty minutes. Jesus, he was so close to the stage. How could that happen?"

"Must have got in before the show started. I been standin' here since the curtain went up."

"Well, thank God for Kelly. Where the hell is Kelly?"

"I'm gonna call my husband," Debbie said.

"You do that," Taylor told her. "I'm going to find Kelly. Jesus!"

They dispersed, and Kelly was alone. Without her shoes or purse, she ran through the dark hallway to the stage door and into the parking lot. It was dark, and the storm had slowed to a thin drizzle of sleet, icing the streets. A dozen young women, hoping for a glimpse of Michael, surged toward the door as she stepped outside. When they saw who she was, they retreated, disappointed. She made it to her car, hopping barefoot across the snow, shivering with cold and delayed shock and a terrible fear that she tried to push to the back of her mind. Not now. She had to drive. She dug the keys out of her pocket and started the engine. Where was Lila? Was she back yet? She raced the Mustang through the streets, her wet, half-frozen feet slipping on the gas pedal.

HE HAD BLOWN IT.

Darl stood in the doorway of a corner grocery store, sheltered from the sleet, and cupped his hand against the wind to light a cigarette.

She was gone.

He had taken a chance, approaching her directly like that. He had known it was risky. But he'd had to try. He was losing his grip on the kid.

The other day, in the basement, Alex had almost given him away. The kid tried to shine the flashlight right on him. When Kelly came down, Darl had hidden in the tunnels and listened. He'd known, when he heard Alex hesitate to lie for him, that the boy could not be trusted much longer.

He was just like James.

So he would have to go, just like James.

And he almost had gone, yesterday afternoon, in an appropriately reminiscent fashion. Now *that* would have brought Kelly home. Darl cursed, thinking how close he had come. If it weren't for Black.

Yes. If Alex had fallen. Think of the guilt she would have felt. It would have been worse than with James. It would have lasted a lifetime. She would have been locked to Darl forever, as she was always meant to be.

He looked down the street, where two police cars were

still parked outside the theater. Yes, they were stupid. They rallied around little blonde Debbie Thompson as though she were the king on the chessboard. Never guessing it was Kelly he was after. His plan to send Debbie into Michael Black's arms had failed, but it was coming in handy now. They'd all be so busy searching for Debbie's stalker, they wouldn't even notice Kelly was gone.

He had seen Kelly racing out to her car in a panic. Completely alone.

He had hoped she could be spared. He had really believed she was different, not like Diane.

But she was the same. They were all the same.

Now there were cop cars pulling up to the Fallon Hotel. They must have found Paul. Let them figure that one out. With any luck, Black would be arrested and spend some time with his rich Arabian ass in jail.

As soon as the cops cleared out a bit, he would return to his rental car. He knew what to do next. He had failed this evening, but he wouldn't fail again.

He smoked three cigarettes while he waited, drawing the smoke deep into his lungs. Finally, he saw the officers return to their vehicles. He watched them through his tinted lenses and smiled. They looked so very small, like pawns.

But he was a knight. A white knight.

And white always moved first.

Chapter Twenty-Nine

Kelly circled her house three times before she stopped. She didn't believe Darl had found this place yet. Otherwise, he would have come straight here, avoided the risky, public theater. But anything was possible. She parked in the driveway. No sign of anyone around. The dark street was deserted.

For a while she kept busy hauling clothing out of drawers and stuffing it haphazardly in suitcases. She hurried, trying to pack as much as she could, the most valuable items. The second Alex got here, they would leave, packed or not. Where was Alex? It was almost eleven-thirty. Lila was late.

She didn't start crying until she entered Alex's room and saw the wooden magician's chest he had found in the Arcana. She had left it open in the middle of the room to air out. How Alex had looked forward to painting it with Michael.

Michael. His beautiful hands, touching her. His total, innocent passion. She had let herself believe in it, like some fool at the end of a romance novel. But this was no romance. No, this was a tragedy she was living out here.

How had she never *seen*?

The stark reality of her life came crashing down on her.

There was no hope now, none. Darl was never going to get better. Even if he was arrested, locked away, there would always be Adam, coming after them. His word against hers. They would have to leave in silence, under cover of darkness. They would have to cut all ties with everyone. She felt a keen sorrow at the thought of those she loved. Even Maggie. Perhaps especially Maggie. So many things were left unfinished between them. But it could not be helped. Kelly would have to disappear completely, for the next ten years at least. A life of anonymity, disguises, car trips in the middle of the night.

But there was no time for self-pity. She had to pack.

WHEN SHE WAS DONE, she paced back and forth across the upstairs hall, between the window at the rear of the small house and the window at the front, watching for Alex—or for Darl. Twelve o'clock. She wrung her hands, feeling sick. Where was Lila? What if Darl had found Lila and Alex? What if he was with them, right now? Or on his way up to the cabin? If only there were some way to reach Lila. She checked the rear window again. An unfamiliar car was pulling up in the back lane.

It was Darl. She recognized his familiar shape as he got out of the car and entered her gate. He was coming down the path leading around the house. Which door was he going to try first? Which one should she try? She ran to the front window and opened it, letting in the winter air. She peered outside. Where was he?

Then she saw Alex. He was trooping up the outside stairs on the other side of the house, heading for the porch door. Lila was below him, looking up at Kelly. Kelly gestured wildly toward the side of the house, where Darl must be. But Lila just waved back, happy to have seen Alex safely inside. She hurried into her car and honked twice, cheerfully, as she drove away. Kelly spotted Darl, moving through the shadows around the front of the house. He had heard Lila's horn. He was heading for the porch.

Kelly dashed down the half-flight of stairs, threw open the porch door and dragged Alex inside. She locked the deadbolt. Safe. But they had to be quiet. She slapped a hand over Alex's mouth.

"Alex," she whispered. Then suddenly the outside porch light came on. Light poured through the stained-glass window, illuminating Eurydice's ruby robes and splashing the walls and floor with color. She hauled Alex up the stairs, out of sight.

She could hear Darl's footsteps on the porch. She heard him rattle the doorknob.

Alex's brown eyes were open in astonishment. His breathing was labored; he was working his lips, trying to break free. "Honey," she whispered. "You just do as I say. I need you to be very, very quiet right now. Do you understand?"

He nodded and stopped struggling. She took her hand from his mouth.

"Is it Dad?" he whispered. "Did Dad find us?" His eyes were wide with fear. He covered his mouth with his own hand.

How much did Alex know?

"Yes," she said. "He's outside in the yard."

There was no time for any more lies.

"Alex," she said, kneeling down beside him. "You have to tell me now. Did your father hurt you?"

"He'll ground me," Alex whimpered. "He'll put me in the basement again if I tell you."

She shook his shoulders firmly. "Alex," she said, "I took you away from your grandpa, remember? I caught you when you fell off the scaffold. I found you when you got lost in the theater. I will keep you safe. Now tell me, what did your father do to you?"

"I can't. He'll kill me. He'll kill *you*. He said he would. He promised." They heard the front doorknob rattle. Darl had moved around to the front of the house. He was going to try every door. "Kelly, he's coming! Hide!"

"The door is locked," she told him. "He can't—"

"He has a key!" Alex wailed. "He made me give him your keys when he put me in the basement."

"In the—?"

The theater basement.

Oh no.

Even now, she could hear the stolen key scraping confidently in the front door lock.

"Come," she whispered. She pulled Alex into his bedroom. Where to hide him? The blue magician's trunk still lay open in the middle of the floor. She picked Alex up and lowered him into its musty interior. "Lie down and be quiet now."

Alex obeyed solemnly. He was shivering. Kelly grabbed a thin blue blanket from his bed and tossed it over him. Darl's footsteps were ascending. She looked at Alex. He lay in the bottom of the trunk, like a child in a small coffin. His eyes stared up at her, completely trusting. With a silent prayer, she closed the lid on him.

She heard Darl close and lock the front door behind him. He was running up the stairs when Kelly stepped out into the hall to meet him, to stall him. She saw the frantic look on his face and the knife in his hand.

"Where is he?"

"Darl—no."

"What are you doing in there?" He pushed past her into Alex's room, grazing her arm with the edge of the blade, scraping a strip of skin from elbow to wrist. She barely felt the physical pain.

"No!"

He turned around, grinning. "He's here, isn't he?"

Darl walked to the closet, opened it, ran his hand through the clothing. He opened the curtains on Alex's window and felt behind them. He got down on his hands and knees to look under the bed.

Kelly saw it just a second before Darl did. The little winter boot, still very wet, lying beside the trunk. It must have fallen off when she shoved him in. Darl smiled. He picked up the boot.

"I remember this," he said. He shook it a little, and water drops sprayed out onto the floorboards. Then he flung it aside. "So," he said. "So he is hiding."

"He's not here, Darl," Kelly said. But even to herself, her voice sounded false, pleading.

One corner of Darl's mouth lifted in sly enjoyment. He looked directly at the trunk. As if in one of those paralyzing dreams, Kelly saw him bend to open it, one hand on the lid, the other hand holding the knife.

She leaped forward.

But she was not strong enough. With one arm, he threw her backward against the wall, knocking the wind from her lungs. She lay there, crumpled and stunned, unable to breathe, but she could still see him. He lifted the lid, victorious at last. He reached down deep inside the trunk and pulled out the blue blanket. Then he tossed it on the floor in disgust. He kicked the trunk with such force that it slid across the floor.

Darl strode to the closet again, this time stepping right inside it, checking the shelves, the ceiling.

"Where the hell is he?" he asked.

But Kelly could not answer. She could not breathe and could not believe what she had just witnessed.

The trunk was empty.

DARL FORCED KELLY through every room, searching for Alex in every cupboard and cranny, babbling about his task. It was all up to him, he complained, always up to him to put things right. To rescue everyone, redeem the situation. If it weren't for him, everything would spin out of control.

By the time they reached Kelly's bedroom, they had looked in every possible corner of the house. Darl glared into the bedroom mirror, as if Alex might be hiding behind the glass.

"Well," he said. "I'll have to deal with you first, then. Once he knows you're dead, he'll come running out from wherever he is." He raised his voice and called out. "Alex! You come out now! No more playing games with Daddy!"

"No, Alex!" Kelly screamed. "Stay wherever you are!"

She felt the knife against her throat. She stopped screaming. She didn't want to antagonize Darl any further.

"Darl," she said. "Let me go. Please. Don't throw everything away. So much has been lost already. Don't sacrifice the only good thing left. The only—"

"Shut up!" She felt the knife blade break the skin at her collarbone.

"Darl! Don't!"

"Shut up. What do you know about sacrifice? *James* was the sacrifice," he said in a low, hollow voice. "You didn't know that? James was the sacrifice."

He turned and faced the mirror again. He addressed his own reflection, as if it were James. "Weren't you?" he said.

Kelly could see her own reflection too. The white face. White throat, with the knife so close. The illusion of James holding her in his arms, holding her hostage. But she knew it was an illusion. Darl didn't. He spoke to his mirror brother.

"It's in the Bible, Jimmy, like Adam always said. You were born to deliver me. Abraham spared his son. And why? *Behold! Behind him a ram caught in a thicket by his horns.* They said—they promised—if I didn't tell, they'd take you instead.

As soon as I started school, they'd let me be. As long as you did what they said. So I had to keep you in line. I *had* to!"

He turned his eyes toward Kelly's reflection. "Jimmy broke all the rules," he said sadly, as if she would understand and sympathize. "No one was supposed to know about me—about what they did to me. What I let them do to James. But he told. He went to Chartrand. Then he told Diane. Then he told you, Kelly. He told you about me."

"But he didn't say anything about you, Darl," she dared to whisper. "Not a word."

"No. He was more devious than that. He drew those pictures, showing everything. As soon as Diane saw them, she knew. She questioned me. She wouldn't let up. I warned her to leave it alone, but she wouldn't. It made her sick, the whole thing. She couldn't stand to look at me. I saw it in her eyes. She was going to leave me, she was going to tell. So I shut her up for good. But that wasn't enough for Jimmy. He kept on making those pictures. He showed them to Leon Chartrand. He kept on showing them to you. He showed them to everybody. Over and over and over. Chartrand finally figured it out. If only you hadn't kept making him go through those damned files! He called me into his office after my shift, said he found something that might be important. He made me look. Asked me what I thought: *Who were the two kids in the picture? What was James trying to tell him?* I told him James already said *enough*, and it killed him. I wasn't going to let Chartrand get me, too."

Kelly felt her spine grow cold. So this was the truth. The one last thing James did not tell, could not let himself remember fully.

She closed her eyes, trying to wash the images away. But all she could see were those drawings. Those pictures that not even James had read correctly. But Darl had seen the devastating truth there. Diane had seen it. And finally Leon, when it was too late. The two little figures. Two.

In every picture, the whole series, the fear was a double fear. The two small twisted children writhed in tandem. Suffering together. James and Darl.

James had not been healing at all. He had reached this one last horrible memory and then he stopped remembering. The stories stopped. No wonder he had seemed so much better just before he died. He had closed the door again. Refused to let the past into his conscious mind.

But the past had continued to surface through James's body, through the hand that held the pencil. So Darl had been forced to move, forced to stop it.

She had to know.

"Darl," she said. "What happened that morning between you and James?"

Their eyes met in the mirror.

"No more questions!" he said. "That's the last question I want to hear from you." He pushed her away from him, shoved her backwards onto the bed so hard she bounced.

He threw himself onto her, holding the knife above her heart. His lips set in a grim line, he stared down at her, his face inches from her own, pinning her there.

She did not try to escape. Right now, *right now* before she died, she wanted to know everything. What happened that morning of June 21? What did James say, up there, by that waterfall? Did they struggle? Did James want to live?

"Tell me, Darl," she said. "Tell me how it happened."

"You want to know?"

"You owe me," she said. She lay rigid, frightened, but she did not look away. She stared defiantly into his eyes. He loosened his grip. He sat up beside her, still holding the knife close.

"Early that morning," Darl said, "I set fire to the house and then—"

"Darl!" Her eyes opened wide. "*You* set the fire?"

He nodded.

"But James—"

"Jimmy never had the guts," he said. "You know that."

Kelly stared.

"But then when we got to camp, I made the mistake of telling him."

"What did he say?" she asked quietly.

Darl laughed. His emotions were fluctuating wildly. "Pitiful little James? He said everything would be all right. I kill our parents—I thought I'd killed them—and he says everything's going to be all right!" He shook his head in disbelief. "He was such a goddamned . . ." He beat his fist against the headboard, in frustration.

"Darl, please. What happened?"

He took a deep breath, began again, angrily. "I thought they were dead. I didn't want to go to jail, believe me. Jimmy said I wouldn't have to. He said he'd go to court with me. He'd testify. I'd walk away, or maybe"—his mouth curled in disgust—"a hospital." He spat the word.

Kelly felt the old pain of grief entering her body again, seeping through her, every vein in her body burning.

"James said he told and he lived through it. Hah! You know what he said? He said you loved him and love was stronger than death. But I knew if I told . . ."

"If you told?" she asked.

"I'd die," Darl said. "I'll die. But James would not shut up. He would not shut up. I was so sick of hearing about love, I ripped the wedding ring off that chain around his neck. So then—" He stopped, began to cry.

She reached up and touched his face. This was such a sad story, this tale of murder. Yet it was the very story she was aching to hear. With a strange sense of inner calm, she realized this story would finally set her free. She caressed Darl's cheek, coaxing it out of him. She gazed at his mouth hungrily, waiting for the words.

"So then—we were standing on the ridge. Up above everyone else. And James—he wouldn't stop talking, so . . ."

"So you pushed him," she said.

"Yes." He placed his hand on top of hers, while she stroked his face.

"It wasn't easy," he said. "He didn't want to go. When he started to fall, he grabbed me. He was holding the front of my shirt. I was losing my balance. We both started to slide and then I—I just kicked him loose of me." His green eyes filled with wonder.

They lay there, staring at each other. The pain that had been coursing through her body dissolved. It left her for the very last time.

Chapter Thirty

Darl jumped suddenly. "What's that sound?"

Kelly heard nothing, but she hoped, if the sound was real, it was Alex getting himself out of the house. Darl stood up. He still held the knife pointed in her direction, but his attention had been drawn to the window. Then she heard it too. But it wasn't coming from the bedroom window. Someone was out on the porch. Someone was rattling the doorknob, but the deadbolt held fast.

"Alex?" Darl called. He stepped toward the window.

Kelly saw her chance. She eased herself to the edge of the bed, stood and ran.

Halfway down the stairs, she heard him coming after her. When she reached the landing, she turned out all the lights with one flick of her fingers, then tore down into the living room, just as he reached the landing behind her. She slipped behind the fireplace and pressed herself against the stone chimney, trying to dissolve into the shadows. The glow of the outside porch light through the stained-glass window provided the only illumination.

There was no escape from this side of the fireplace, unless Darl made a mistake and headed toward the kitchen. If he did that, she could make it to the front door. But if he came around the piano, he would block her exit.

Kelly prayed for him to turn right, and he turned left.

She could see the dark shape of him coming at her.

"I have to, Kelly," he said.

She was cornered.

Just when he stood two feet in front of her, and she was prepared to fight to the death, there came a crash from above. Kelly and Darl both whirled around. A sickening, splintering noise, and Kelly saw the stained-glass window shatter, a hand coming through it, right through Eurydice's heart. The hand came again, cracking her glass lips open. Then the silhouette of an entire body hurled itself against the window. Orpheus and Eurydice broke into pieces, and a dark figure flew into the room, landed on the floor amid the broken shards, and rolled right into Darl, who was knocked to the ground, still holding the knife. The two of them struggled for a moment, in confusion.

In the dimness, Kelly could make out Darl's arm, stabbing blindly. A high, agonized cry. Then his attacker stood up and flicked on the light switch.

It was Angel.

Holding Paul's gun.

She fired.

Darl rolled over and clutched his stomach. Kelly pressed up against the wall, holding her hands over her face. She didn't want to see this. But she looked.

They were both still. Darl moaned quietly, his wiry body clenched in a fetal position. Angel stood, reeling, gripping the gun, the whole left side of her face covered in cuts. Her wrist and shoulder bled profusely from her stab wounds. She breathed heavily. Everything was eerily, suddenly quiet.

Kelly moved forward. "Ange," she started to say. But Angel held up a hand to silence her.

"Paul was right," Angel said to Darl. "You bastard. When

I got back home and found him gone, found out your parents were dead—"

"Dead?" asked Kelly. "Both of them?"

"Dead as doornails," Angel said. "Just like Paul." She held the gun with both hands, pointing it at Darl's head.

Darl retched and began to shiver.

"I got in my car and booted it back down here. When I got to the theater, there was cops everywhere. An ambulance. They were zipping my husband into a body bag. So I came here, and I heard you through the window. I heard everything, Darl! That bullet you got in your gut is for James," she said. "And this one—"

Darl opened his eyes. "Kelly," he said, as if surprised to see her. He sounded confused. "What happened to your arm?" He pointed to the long scrape he'd made with the knife.

"This one's for Paul." Angel took careful aim.

Darl looked up. He knew exactly what was happening, now. He saw.

For a few seconds Kelly thought she glimpsed the old Darl, the one she thought she knew, her protector. His green eyes filled with regret, sorry he couldn't save her from this one last thing.

And then Angel fired again.

"Too much death," said Angel. She addressed his body, which did not move. His eyes stared, unseeing. "Too much blood." She looked down at her wounded shoulder, staggered, but regained her balance.

"It's a good thing he did this," she said to Kelly. She indicated her own stab wounds, her bloody arm.

Her face had gradually lost color, and now she was white as ash. She was about to faint. But first she turned to Kelly with a weak grin and said, "Self-defense." Then she hit the floor.

Chapter Thirty-One

Sam and Lila sat with Angel and Kelly at Kelly's kitchen table back in Winnipeg. It was late at night. The two sisters were weary and drained from a week of dealing with legal, official details, funeral details. Of telling Alex that Daddy was very sick and Daddy died.

For now, Alex slept.

Kelly wondered how much Alex heard when he hid in the trunk. After the shooting, when she staggered upstairs, calling out Alex's name, the first thing she did was open the trunk. And there he was—curled up in the false bottom. The trunk had truly been magic. She bundled him in the blue blanket and carried him down the stairs, over the shards of colored glass, shielding his eyes from the destruction, the two bleeding figures on the floor below. She stepped right through that broken window with Alex in her arms. And ran for help.

Kelly looked at the friends sitting around the table: Sam and Lila, and Angel in her white sling, like one white wing resting lightly on her shoulder. She realized how little she'd known her own sister.

She thought of Lila's words on Hallowe'en night. Her

prediction: *someone you know and yet you do not know.* Kelly had laughed it off, but it was true. True of all of them. Paul, who risked his life for her, and lost. Alex, who so easily concealed his suffering from her. Darl, the one she thought she knew. She hadn't seen any of them, really. She hadn't been looking at them.

She had always been looking back. Looking for James. Turned so ardently in his direction she couldn't see what was going on in front of her.

She looked down at her own hand, with its double lifeline, its double wedding bands. Soon, she knew, it would be time to remove both these rings from her finger.

She excused herself and went upstairs to Alex's room and watched him sleeping. He'd kicked off the covers, and she tucked him in again. She thought of James's pictures of his own childhood, that crooked, evil house. At last, unexpectedly, Kelly had been given a chance to do what she had long wanted to do, to reach back in time, reach down into that dark house, into that pit of fire, and pull out someone alive.

EVERYBODY BELIEVED MICHAEL would show up. Lila certainly believed it. She told Angel all about him and Angel believed it. Alex overheard them and he believed it, too.

But Kelly thought she knew better. She knew what happened to the Little Mermaid in the real story, the original. The poor mermaid could not walk in the world of the prince. To enter his world, she had to have her tongue cut out, and when she walked on land, she felt sharp knives thrusting into her feet. The prince in the story, no fool, married one of his own kind.

She remembered what Rocko said about Michael once, that he was too simple, too content with his own life to understand tragedy. "Which is why he doesn't get *Hamlet*," Rocko said.

Kelly guessed Michael wouldn't get her story either, her terrible story of secrets and death. How would he react to a dead body in his hotel room, blood on the carpet? What rumors flew around Minneapolis, now, about her? It was a story all too scandalous and complicated for Michael. Driving a car was too complicated for Michael, for goodness' sake. She could never tell him.

So she did not return his calls. She asked Lila not to call him. He could easily find out where she lived, but she knew he would not want to be involved in all this ugliness, this death. He would not come.

Nevertheless, she stood watching at her front window early Monday morning, the one day of the week she knew the Arcana would be closed, the play not performed. A delicate snow descended over the yard, the white flakes catching on the branches of the young poplars.

James wanted to live, she whispered. She held on to that shining truth. *James said love was stronger than death. And perhaps, after all, it is.* If Angel could fly through glass, if James could break through from the other world, to warn her, then surely the wall between one person and another was fragile as a skin of water. Love could part and open it, as the body could part the surface of a river.

If Michael came this far, she thought, if he came walking toward her, right now, through the lightly falling snow, she would risk it.

She would tell.